DATE			

THE
WOMAN
WHO FELL
FROM
GRACE

THE
WOMAN
WHO FELL
FROM
GRACE

David Handler

A Perfect Crime Book
DOUBLEDAY
NEW YORK   LONDON   TORONTO   SYDNEY   AUCKLAND

FIC

A PERFECT CRIME BOOK

PUBLISHED BY DOUBLEDAY
a division of Bantam Doubleday Dell Publishing Group, Inc.
666 Fifth Avenue, New York, New York 10103

DOUBLEDAY is a
trademark of Doubleday,
a division of Bantam Doubleday Dell
Publishing Group, Inc.

Book design by Tasha Hall

All characters in this book are fictitious,
and any resemblance to actual persons, living or
dead, is purely coincidental.

Library of Congress Cataloging-in-Publication Data

Handler, David, 1952–
    The woman who fell from grace / by David
Handler. —1st ed.
        p.   cm.
    I. Title.
PS3558.A4637W6   1991
813'.54—dc20   91-9730
                                                CIP

ISBN 0-385-42115-X

3   5   7   9   10   8   6   4   2

THE
WOMAN
WHO FELL
FROM
GRACE

For Stella
who has been nice enough
to stay behind

It's being hailed as the ultimate American novel, and maybe it is. It's huge, loud, sentimental, and its pants are on fire. It's also a rollicking good time. I devoured it in greedy bites and would happily come back for seconds.

—from Dorothy Parker's review of *Oh, Shenandoah* in the Sunday *New York Times,* June 2, 1940

Chapter One

I was standing in the lobby of the Algonquin Hotel seeing double. Two utterly distinguished, utterly identical elderly gentlemen sat there before me sipping on martinis at one of the small, round lounge tables. They had the same handsome, patrician face—eyes blue, brows arched, nose long and rather sharp, chin cleft, hair silver and wavy. They wore the same double-breasted navy blazer, white cotton broadcloth shirt, yellow-and-burgundy-striped silk tie. They looked up at me at the same time. They smiled at me at the same time. Same smile. Same teeth. White.

I had to blink several times to make sure I wasn't having an acid flashback from the summer of '70, the one I can't remember too much about, except that I wanted to move to Oregon and raise peaches. I even shot a glance down at Lulu, my basset hound, who was looking uncommonly pert that season in the beret Merilee had bought her in Paris. Lulu was blinking, too.

"Frederick, Mr. Hoag," said one, as I dumbly shook his long, slender hand.

"Edward, Mr. Hoag," said the other, as I shook his.

"Won't you please join us, sir?" they said in perfect harmony.

Harmony because their voices were different. Each spoke with the gentle, courtly accent of the Southern aristocrat. But while Frederick's voice was husky, Edward's was softer, higher pitched. A small distinction, but I had to grab on to something, anything, to keep from hooting. I joined them. Lulu turned around three times at my feet and curled up with a contented grunt. She likes the Algonquin. Always has.

It was after five and the place was filling up with the pasty-faced English tourists and assorted New York literary fossils and bottom feeders who usually hang around there. Peter Ustinov was giving a radio reporter an interview on the sofa next to us, and a whole new meaning to the words *couch potato*. Rog Angell was busy demonstrating the hitch in the Straw Man's swing to two other owlish *New Yorker* editors. Pretty much everybody else in the hotel was staring at Eddie and Freddie, who might have been retired diplomats or rear admirals or a new set of Doublemint Twins for the Depend-undergarment set, but who were actually the Glaze brothers of Staunton, Virginia, the exceptionally shrewd keepers of the *Oh, Shenandoah* flame. It was the Glaze brothers who had just engineered the record-shattering $6.2-million auction for the most eagerly awaited literary sequel of all time, the sequel to *Oh, Shenandoah,* the epic romance novel of the American Revolution penned in 1940 by their mother, Alma Glaze. *Oh, Shenandoah* wasn't the greatest novel in the history of publishing, but it certainly was the most popular. More than 30 million readers in twenty-seven different languages had gobbled up the thousand-page saga through the years. Ten times that many had seen the Oscar-winning movie, which in the opinion of most critics ranked as the greatest Hollywood blockbuster of all time, greater than *Gone With the Wind,* than *Citizen Kane,* than *Yes, Georgio.* For decades, fans had been clamoring for a sequel. Now they were going to get one.

"So glad you could make it, Mr. Hoag," Frederick rasped as he rang the bell on our table for our waiter.

"My pleasure. And make it Hoagy."

"As in Carmichael?" asked Edward softly.

"As in the cheese steak."

"Would that be the one they serve in Buffalo?" Frederick inquired.

"Philadelphia. It's chicken wings they do in Buffalo."

"And I'm sure they do them exceedingly well," said Edward graciously.

Our waiter, Frank, hurried over and said how nice it was to see me again. The Glaze brothers ordered another round of martinis. I tagged along, heavy on the olives. Lulu had her usual. After Frank went off, Edward leaned over and scratched her belly roughly, as if she were a hunting dog. She's more the champagne-and-caviar type. She snuffled in protest.

He immediately made a face. "My goodness. Her breath is somewhat . . ."

"She has rather strange eating habits."

Frank returned with our drinks and a plate of pickled herring and raw onion for Lulu. She attacked it at once. The brothers watched her. They sipped their drinks. They glanced at each other. I watched them, beginning to detect the subtle differences. Frederick had a more relaxed set to his jaw and shoulders, an easier manner. Edward appeared more formal and reserved. The shy one.

It was Frederick who began. "Exactly how much do you know about this project of ours, Hoagy?"

"Very little. I've been away."

He leaned forward eagerly. "With Merilee Nash?"

"Frederick, please," scolded Edward. "You're being nosy."

"It's okay," I assured him. "I'm used to being a public laughingstock. It's kind of a nice feeling, after a while."

"I shall bring you up to date, if I might," said Frederick. "As you may know, our mother, in her last will and testament, specified that no sequel to *Oh, Shenandoah* would be authorized until some fifty years after her death, which is—"

"Which is to say *now,*" interjected Edward.

Frederick shot him a cool glance, then turned back to me. "Sometime before her death, Mother had in fact outlined the plot for a second volume, which was—"

"Which was to be called *Sweet Land of Liberty,*" Edward broke in.

Frederick shot him another cool look. He clearly didn't like it when Edward interrupted him. Something told me that Eddie had been doing it for sixty years. "*Which,*" Frederick went on, "she then tucked away in the safe in the library of Shenandoah, our family's estate, where it has remained, sealed, until—"

"Until a few weeks ago," Edward said. "When it was, at long last, opened."

Frederick calmly pulled a slim gold cigarette case from the inside pocket of his blazer, removed a cigarette, and lit it with a gold lighter. He politely blew the smoke away from me. He blew it directly toward Edward, who scowled and waved it away, irritably.

"The safe's opening," Frederick continued, "took place live on national television. That Geraldo Rivera person. Perhaps Mr. Rivera is a friend of yours . . . ?"

I popped one of my olives in my mouth. "Not even maybe."

"Horrible little man," sniffed Edward.

"Garish display," agreed Frederick. "Mave's idea, naturally."

"Naturally," said Edward.

Mave was their younger sister, Mavis Glaze, the socialite who wasn't quite so famous as their mother but who was damned close. Ever since the late seventies, when the PBS affiliate in Washington, D.C., asked her to host a little half-hour, weekly show on social graces called *Uncommon Courtesy.* Something about the stern, matronly way she said "Courtesy is most decidedly *not* common" had tickled Johnny Carson's funny bone. He began to make her the butt of his nightly monologue jokes, and then a frequent guest on *The Tonight Show,* and before long her show had gone national and Mavis Glaze had become the Jack Lalanne of manners with a chain of more than seven hundred etiquette schools. To get Mavis Glazed was to emerge civil and poised, the perfect hostess, the perfect guest. "Civilization," declared Mavis over and over again in her endless TV commercials, "starts here." She ran her empire from Shenandoah, the historic 5,000-acre estate that had been in the Glaze family since the days when Virginia was the jewel of the colonies. Shenandoah was where Alma Glaze's epic had been set. The movie had been filmed entirely on location there. Part of the time now it was open to the public, and the public came by the busload to see it. They felt a special kind of love for the place. Shenandoah was America's ancestral home. It was even more popular with tourists than Monticello, Thomas Jefferson's home, situated across the Shenandoah Valley outside of Charlottesville. Jefferson was only our nation's most brilliant president. He never won an Oscar.

"Given Mave's own prominence," Frederick went on, "we all felt that she—"

"*We* being my brother and I," Edward broke in, "as well as the publisher and Mave . . ."

"That Mave should author the sequel." Frederick casually brushed some cigarette ash from the sleeve of his blazer onto the sleeve of Edward's. Edward reddened and flicked it onto the floor. "It seemed only natural," Frederick concluded.

I nodded, wondering how long it would be before one of them had the other down on the carpet in a headlock, and which one I'd root for.

"The understanding," explained Edward, "was that we find a professional novelist to do the actual writing. Someone gifted enough to meet Mother's high literary standards, yet discreet enough not to divulge their association with the project."

"Or the contents of Mother's outline," Frederick added. "Just exactly what happens in *Sweet Land of Liberty* is a well-kept secret, Hoagy. We've planned it that way to heighten reader anticipation. The tabloids would happily pay one hundred thousand dollars to steal our thunder."

I nodded some more. It's something I'm pretty good at.

"We all felt a novelist successful in the romance field would be most appropriate," said Edward. "The publisher came up with a list of several." He rattled them off. Two were million-plus sellers of historical bodice-rippers in their own right—Antonia Raven and Serendipity Vale, whose real name was Norman Pincus.

"Unfortunately," lamented Frederick, "none of them has worked out."

"How many have you gone through?" I asked. You can only nod for so long.

"Five of them left the project after one day," replied Edward. "Amply compensated for their time, of course. To assure their silence."

"Three more didn't make it to the end of the first day," added Frederick.

"Pretty surprising that any red-blooded writer would walk away," I said, "considering how much money is involved."

"They didn't walk, sir," said Edward. "They ran."

"Mavis," explained Frederick, choosing his words carefully, "is, well, *Mavis*. She's . . . She can be, perhaps, a bit . . . high-strung. Demanding. Magisterial . . ."

"She makes Nancy Reagan look like Little Red Riding Hood," Edward blurted out.

"A prize bitch," acknowledged Frederick. "But she's our baby sister and we love her."

Edward nodded emphatically. At least they agreed on that.

"Sounds like what you need," I suggested, "is someone

who's used to being screamed at. Why don't you ask around up at Yankee Stadium?"

"What we need," said Edward, "is someone who can retain the flavor and spirit of *Oh, Shenandoah*. Otherwise, Mother's fans will be terribly disappointed. Unfortunately, Mave has, well, some ideas of her own. Ideas that are nowhere indicated in any of Mother's notes, though she insists they are indeed Mother's very own." He glanced uneasily over at Frederick, colored slightly, and lowered his voice. "Ideas she says Mother has personally communicated to her. While she sleeps. In her dreams."

I tugged at my ear. "What kind of ideas are we talking about?"

"Queer ones," Edward replied gravely. "Very, very queer."

"According to the terms of our contract with the publisher," said Frederick, "the estate has final say on the contents of the manuscript. We insisted upon it. If Mavis gets her way, Hoagy, and she always does, I have no doubt that the publication of *Sweet Land of Liberty* will rank as one of the greatest embarrassments in the history of American publishing. Not to mention a major financial disaster."

"You're her brothers," I said. "Won't she listen to you?"

"Mavis doesn't have to listen to us if she doesn't choose to," replied Edward. "And she generally doesn't choose to. You see, Hoagy, Mother believed in a system of matriarchy. We three children took her family name, Glaze, not father's, which was Blackwell. And when she died, she left Shenandoah and the entirety of her fortune to Mave and Mave alone. Frederick and I merely serve her in an advisory capacity. I happen to practice law. Frederick is an investment counselor. Protecting the financial and legal interests of Shenandoah and Mavis does occupy much of our time, and Mave does pay us quite generously for it. But it is she who has final say in all estate matters."

"And when she dies," added Frederick, "Shenandoah will

pass on to her own first daughter, Mercy. Mave's husband, Richard, the gallant Lord Lonsdale, gets nothing."

"What does he do with himself?" I asked.

"Come when Mavis calls him," Frederick replied drily. "Tail wagging."

"Do they have any other children?"

"Just Mercy."

"And you gentlemen?"

"We are both bachelors," Edward said. "Without issue."

I drained my martini. Another appeared at my elbow instantly. "Sounds like one big unhappy family."

"Just like any other," agreed Edward pleasantly.

"Does your publisher know what's going on?"

"Only that we're having a bit of trouble finding a writer," replied Edward. "Not why. They are, however, getting nervous about our deadline. They expected the book to be well under way by now. They impressed upon us yesterday the amount of pressure they are under. Huge sums of money have been committed. The paperback publisher is waiting impatiently in line, as is the movie studio."

"They recommended you," said Frederick. "As a sort of specialist."

"I suppose that's one word for what I am."

"They said there isn't a celebrity alive, including Mavis, who you can't lick."

Edward shuddered. "What a horrible image, Frederick."

Frederick stared at him a moment. Then turned back to me. "You're our last and best hope, Hoagy. We're desperate. Will you fly down to Shenandoah and talk to Mavis?"

I sat back in my chair. "I should warn you there aren't many people who are good at what I'm good at. It's a rare talent. In fact, I'm the only one who has it."

"Not exactly bashful, are you, sir?" said Edward stiffly.

"You want bashful, get J. D. Salinger. He'll cost you a lot less money than I will."

"Certainly we can hammer something out," Frederick ventured. "We're all reasonable men, aren't we?"

"You might be. I'm not."

Frederick cleared his throat. "Frankly, money happens to be the least of our worries right now. Get Mave to stop communicating with the dead. Deliver a novel that Alma Glaze would have been proud to put her name on. Do that and we'll meet your price, no matter how unreasonable. Satisfied?"

"Every once in a while, if I try real hard." I sipped my martini. "Okay, we'll fly down there."

"Excellent," exclaimed Frederick, pleased.

Edward frowned. "By 'we' I trust you're not referring to Lulu here."

A low moan came out from under the table. I asked her to let me handle it.

"I am," I replied. "I tend to do most of the heavy lifting, but we always work together. We're a team."

Edward smiled. "Like Lunt and Fontanne?"

"I was thinking more of Abbott and Costello."

"I understand," said Frederick, "but there is the matter of the Shenandoah peacocks. Our trademark. They've lived on the north lawn for more than two hundred years. Their wings are clipped to keep them from flying away or—"

"Or crapping on anyone's head," Edward broke in.

Frederick lit another cigarette and blew the smoke Edward's way. Those boys were at it again. "That makes them exceedingly vulnerable to predators—dogs, cats, raccoons, foxes. The grounds are kept carefully guarded, and no animal of any kind, no matter how well trained, is ever allowed on the property. I'm sure you can appreciate that."

"Gentlemen, the sole predatory act of Lulu's life was a growling contest she got into in Riverside Park with a eight-month-old Pomeranian named Mr. Fuzzball. She needed eighteen stitches when it was all over."

They mulled this over a moment, lips pursed. They looked at each other. A silent message passed between them. "We have your word, as a gentleman, that she'll not harm the peacocks?" asked Edward.

"You have my word, as a gentleman, that she'll be deathly afraid of them."

"Very well," said Frederick reluctantly. "We'll finesse Mavis on this particular point. Just try to keep Lulu under cover, if you can."

"That's no problem. In a rainhat and sunglasses she easily passes for Judd Hirsch. When do we leave?"

Chapter Two

We left early the next week. I had stuff I had to do first. It was nearly April. My Borsalino was due for its 30,000-mile overhaul at Worth and Worth. I had to take the wool liner out of my trench coat and put my winter clothes in storage and fill the prescription for Lulu's allergy medicine. I had to read the damned book, all 1,032 pages of it.

Partly, *Oh, Shenandoah* was the story of how the American Revolution shattered forever the privileged lives of colonial Virginia's landed British gentry. But mostly it was a love triangle, heavy on the violins. Flaming-haired Evangeline Grace, the beautiful, headstrong young daughter of a wealthy tobacco planter, was torn by her love for two men. John Raymond, handsome son of the colonial governor in Williamsburg, was a brilliant law student, a sensitive poet, a budding statesman. The other, a dashing, hot-blooded Frenchman named Guy De Cheverier, was a fearless adventurer, a ruthless brigand reviled by polite society. It was their story. It was the story of the great Virginia plantations—of colorful horse races and grand balls, of velvet waistcoats and powdered wigs, and smiling, happy slaves. And it was the story of the Revolution. De Cheverier would become a daring war hero who time and again led his brave, loyal men into victorious battle against the Redcoats. Raymond would break with his English father to become an architect of the Revolution at the side of his William and Mary law classmate Tom Jefferson. Real figures from American history were sprinkled throughout the novel— George Washington, Benjamin Franklin, James Monroe, James Madison. Alma Glaze did her homework. She drew her portrait of Shenandoah Valley plantation life from local historical records and supposedly, her own family's illustrious past. Still, it was the love triangle, the battle between Raymond and De Cheverier for Vangie's hand that carried the reader's interest across so many pages. Which one would she marry? In the end, she couldn't decide, and since neither was willing to bow out gracefully, the two of them fought a duel for her hand, Vangie to marry the winner. Who won? Alma Glaze never told us. All she left us with was that famous closing line: "As one man fell, Evangeline stepped forward, eyes abrim, breast heaving, to embrace both the victor and the new life that surely promised to be her grandest adventure." For fifty years, readers had been arguing over what the hell that meant. That's why there was so much interest in the sequel.

Naturally, it's hard to read it nowadays without seeing the faces of the actors who played the roles in the lavish Sam Goldwyn production, the only movie in Hollywood history ever to sweep Best Picture, Best Director (William Wyler), Best Screenplay (Robert Sherwood), as well as Best Actor and Actress. Warner Brothers loaned Goldwyn Errol Flynn to play De Cheverier. For the coveted roles of Evangeline Grace and John Raymond, Goldwyn cast the gifted young British stage performers Sterling Sloan and Laurel Barrett, who also happened to be husband and wife in so-called real life. Neither had appeared in an American film before. Sloan was fresh off his acclaimed Hamlet in London's West End and being touted as the new Olivier. The fragile, achingly beautiful Barrett, the woman who beat out every top actress in Hollywood to play Vangie, was a complete unknown. Both won Oscars for *Oh, Shenandoah.* Sloan's, of course, was awarded posthumously. He dropped dead of a ruptured brain aneurysm only hours after wrapping the film on location in Virginia. His death at age thirty-two destroyed Barrett. She suffered a nervous breakdown soon afterward. She was in and out of institutions for depression right up until she died in 1965 at the age of fifty-two, her life made, and seemingly unmade, by her *Oh, Shenandoah* triumph. She wasn't alone in that.

Alma Glaze herself encountered outrageous swings of fortune, good and bad. A small, rather flinty woman given to wearing orthopedic shoes and severe hats, she was the only child of the Shenandoah Valley's most distinguished old family, and wife to a successful local banker. She began work on her first and only novel one summer while she was recovering from pneumonia. She spent seven years on it. When she finally finished it, she gave it to a childhood friend who taught literature at Mary Baldwin, a small, proper nearby women's college. The friend sent it on to his brother, an editor for a New York publishing house. The rest is publishing history. *Oh, Shenandoah* sold an incredible one million copies in its first six months, sometimes as many as sixty thousand copies in one day. Still, Alma Glaze wasn't able to savor its success for long. The day she was awarded the Pulitzer Prize for literature was the same day her husband died of tuberculosis, leaving her a forty-two-year-old widow with three children. She sold the film rights to Sam Goldwyn for the then-whopping sum of $100,000. And though the movie's success would surpass even that of the book, she was again unable to enjoy it. The week after it premiered, she was run over by a hit-and-run driver while she was crossing a street in Staunton, Virginia, her hometown. She died instantly.

And now it was a raw March morning fifty years later, and I was squeezed into a tiny, stuffy De Havilland Dash four-prop that was riding the turbulence on down to Charlottesville from New York, by way of Baltimore. My complimentary honey-roasted peanuts and plastic cup of warm orange juice were bouncing around on the tray before me. Lulu was on the floor under me, making unhappy noises. My mind was on how I never expected things to turn out this way. This wasn't me. This was someone else sitting here getting airsick. Not me. Never me.

If you're a serious fan of the gossip columns, and of American literary trivia, you may remember me. It's okay if you don't. It has been a while since the *New York Times*, upon reading my first novel, *Our Family Enterprise*, labeled me "the first major new literary voice of the '80's." Ah, how sweet it had been. The best-seller list. The awards. Fame. Marriage to Merilee Nash, Joe Papp's hottest and loveliest young leading lady. The eight art-deco rooms overlooking Central Park. The red 1958 Jaguar XK150 convertible. The gaudy contract for book two. But then there was this problem with my juices. They dried up. The creative kind. All kinds. Merilee got the apartment and the Jag, the Tony for the Mamet play, the Oscar for the Woody Allen movie. Briefly, another husband, too, that fabulously successful playwright Zack something. I got Lulu, my drafty old fifth-floor walk-up on West Ninety-third Street, and my ego, which recently applied to Congress for statehood.

My juices did come back. Somewhat. There was a slim second novel, *Such Sweet Sorrow*, which managed to become as great a commercial and critical flop as my first was a success. Merilee came back, too. Somewhat. These days we're two intelligent semiadults who are content not to ask questions anymore and to just go ahead and make each other miserable. Actually, we get along fine as long as we're not together. I still had my apartment. She still had her eight rooms on Central Park West and her eighteen acres in Hadlyme, Connecticut, where right now she was busy playing in the mud while the offers rolled in. No plans for a merger. We know better than that.

I'd just spent the last three months in a small boat on the Aegean, subsisting on grilled fish and iced retsina and fasting from the neck up—no books, no magazines, no newspapers. No ideas, except my own. Slowly, a third novel had begun to take shape. But it would take me a good three years to write, and I had no publisher for it and no money left. That meant I had to fall back on my second, decidedly less distinguished calling—pen for hire. I've ghosted three celebrity memoirs so far. Each has been a best-seller. My background as a writer of fiction certainly helps. Good anecdotes are vital to the success of any memoir. The best way to make sure they're good is to make them up. It also helps that I used to be a celebrity myself. I know how to handle them. The lunch-pail ghosts don't. That's why the Glaze brothers had turned to me.

On the downside, ghosting has proven hazardous to my health. Not to mention the health of others. People have this way of dropping dead around me. Consider yourself warned. Also consider this before you get any ideas: If you're in trouble, if you need help, if you don't know who to call, don't call me. I'm not a hero. Besides, you can't afford me.

We left the storm behind as we flew further south. There was nothing but blue skies over Virginia. I was one of four men who got off at Charlottesville, and the only one who wasn't wearing mint-green golf slacks. The air was softer and more fragrant than in the North, the sun bright and hot. I was halfway to the small cinder-block terminal when I suddenly realized I was alone. Back across the runway I went and up the steps into the plane.

She was still under the seat, trembling as badly as she does when she's about to get a s-h-o-t. She flat out didn't want to get off the plane. She does like to fly. In fact, she's already amassed enough frequent-flyer miles to qualify for a free coach flight all the way from New York City to Lansing, Michigan. This, however, was a little much. I asked her what the problem was. All I got in response was whimpering. I told her to come. She refused. I'm bigger. I dragged her out from under the seat, hoisted her up, and carried her, thrashing and moaning in protest, out the cabin door.

"Terrible twos," I explained to the stewardess.

My rented Chevy Nova smelled as if somebody had once stuffed it full of Styrofoam peanuts. I stowed my gear in the trunk, tossed my trench and Borsalino in the backseat, and took off the jacket of the gray cheviot-wool suit I'd had made for me in London at Strickland's. I shoved the driver's seat back to accommodate my legs and rolled down the windows so Lulu could stick her large, black nose out and wail unhappily at the parking lot. I reminded her I'd gone to a lot of trouble to get her invited along, and if she wasn't going to behave, she could spend the next three months in a kennel with a lot of strange, mean pit bulls. She shut up.

I worked the Nova out of the airport and through the outskirts of Charlottesville, seat of Albemarle County, lush Eden where Jefferson built Monticello and Monroe built Ash Lawn, and where the haves still breed horses and cattle and themselves in plush country comfort.

Spring came earlier here. The cherry trees were already blossoming a gaudy pink. The tulips and daffodils were open, the grass was thick and green, and the forsythia bushes were explosions of mustard yellow.

I picked up Route 64 outside of town and coaxed the Nova up to eighty, where it handled smooth as a Maytag in the spin cycle. The highway climbed through the Blue Ridge Mountains. Then it tumbled down and before me spread the valley with its gently undulating patchwork quilt of fertile green farmland and red clay soil, its tree-shaded brick manor homes, its calm. Clumps of cattle munched away on the grass and the Alleghenies rippled endlessly across the sky. There may be prettier places on earth than the Shenandoah Valley, but I haven't seen one.

I got off the highway at Staunton, the historic little town where they don't pronounce the *u* and where two world-famous celebrities, Alma Glaze and Woodrow Wilson, were

born. It's a gem of a place—steep, hilly streets of turreted Victorian mansions shaded by magnolias and redbuds, a restored
turn-of-the-century business district, and a pleasing absence of
the Yushie influence. Nary a sign of the young urban shitheads
in their spandex workout togs. No take-out stir-fry emporium
called Wok 'n' Roll. No singles Laundromat called *dirtysome-
thing*. The tallest building in town was the Hotel Woodrow
Wilson, and it was built in 1925. Eleven stories, not counting
the neon sign on the roof.

It was just past five. Workers were streaming out of the
office buildings and the Augusta County Courthouse for their
cars. They were smiling and laughing. No scowls. No snarls.
No one was riding on my tail. No one was blasting his horn.
They must put something in the water.

The Glaze brothers' directions took me through town on
Beverley Street past the Dixie Theatre, the vast, fabled, old
silent-picture palace where *Oh, Shenandoah* had its original
worldwide premiere. Workmen were busy sprucing the place
up. A newly restored 70mm print of the film classic was being
screened there in a few weeks as part of the fiftieth anniversary celebration. It was going to be a major deal. Surviving
cast and crew members were even going to be flown in. Not
that very many biggies were still around. The three stars and
Goldwyn and Wyler were long gone. So was most of the all-
star supporting cast. Raymond Massey, who played Thomas
Jefferson. David Niven, who was the smug British colonel,
Edgerton. Ethel Barrymore, Donald Crisp, Walter Huston,
Linda Darnell. About the only surviving cast member I could
think of was Rex Ransom, who played James Madison. I was
hoping Rex came. I wanted to meet him for reasons that had
nothing to do with *Oh, Shenandoah* and everything to do with
my childhood.

I turned onto a narrow country road outside of town that
twisted its way back through poultry farms and fenced pasturage. Fields of winter rye were being plowed under for fertil-
izer. The air was redolent of loamy soil and cow pies. Some

black Angus grazed alongside the road. Lulu barked gleefully at them, secure in the knowledge they couldn't catch her as we sped past. Such invincibility did not, however, extend to her sinuses. Her hay fever was already making her sniffle. I'd have to give her a pill when we got there. I didn't want her developing breathing problems again. She snores when she has them. I happen to know this because she likes to sleep on my head.

Occasionally, a blue sign assured me I was on the right road for Historic Shenandoah. After about ten miles, the road came to an end at a white paddock gate, which was closed, and another blue sign, a big one. I had arrived. Historic Shenandoah was open for guided public tours Mondays, Wednesdays, and Fridays from nine to three and all day Saturday. The public was not welcome at any other time, such as now. The closed gate and the six-foot brick wall topped with electrified barbed wire made that quite clear. So did the surveillance camera. There was a phone at the gate. I picked it up and got a recording that told me everything the sign told me, then told me that if I had any other business to please hold on. I held on. The stirring Muzak version of "Vangie, My Love," from Max Steiner's *Oh, Shenandoah* movie score, began tickling my ear.

Until there was a click and a woman's voice: "Help ya?"

"Stewart Hoag. I'm here to see Mavis Glaze."

"Y'all want to drive right on up past the gift shop to the main house. Somebody'll be there to meet ya."

The gate swung open. I drove through. It closed behind me automatically. Evenly spaced ash trees lined the drive on both sides as it snaked up through fenced pasturage for several hundred yards before it arrived at a parking lot. There were picnic tables here and rest rooms and a log-cabin gift shop, where the people who were willing to spend five dollars a head to see the house where *Oh, Shenandoah* was filmed could spend even more on *Oh, Shenandoah* picture postcards, pens, pins, plates, peacock feathers, place mats, paintings, and posters, on *Oh, Shenandoah* cuff links, candlesticks, cookie molds, and cookbooks, on the many different renditions of "Vangie,

My Love," which had been recorded through the years by everyone from Bing to Burl to Billy. Idol, that is. The parking lot was empty now, the gift shop closed. A pair of black custodians were sweeping up. They didn't look up at me as I drove past. The drive worked its way through some dense forest now, climbing as it did. Then the trees opened out in a huge semicircular forecourt of crushed stone, and there it was before me, up on a terraced rise so it could look down on the valley. Shenandoah was a mid-Georgian mansion of red brick built in the 1750s in the Palladian style. In fact it was considered the finest Palladian mansion of the British Colonies still intact. The main house was two stories high with a two-tiered portico and a mansard roof. Smaller, matching two-story dependencies flanked it in the forecourt and were connected to it by covered arcades. Broad stone steps led up to the front door, the one where a sobbing Vangie embraced De Cheverier after his bloody triumph over Edgerton. A short, massively built woman in her sixties stood there waiting for me in a pastel-yellow pantsuit that wouldn't have looked good on Elle Macpherson. On her the effect was that of a banana that had two Bosc pears stuffed inside it. She had curly white hair and Popeye forearms and so many jowls her chin seemed to be melting into her neck. She came down the steps to greet me, her skin flushed with perspiration. She was squinting at me.

"Welcome to Shenandoah, Mistuh Hoag," she said, her voice surprisingly high-pitched. She stuck out her hand. "I'm Fern O'Baugh, the housekeeper, cook, whatever."

We shook hands. She nearly broke mine. A lot of her may have been fat, but her forearms weren't.

"Make it Hoagy."

"As in Carmichael?"

"As in the cheese steak. The one they don't do in Buffalo."

She squinted up at me curiously. Then a big jolly laugh erupted from her and she began to shake all over. "My, my," she gasped. "I do love a man with a sense of humor. Y'know, I've read about you many times, Hoagy, in *People* magazine.

All about your stormy marriage to Miss Merilee Nash, the woman who has everything except love."

"More fiction than fact, I assure you."

"Glad to hear it," she said brightly. "Because, honey, you come across in print like a real beanbag."

"Fern, I think we're going to get along just fine."

She erupted into another laugh. Then she took two steps toward my suitcases, tumbled right over Lulu, and sprawled heavily to the ground with an "Oof." I gave her my hand to help her up. My knees buckled but somehow held.

"My, my, I'm sorry, darlin'," she said, squinting down at Lulu. "I'm blind as Mistuh Magoo without my glasses. Should be wearing 'em, but they're such a bother." They were on a chain around her neck. She put them on and peered down at Lulu, who peered back up at her. "I do declare," Fern cried, astonished. "You're a little puppy dog! I thought you just had to be a big ol' puddy cat. Sure do smell like one."

"She has rather strange eating habits."

"But what's that there blue pancake she's got on her head?"

Lulu snuffled, insulted.

"A present from her mommy," I explained.

"Now, Hoagy, I must have your word she'll stay off the north lawn. She riles the peacocks and Mavis'll shoot her and me both."

"Not to worry."

"Good." Fern snatched up my suitcases as if they were empty and started up the steps with them. She was quite light on her feet for someone so round. "Too bad you didn't get an earlier flight," she said to me over her shoulder. "You just missed her."

I stopped. "What do you mean I missed her? We have an appointment. That's why I'm here."

"I know, but she flew up to Chicago to appear on the Miss Oprah Winfrey television show. Special program on the death of politeness in the modern American family. Last-minute thing. Mave felt sure you'd understand."

"Oh, I do," I said stiffly. "And when will she be back?"

"Sometime after midnight. Give you time to get settled. Now don't you go getting heated up about Mavis. She's the duchess. Anybody wants to get along with her learns that right off, or gets chewed up and spit out. That's the way it is." She glanced at me uneasily from the doorway. "Now I can just *tell* what you're thinking. You're thinking, 'That's the way it *was*, ma'am.' You're thinking, 'She hasn't met *me* yet.'"

"My thoughts don't tend to be that hard-boiled, generally. Runny is more like it."

"Well, you just stick that business in your back pocket and sit on it. No offense, but you don't look nearly tough enough to me. In fact, you don't look tough at all." She checked me over. "Got a nice tall frame on you, but they ain't been feeding you enough up there in New York. How you stay so skinny?"

"Good breeding."

"I'll have to start putting some meat on your bones. I can do French tonight, Italian, you name it."

"Southern will more than do."

"Fine. I'll fry us up a few chickens. It's just you and me. Richard went with Mave, and Mercy has a late class. You allergic to anything I should know about?"

"Only assholes."

She grinned up at me. "We *are* gonna get on fine."

We went inside.

The broad entrance salon extended straight through the center of the old house to the glass doors at the back, which were thrown open to let in the late-afternoon breeze. The north lawn out back was being cut by a gardener on a tractor mower. The aroma of fresh-cut spring grass spiced with wild chives wafted in the doors, finer than any perfume. The salon was paneled in tulip poplar with crown molded-wood cornices. The floor was irregular, wide oak boards. A narrow staircase with a walnut railing led up to the second floor. The furnishings were spare—a tall clock, a Chippendale table, a deacon's bench. Glaze-family oil portraits hung from the walls along with old maps and documents. One was the original royal land patent from the 1700s.

Two pedimented doorways on either side of the entrance salon opened into the four downstairs rooms. Fern led me through them. They were large, airy rooms with twelve-foot ceilings and tall windows overlooking the gardens. The walls were painted eggshell white throughout, with raised plaster molding and colonial-blue chair rails, except for in the library, which was paneled like the entrance salon. All four rooms had stone fireplaces. Again, the furnishing was spare, and Chippendale. The two front rooms were parlors, one formal, the other a sitting room. The sitting room was where John Raymond proposed to Vangie in the movie. The two rear rooms were the dining room and the famous library, where Alma Glaze wrote *Oh, Shenandoah* in longhand seated before the windows at a small writing table. There was a velvet rope in front of the table to keep visitors from touching it and the writing implements arrayed upon it. Her original manuscript lay there in a glass case in the middle of the room. Aside from this, and the obvious presence of electricity, the downstairs was just as it had been more than two hundred years before.

"The main house is only used for formal occasions nowadays," Fern declared. "Mostly, it's here for the tourists. They see the downstairs, the master bedroom upstairs, and Miss Alma's own room from her girlhood, which they used for Vangie's in the movie. The rest of the upstairs is still in need of historical restoration. The Glaze family was still living up there until the 1920s, when they remodeled the east wing and moved out there. That's where they live now. Keep their privacy that way. We lead visitors from here over to the old kitchen wing, and then the historic service yard and then on out. C'mon," she commanded, smacking me in the shoulder with the back of her hand. "I'll give ya the quick tour."

Lulu and I followed her through a narrow door off the

dining room and down a short wooden stairway to a damp, cellar passageway.

"They'd bring the food from the kitchen along here to the table," she explained, puffing as we made our way down the long, dark corridor, passing the wine cellar and then the root cellar. "Quite a trek, but they always had the kitchens a distance away from the main house in the old days, on account of the heat and danger of fire."

The sunken corridor eventually came up outside the old kitchen. A low railing kept people from going inside. The kitchen ceiling was very low and soot-blackened. There was a vast open hearth with a baking oven and a cast-iron crane with heavy cast-iron pots hanging from it. A pine table sat in the middle of the room heaped with antique kitchen implements. Dried herbs hung from pegs. The floor was dirt.

"Whole lot of sweaty, hard work," observed Fern. "But believe me, the food come outta here tasted a sight better than what you get outta one of those microwaves. The cooks slept upstairs. Kitchen fire heated the whole place." She smacked my shoulder again. "C'mon."

I followed her, rubbing my shoulder. I'd have a welt there by morning. Outside, eight or ten rough, old, wooden outbuildings were clustered around a big kitchen garden. A gaunt old man in baggy, dark-green work clothes and a John Deere cap was slowly turning over the garden soil with a spading fork.

Fern pointed to the buildings. "That was the toolhouse, cobbler's shop, counting house, smokehouse, joinery, blacksmith . . . They didn't have no shopping mall to run down to in those days. Had to do everything themselves on a plantation this size. Be resourceful. That's what's wrong with people today—don't have to use our brains anymore. Nothing but a mess of jelly up there now."

"That would explain prime-time television."

She let out her big, hearty laugh. "Want y'all to come meet Roy. He's caretaker, head gardener."

"It must take a big staff to run this place," I said as we started over to the old man with the fork.

"All of it's day help from Staunton," she replied. "Custodians, housekeepers, gardeners, tour guides—everybody except for me and Roy. He has an apartment over the garage. Does his own cooking. Is good for maybe three, four words a year. Roy? Say hello to Hoagy. He'll be living here awhile. The short one's Lulu."

Roy was close to eighty, and mostly bone and gristle and leather. His face and neck were deeply tanned and creased, his big hands scarred and knuckly. He had a wad of tobacco in one cheek.

"Glad to meet you, Roy," I said, sticking out my hand.

He gave me a brief glance. His eyes were deep set and pale blue and gave away about as much as the ones you see on a sea bass under a blanket of shaved ice at the fish market. He spat some tobacco juice in the general direction of my kid-leather ankle boots, the ones I'd had made for me in London at Maxwell's. Then he went back to his forking. My hand he ignored.

Lulu growled at him from beside me.

We chose not to linger.

"Don't mind Roy," advised Fern as we started back to the main house. "At first, I thought he was rude. Then I decided he was slow. He ain't neither. He just hasn't got anything to say. Been working here forever, and I never have figured out why, since he's not exactly what you'd call competent. Of course, one thing you're gonna discover is things don't always make sense around here."

"Sounds not dissimilar to everywhere else."

We took the covered brick arcade back to the old house. Six of the Shenandoah peacocks were out on the lawn now, strutting and preening. One of them honked at us, a flat, derisive Bronx cheer of a honk.

"That's Floyd," declared Fern. "He's the biggest."

Not that any of them were exactly small. They were big as tom turkeys. Their electric-blue necks were nearly three feet long, and their train of tail feathers was twice that. They were aware of us watching them. They watched us back. They didn't look very friendly. One of them spread his fan of plumage for us to see. It was not unimpressive.

"That's Wally. He's all ham."

I felt something at my feet. Lulu was crouched between my legs, trembling.

Fern looked down at her and laughed. "I guess we don't have to worry about her at that."

The great lawn sloped downward from the back of the house. A circular footpath ringed it, the border beds planted with tulips and daffodils. Beyond were orchards, a pond and gazebo, the family cemetery, where Alma Glaze was buried. For a backdrop there were the Alleghenies. The sun was setting over them.

"If you're going to live in a museum," I observed, "this isn't a terrible one."

"Mavis, she feels America has a right to see Shenandoah," Fern said with more than a trace of pride. "After all, it's a national treasure. Family doesn't make a nickel off the proceeds, y'know. All goes to the Society for the Preservation of Virginia Antiquities, of which Mavis happens to be president."

"Been here long, Fern?"

"Thirty-five years," she replied. "Longer, if you figure in the movie. I was in it, y'know. What's wrong, honey? Don't I look like your idea of a movie star?" She laughed hugely. It had been a long time since I'd met anyone who laughed so easily and often. "Fact is, damned near everybody in town was in it, with all them crowd and battle scenes. But me, I was picked out of fifteen other girls in the tenth-grade class to play Vangie's little sister, Lavinia. Had me one whole line of dialogue, too: 'Why, thank you, Mistuh Randolph,'" she declared with a dainty curtsy. "Miss Laurel Barrett, she was a fine actress and lady, and very, very kind to me. I sure felt sorry she had so much misery in her life. . . ." She looked up at me very seriously for a moment as if she wanted to tell me something. But then she changed her mind and went and got my suitcases.

There was less grandeur in the east wing. The ceilings were lower, the floors carpeted, the decor 1950s English country estate, complete with chintz-covered furniture and flowery wallpaper. Lots of peacock art, too. Framed peacock watercolors. Vases of peacock-feather arrangements. Peacock needlepoint pillows. You'd be surprised just how little it takes to make a really powerful peacock statement. A short hallway led to the kitchen, which was big and modern and cluttered. A round oak table piled with papers sat in the middle of it. Fern's bedroom and a suite of offices were off the kitchen.

"This here's kind of the nerve center of the estate," Fern explained. "Though I reckon you'll find wherever Mavis happens to be at the moment is the nerve center." She laughed. "She and Charlotte do their business here. Charlotte is her assistant. Nice quiet girl. Handles her correspondence, her schedule, and so forth. She's up in Chicago with Mave and Richard right now."

We went out the kitchen door to an L-shaped brick courtyard that was the modern service yard. There was a three-car garage, a garden shed, a workshop. The tractor mower was parked here next to a pair of battered pickups. At the far end of the courtyard was a row of low, attached, wood-framed cottages that looked quite old.

"Guest rooms," Fern informed me as we headed toward them.

"Converted carriage houses?" I asked.

"Slaves' quarters," she replied matter-of-factly.

"Perfect."

Mine had a small sitting room that faced onto the courtyard. There was a pine student's desk, matching easy chair and love seat, and a fireplace. Lulu promptly tested the easy chair for fit. It passed.

"I put in that little fridge you asked for," Fern pointed out. It was over next to the desk. "Stocked it with milk, imported mineral water, and anchovies, like you wanted. What y'all do with cold anchovies anyway?"

"You don't want to know."

A spiral staircase led up to the bath and sleeping loft. The bed had a skylight and ceiling fan over it, and a fine old quilt on it.

"We'll be more than comfortable here," I assured her.

"Y'all need anything, just let me know," she said. "I'll be in the kitchen. Come on in and eat when you're ready."

The place was a bit stuffy. I left the screen door open while I got settled. Lulu busily cased the place, large black nose to the floor. She wasn't crazy about the spiral staircase. The steps just weren't made for someone with her body and her nonlegs. She had to descend sort of sideways, with a *hop-thump-thump, hop-thump-thump.* She sounded like a bowling ball going down. Before I did anything else I opened up a tin of chilled anchovies and wrapped one tightly around one of her allergy pills. She devoured this with a single chomp. She prefers them chilled—the oil clings to them better. Then I unpacked her bowl and spooned a can of her Nine Lives mackerel for cats and very weird dogs into it and set it by the front door. While she dove in, I opened the bottle of aged Macallan single malt I'd thoughtfully brought along, and I poured two fingers in a water glass. I sipped it as I unpacked my faithful late-fifties-vintage, solid-steel Olympia manual portable, my electric coffeemaker, my tape player, my tapes. I'd brought Erroll Garner with me. Something had told me it was going to be his kind of project. Then I went upstairs and hung up my clothes and changed into a polo sweater of black cashmere and a pair of old khakis that were soft as flannel.

Lulu was waiting for me at the bottom of the staircase with a mournful expression on her face, mournful even for her. When I asked her what her problem was, she whimpered and glanced over in the direction of her supper dish, greatly distraught.

A kitten was finishing her mackerel.

"Well, what do you expect me to do about it?" I demanded. "You're the huntress, not me. Defend your turf."

She did try. She growled at the kitten. Even bared her teeth, a sight known to throw sheer terror into the hearts of more than a few baby squirrels. The kitten just ignored her—it was pretty pathetic—while it licked the mackerel bowl clean.

It was maybe four months old and on the scrawny side. Its ears stuck straight up and made it look a little like a bat. Gray mostly, with white belly and paws and a gray-and-black-striped tail. Its eyes were a yellowish green. I suppose it was cute, if you happen to care for cats. I don't. I've never understood the strange power they hold over people. All they ever do is sleep or hide behind the furniture. People who live in apartments even let them shit in the house.

There weren't supposed to be any cats around Shenandoah. I wondered whom it belonged to.

Its meal completed, it arched its back and leisurely came over to me and attempted familiarity. Rubbed against my leg. Bumped my ankle with its head. Made small motorboat noises. This business got Lulu growling again. I reached down and picked the damned thing up and showed her—it was a her —the screen door. I latched it behind her. I'd have to remember to keep it latched in the future, or Lulu would starve.

This kitten didn't know how to take a hint. She tried to push the screen door open again. When she failed, she started yowling out there in the growing dark. I had to shoo her off. She darted under one of the pickups, her eyes glowing.

I poured myself another Macallan. I was unpacking my briefcase when someone tapped at the screen door. I went over to discover a midget human life-form, type male, standing out there looking warily up at me. I opened the door. He was maybe eight years old, with a mess of dirty-blond hair and freckles and narrow shoulders. He wore a blue sweatshirt cut off at the elbows, soiled khakis, and high-topped sneakers.

"Thorry to bother ya, mithter," he said. He was missing a couple of front teeth. "Can I . . ." He looked nervously over his shoulder at the house, then turned back to me. "Can you keep a theecret?" he whispered urgently.

"I doubt it," I replied. I ought to tell you right off—I like cats a lot more than I like kids. Kids I rate dead even with large, spiny reptiles. "What kind of secret?"

He hesitated, swallowed. "Y'all theen Thaydie?" he asked gravely.

I frowned. "Thaydie?"

"Not Thaydie," he said, shaking his head. *"Thaydie."*

"Sadie."

"Have ya?"

"That all depends," I said, tugging at my ear. "Is she small and furry? Has a tail?"

He nodded eagerly.

"Under that pickup over there."

He scampered over to the truck, knelt, and talked her out softly. Then he carried her back to me, hugging her tightly to his small chest. "Thankth, mithter. Thankth a whole lot."

"No problem. I'm a big believer in happy endings."

He glanced inside at my sitting room through the screen door. "Y'all have a *dog*? Wow!" Thrilled, he barged inside, handed me Sadie, and bounded over to Lulu.

"Sure thing," I muttered. "Come right on in."

"What'th her name?"

"Lulu."

"Hey, Lulu." He fell to his knees and began stroking her.

She suffered this quietly. She isn't crazy about kids herself. Most of them tend to tug on her ears and call her Dumbo. Sadie, meanwhile, began wriggling in my arms. When I tightened my hold on her, she bit my thumb. Her teeth were razor sharp. Wincing, I put her down on the sofa.

"I thought cats weren't allowed here," I said as she made herself at home.

"She's *mine*!" he cried, suddenly terrified.

"Okay, okay. She's yours."

He relaxed. "She'th a thtray. I found her. Been hidin' her,

feedin' her from my plate. Don't tell the witch, okay? She'll take her off to the pound to get murdered, for sure."

"The witch?"

"That ol' Fern."

"Seems pretty nice to me."

"I *hate* her."

"I'm Hoagy by the way."

"I'm Gordie. Live in the cottage next to ya, Mithter Hoagy."

"Make it plain Hoagy, seeing as how we're neighbors."

He gave Lulu a final pat and jumped to his feet. "Wanna play catch? I can throw a thpitter."

"Darn. I didn't think to bring my mitt down with me."

"Wanna watch a movie? Got me a tape with my favorite actor in it."

Before I could reply, someone outside called out his name. It was Fern.

"Oh, no!" he gasped, shoving Sadie at me. "Hide her, quick! She'll *kill* her!"

"Gordie?" called Fern from my doorway. "You in here?" She put her glasses on and saw he was and came in after him.

I hid Sadie under my sweater, wondering just how I'd gotten myself into this.

"Gordie, you're supposed to be taking yourself a bath," Fern barked, every inch the drill sergeant. "You ain't supposed to be bothering Hoagy here."

"He wasn't," I assured her.

Gordie said nothing. Just stood there stiffly.

She pointed a finger at him. "Bathe yourself, Gordie. Or I'll be in to do it for ya, hear me?"

He still said nothing. His manner had changed noticeably in her presence. He'd withdrawn into himself. His face was now a mask, betraying nothing.

Exasperated, she grabbed him by the shoulders and shook him. "You hear me!"

"Yeth'm," he finally said softly and obediently.

"That's better. C'mon, Hoagy." *Thwack.* "Dinner's waiting."

"I'm right behind you."

Gordie relaxed as soon as she left. I gave him Sadie back. "Thankth, Hoagy," he said. *"You* take baths?"

"Frequently."

He shrugged, disappointed. "Well, 'night."

"Good night, Gordie. Who is your favorite movie star, anyway—Arnold Schwarzenegger?"

"Naw. *McQueen.*"

"That makes two of us," I said.

"Really?" he cried.

I nodded approvingly. "You're okay, Gordie. You're definitely okay. Too bad you're a kid."

The big round kitchen table was heaped with a platter of fried chicken, bowls of coleslaw, macaroni salad, mashed potatoes, black-eyed peas, stewed tomatoes, a basket of corn bread.

Fern was filling two chilled mugs with beer. She squinted at me blindly when I came in. "That you, Hoagy?"

"Looks good," I said, partly to identify myself, and partly because it did.

"Well, sit and get at it, honey. Just save a little room. I made an apple pie this morning, and there's vanilla ice cream. We make our own. Vanilla, strawberry . . ."

"Licorice?" I asked, daring to hope. It's my favorite, and damned hard to find.

"Licorice? Why would anyone want to eat that?"

"I can't imagine."

I sat and got at it. We both did. The chicken was crisp and moist, the salads homemade, the corn bread fresh baked and laced with hunks of bacon. It wasn't a common meal. I told her so between bites.

"Got a husband, Fern?"

"That a proposal?" She erupted in her big jolly laugh. "Naw. Never have."

"Gordie. Who is he?"

"He's the VADD poster boy," she replied. "Picture's plastered up all over the state. Them public service posters for Virginians Against Drunk Driving. Poor thing's parents were killed by one a few months ago. Local working people. Gordie had no other living family, so Mavis decided to adopt him. She feels very strongly about drunk drivers. They've never known for sure, but it's generally believed her own mom, Alma, was run over by one. Mavis helped start VADD. The proceeds from the golden-anniversary celebration are going toward it."

"She sounds mighty into her causes."

"Mavis don't know how to do things halfway. And she's got a darned good heart, too, deep down inside. People around here thought it mighty kind of her to take Gordie in as her own. I kinda like having him around to fuss over, you want to know the truth. I'm just sorry there isn't more for him to do around here. No other kids to play with. He gets bored. Real quiet, too. Can't hardly get a word out of him."

"Could have fooled me."

"He talked to you?" she asked, surprised. "Wonder how come."

"Just my good fortune, I guess."

She got us a couple of fresh beers from the fridge and filled our mugs.

"If he's a member of the family," I said, "how come he's living out there in a guest cottage?"

"No room for him in here," Fern replied, cleaning her plate. "Mavis has got her gymnasium in the spare bedroom upstairs. She works out like a demon. I offered to give up my room down here for him. She wouldn't hear of it. But, hey, he bothers you, let me know. I'll move him somewheres else." She drank deeply from her mug, then she sat back with a contented sigh. "So it's not true what they say about you in all them articles?"

"What do they say?"

She narrowed her eyes at me shrewdly. "That you solve murders."

"Oh, that. Not true. I attract them. A flaw of some kind in my character. I wish I knew what." I had some of my beer. "Why do you ask?"

Fern took a deep breath and plunged ahead. "Cause I think somebody was murdered here. Sterling Sloan, the star of *Oh, Shenandoah*. I think he got himself murdered here fifty years ago next month, and that whoever did it to him got away with it."

Chapter Three

"Sterling Sloan," I pointed out, "died of a ruptured aneurysm in his brain."

Fern puffed out her cheeks. "That's what they *said*, to sweep the whole mess under the rug. But I know otherwise."

"What do you know?"

"I know I was there on that set," she said, leaning forward anxiously. "I know I saw something. Something I've never dared tell another living soul about."

"Why tell me?"

"Because I think I can trust you. And because it has to come out now. Don't you see?"

I tugged at my ear. "I'm afraid I don't."

"Other people know what really happened. She knew. Miss Laurel knew. Why do you think she went so nuts?"

"She was an actress. Kind of goes with the territory."

Fern shook her head. "The others, they'll be coming here for the fiftieth anniversary. Aren't many of them left. Most of 'em are gone now, the secret buried with them. Don't you see,

Hoagy? It's now or never. This is the last chance to see the plain truth come out."

"The truth is anything but plain," I said. "It's a very confusing business, and the closer you get to it, the more confusing it gets."

"But you'll help me, won't you?"

I hesitated. "Well . . ."

"Don't say you aren't intrigued," she said, grinning. "I can tell you are by the way you look."

"And how do I look?"

"Profound. Disillusioned. Bored."

"I always look this way. That breeding thing again."

"Look here," declared Fern. "I ain't no crank from down on the farm thinks she seen flying saucers shaped like cigars. I ain't crazy."

"I didn't say you were, Fern. It's just that—"

A car pulled up outside in the courtyard. Fern stiffened, raised her index finger to her lips. The engine shut off. The car door opened, closed. There were footsteps. Then the kitchen door opened and in walked a tall young blonde clutching a pile of books. She was pretty, in a neat, correct, Laura Ashley flowered-print-dress sort of way, complete with lace collar and puffed sleeves. She would never exactly be willowy. She was a bit sturdy through the legs and hips. But there was a healthy pink glow to her cheeks, a youthful brightness to her blue eyes, a clean lustrousness to her hair. And there was what is, for me, the most attractive quality any woman can possess—she knew who she was. She was Mercy Glaze, the girl who would inherit Shenandoah.

"Say hello to Stewart Hoag, Mercy," said Fern as she dished up our pie. "Goes by Hoagy."

Mercy looked me over briefly and offered me her hand. "Pleased to meet you," she said, manner forthright, grip firm. No Southern coquette this.

"Likewise," I said.

Mercy dropped her books and purse on the counter,

grabbed a leftover drumstick from the chicken platter, and started to bite into it.

"Get yourself a plate and napkin and sit down," commanded Fern. "You're a lady, not a field hand."

"Tastes better this way," Mercy insisted, attacking it happily.

"Mavis would kill you if she saw you," Fern said.

"So don't tell her," Mercy said.

Fern promptly whipped a Polaroid camera from a drawer and aimed it at her.

Mercy froze, genuinely alarmed. "You wouldn't."

"I *would*," Fern vowed.

Mercy rolled her eyes and flounced over to the cupboard, every inch a suffering teenager now. She got a plate and napkin and sat across the table from me. "You're the writer who's going to get along with Mother?"

"That's the idea. Any advice?"

"Yes," she replied, nibbling at the chicken leg. "Place your foot firmly on her neck and keep it there."

"That'll work?" I asked.

"I honestly couldn't say," she replied. "But it sure would be fun to see someone try it."

"Polk Four phoned for you a while ago, honey," Fern told her, setting my pie and ice cream before me. For my benefit she added, "Polk's her fiancé."

"He is not," Mercy said petulantly. "He just thinks he is."

"Polk Four?" I inquired, tasting my dessert. I was not disappointed.

"Polk LaFoon the Fourth," Fern explained. "He's Augusta County sheriff like Polk Three and Polk Two before him. Handsome as Mistuh Bob Stack in his uniform. And he's smart, too. Got his law degree from Duke. Gonna be our attorney general someday. Maybe even governor"—she winked at me—"if he marries right."

"I swear, Fern," declared Mercy. "You are getting absolutely senile, the things come out of your mouth." She turned to me, frowning. "You're not the same Stewart Hoag who wrote *Our Family Enterprise,* are you?"

"I am."

She looked a bit awestruck now, poor child. "I-I read you in modern lit."

"You don't say. Large class?"

"I guess there were about eighteen of us. Why?"

"Just calculating my royalties."

"You're a real distinguished American author," she pointed out.

"Careful. My head swells easily."

"To tell you the truth," she confessed, "I didn't realize you were still alive."

"That's more like it, though you could bring me back down a little easier in the future."

She giggled. Fern busied herself at the sink, noisily.

"So you do this sort of work, too?" Mercy asked, fascinated.

"Yes. I'm kind of the Bo Jackson of publishing."

"But isn't this, well, beneath you?"

"Nothing is beneath me," I replied, "with the possible exception of screenwriting."

"I guess I don't understand why you bother."

"Just finicky, really. I won't eat out of garbage cans."

"Oh." Chastened, she poured herself coffee. "You must think I'm awfully sheltered and insensitive and stupid."

I gave her a frisky once-over. "That's not what I'm thinking at all."

She blushed and lunged for her books. "Well, I've got a paper due tomorrow," she said, starting for the stairs with her coffee. "Know anything about Spenser's *Faerie Queen?*"

"Yes. Understanding it won't come in handy later in life."

"That's not what this little girl needs to hear," Fern cautioned.

Mercy sighed. "I'm not a little girl, Fern. I'm twenty-one years old."

"Don't remind me," said Fern. "I was a middle-aged woman when you was born. I hate to think what that makes me now."

"Enjoy your Spenser," I said.

She smiled and said it was nice meeting me. Then she went off to her room.

"Seems like a nice girl," I observed.

"Keep your hands off or Mavis'll cut 'em off," Fern warned. "With a hatchet."

"Not to worry, Fern. I'm not looking these days."

"Look all you want. Just don't touch."

I brought my dessert plate to her at the sink. "Thanks for the best meal I've had in a long time."

"You don't believe me about Sterling Sloan, do you?" she demanded, peering up at me. "You think I'm some crazy old lady."

"That's not the case at all, Fern," I replied tactfully. "I'm flattered that you confided in me. I'm just not your man. I came through the gate in a Chevy Nova, not on the back of a white horse. You need someone with a square jaw and fists of stone and a resting pulse rate of fifty-six. You need a hero."

"I reckon so," she said, crestfallen. "I just don't know who . . . I mean, you were my best hope."

I sighed inwardly. One hundred percent marshmallow, through and through. "I'll sleep on it. How's that?"

She brightened considerably. "That's more like it!" *Thwack.* "Only don't sleep too late. You got an audience with Mavis at nine o'clock sharp in the old library. She has fits if people are even a minute late."

"I thought the old house was only used for formal occasions."

"Believe me, honey, meeting Mavis Glaze *is* one."

Her phone rang several times before she finally picked it up. My heart began to pound at once when she did. It always does when I hear that feathery, dizzy-sounding, teenaged-girl's voice that belongs to her and no one else.

"Did I wake you?" I asked.

"No, I'm sitting up with Elliot."

"Something serious?"

"I don't know, darling. He simply wouldn't touch his food all day."

"Maybe he just wasn't hungry, Merilee."

"Hoagy, pigs are *always* hungry. No, I'm afraid Elliot's not himself, the poor dear."

She had named him after her first agent. And people say there's no sentiment in show business.

"Call me old-fashioned, Merilee, but I still don't believe in giving a name to someone you intend to eat."

"Mr. Hoagy! How could you be such a-a *barbarian*!"

"Merilee . . ."

"Elliot happens to be a member of this household, sir! And he's certainly more of a gentleman than you'll ever be."

"Merilee . . ."

"What!"

"Hello."

"Hello yourself. Did you find out yet?"

"Find out what?"

"Who Vangie marries at the end of *Oh, Shenandoah,* silly."

"Not yet. Do you really care?"

"Are you serious? I've only read that book eight times and wept uncontrollably every single time. And the *movie,* merciful heavens . . . Now listen, Hoagy, when you do find out, don't tell me who it is. I'm serious. I'm such a blabber-mouth I'll spread it all over town and get you in deep doo-doo."

"Okay," I said.

Stunned silence. "What did you say?" she demanded.

"I said okay."

"*Mister* Hoagy!"

"Just agreeing with you, Merilee."

"I'm not so sure we can be friends anymore."

"Is that what we are?"

"How's sweetness?" she asked, neatly slipping my jab.

Lulu whimpered from next to me on the bed. She always knows when her mommy is on the phone. Don't ask me how.

"Her usual obnoxious self. Have you called the vet about Elliot?"

"Not yet. I don't want to be one of those overprotective city slickers who they all hoot at. I will if he isn't better in a day or two."

"Well, look on the bright side."

"Which is . . . ?"

"He could stand to take off a few hundred pounds."

"Very funny."

"What do you remember hearing about the filming of *Oh, Shenandoah*?"

Merilee is a big fan of show-biz gossip, as long as it isn't to do with her, of course. She often befriends elderly fellow cast members and eagerly soaks up their reminiscences of Hollywood's golden age.

"Way over budget," she replied. "Tons of pissy fits, bad weather, last-minute rewrites. First two directors got fired by Goldwyn in preproduction before Wyler finally took it over . . . Or are you more interested in who was doing the big, bad naughty with who?"

"I've missed your quaint little expressions."

"It seems to me," she recalled, "it was one of those shoots where everyone was hopping into the feathers with everyone else. Of course, that always happens on location, particularly with a love story."

"Why is that?"

"We can't tell the difference between real and make-believe, darling. That's what makes us actors."

"Which am I?"

"I like to think of you as a bit of both."

"Why, Merilee, that's the second-nicest thing you've ever said to me."

"What was the nicest?"

" 'You're not the sort of man who I can see wearing anything polyester.' "

"As I recall," she said, "neither of us was wearing anything, period, at the time."

"Merilee Nash! You've been getting seriously ribald since you started hanging around with farm animals."

"So that explains it."

"Anything about Sterling Sloan?"

"Well, he died."

"I know that. I was wondering if there was any chance it didn't happen the way they say it did."

She was silent a moment. "Oh, no, Hoagy . . . You're not getting into something weird again, are you?"

"No chance. Housekeeper here just has some crazy idea."

"I certainly don't remember hearing anything." She mulled it over. "I'm skeptical, frankly. *Oh, Shenandoah* has commanded so much attention through the years. If there'd been even a hint of scandal about Sloan, the sleaze-biographers would have been all over it by now."

"That's kind of what I was thinking."

"Of course, I could ask around for you. Some of the old-timers might remember if there was scuttlebutt. Want me to?"

"If you don't mind."

"Not at all. It'll give me an excuse to call them. Comfy down there?"

"Aside from a lousy set of rental wheels."

"Possibly you're a bit spoiled in that department."

"Possibly that's not the only department I'm spoiled in."

We were both silent a moment.

"I'd better get back to Elliot," she said softly. "Hoagy?"

"Yes, Merilee?"

"What was her name?"

"Whose name?"

"The girl you met tonight."

"I . . . what makes you think she was a girl and not a woman?"

"A woman can tell."

"Why, Merilee, if I didn't know you better, I'd swear you were jealous."

"I'd swear I was, too."

"You never have been before."

"I wasn't forty before," she declared, sighing grandly. "And more important, neither were you. Sleep tight, darling." And then she hung up.

I undressed and climbed into bed. I was working my way through a collection of James Thurber stories, which is something I do every couple of years to remind myself what good writing is. I had just gotten settled in when I heard a car pull up in the courtyard outside. I turned out my bedside lamp and pulled back the curtain.

A big Mercedes 560 SEL sedan was idling out there in the moonlight with its lights on.

Two women got out, one tall, almost regal, the other short and thin. The driver pulled the Mercedes into the garage while the two women spoke briefly. Then the tall one went in the kitchen door of the east wing, closing it behind her. The other woman got into a red Pontiac LeMans that was parked there and started it up. The Mercedes's lights went off in the garage. A man got out and closed the garage door and went over to the LeMans. He was stocky, with a heavy torso and short legs. He said something to the woman in the car, gestured for her to roll her window down. Instead she began easing the car out of the courtyard toward the driveway. He was insistent—ran out in front of her, waved his arms for her to stop. She wouldn't. In fact, she floored it and made right for him. She wasn't kidding around, either. He had to dive out of the way or she'd have run him over as she sped on down the drive. He landed heavily and lay there a moment. Slowly, he got to his feet and brushed himself off. He stood there watching the driveway for a long moment before he went in the house.

I turned over and went to sleep, Lulu comfortably ensconced in her favorite position. I didn't stay asleep long. She woke me at three, pacing the bedroom floor, whimpering like she had on the plane. I told her to shut up and come back to bed. She wanted me to let her out. These things happen. I did, after reminding her to stay away from the peacocks. Then I went back upstairs to sleep.

I dreamt I was being smothered by peacock feathers.

A steady tapping at the cottage's front door woke me. Grandfather's Rolex said it was seven-thirty. I padded downstairs and opened it. A covered breakfast tray was waiting there for me on the doorstep. So was Sadie, my new friend, who sat poised on her haunches a foot away, staring at it intently. Lulu was stretched out a few feet from her, staring at her staring at it. Lulu and the tray came inside with me. Sadie did not.

There was a copy of that morning's *Staunton Daily News Leader* to go with my scrambled eggs, country ham, grits, toast, juice, and coffee. The food was excellent. So was the news. Crime in Augusta County was down 11 percent over the past three months, according to Sheriff Polk LaFoon the Fourth. And veteran Hollywood actor Rex Ransom was definitely planning to attend the *Oh, Shenandoah* fiftieth-anniversary gala. Already my day was made. When I finished eating, I climbed into a hot tub and lolled there. I was still there at nine, when I heard someone pounding on my front door, and at nine-fifteen, when someone pounded on it again, louder. When I got out, I stropped grandfather's pearl-handled straight edge and shaved and doused myself with Floris. I dressed in my charcoal silk-and-wool tickweave suit with calfskin braces, a white Turnbull and Asser broadcloth shirt, lavender-and-yellow bow tie, and my brown-and-white spectator balmorals. I emerged with my breakfast tray a few minutes before ten. That damned cat was still there on my doorstep. Gordie was sitting on the ground nearby tossing a ball against a wall and catching it in his mitt on the comeback. The red LeMans from the night before was parked by the kitchen door.

"Mornin', Hoagy," Gordie said glumly.

"Something wrong?"

"Thaydie's awful hungry," he replied. "Jutht wish I had a little milk to give her . . . I mean, she'll *thtarve.*" His lower lip began to quiver.

I sighed. This was turning into a miserable job. Truly miserable. "I have some milk in my fridge," I said grudgingly.

His face lit up. "Really?"

I went back inside and filled my empty coffee cup with milk and put it out for her. She lapped it up hungrily.

"Gee, thankth, Hoagy," Gordie exclaimed.

"No problem."

"Wanna play catch?"

"Don't you have school or something?"

"I'm on thpring break. Throw me one? Jutht one? Huh?"

"All right, one fly ball. Go deep."

He tossed me the ball and dashed across the courtyard toward the lawn. It was an old hardball, worn and frayed. The sight of it in my hand triggered a memory. Of another worn, frayed hardball, another little boy, another tall, distant man. A powerful and most unexpected wave of nostalgia crashed over me. Nostalgia isn't generally my style. Especially for that time and that tall, distant man.

Gordie was waiting for me, pounding his mitt. I waved him deeper. Then I wound up and aired out the old javelin shoulder. I sent the ball high in the air, way over his head. The little guy went after it. He was quick. He was there waiting for it when it came down, mitt held high.

"Wow," he hollered, trotting back to me with it, "I ain't never theen anyone throw a ball tho far in my whole life!"

"It's all in the mechanics," I said, wondering just when the pain would stop shooting through my shoulder. "Not a terrible grab, by the way."

"Thankth. Throw me another?"

"Later. Maybe."

Inside, Fern was doing the breakfast dishes. Someone was typing in the adjoining office.

She squinted at me disapprovingly when I handed her my tray. "Honey, Mave's been waiting over there for you nearly one hour. I knocked on your door twice. You deaf or you just got a death wish?"

"None of the above."

She shook her head sadly. "Been nice knowing you."

"Care to place a wager on that?"

"What kind of wager?" she asked, grinning at me.

"You have to make me licorice ice cream."

"And if I win? Because I don't plan to lose. And honey, I sure don't eat nothing gray."

"Ten bucks?"

We shook on it. Then I headed for the old house to meet Mavis Glaze.

Chapter Four

S he was smiling.

Mavis Glaze always smiled. Her face was frozen that way. It happens sometimes when you have one lift too many. The skin was drawn across her cheekbones tight as Saran Wrap pulled over a bowl of leftover fruit salad. There was, however, no smile in the hard blue eyes that stared out at me from behind the writing table where her mother had created *Oh, Shenandoah*. The eyes were cold steel. She sat stiffly, her hands folded tightly before her on the desk, knuckles white. Every muscle in her tall, lean body seemed taut. You could have plucked an F-sharp off the cords in her neck. The lady wouldn't bend in the wind—she'd snap. Even her copper-colored hair was drawn into a tight, *tight* bun. She had the same long blade of nose and cleft chin her brothers had. On them it looked better. She was not a pretty woman, though she was, for sixty, a handsome one. She was elegantly dressed in a double-breasted pantsuit of cream-colored raw silk with a white silk blouse. Her nails were painted salmon, as was her mouth. She wore no other makeup.

She glanced down at her wristwatch, then back up at me. "You are precisely one hour late, Mr. Hoag." She enunciated every syllable as if she were speaking to a small, slightly deaf native boy. "My brothers led me to believe that you were a professional. Sadly, they were mistaken. Your behavior is anything but professional. It is unacceptable."

"That makes us even."

She glared down her nose at me. "I seriously doubt that," she said witheringly.

"We had an appointment yesterday afternoon," I said. "You didn't keep it. You didn't have the courtesy to reschedule it or to contact me so I could make other arrangements. You just kept me hanging around here, wasting my time. You're lucky I'm here at all. And if you don't start talking to me like your collaborator instead of the guy who pumps out your septic tank, I won't be."

Her blue eyes widened slightly. Otherwise she didn't react. Until she abruptly grabbed one of the tulips out of the vase on the desk and snapped its stem in half. "Get out, Mr. Hoag. Get off my property at once. If I find you anywhere near Shenandoah in one hour, I shall call the sheriff and have you arrested."

"You'd better call your brothers, too, while you're at it. They'll have to break it to your publisher that we didn't hit it off. I'm afraid it won't go down too well, since I was kind of your last shot."

"Last shot?" She bristled. "Whatever do you mean?"

"You're the laughingstock of the entire publishing industry, didn't you know? You're blowing the biggest sequel in history, and dragging your publishing house down with you. They're very unhappy. And they're going to be even more unhappy about this. But that's your business, not mine. Nice meeting you, Mavis. Actually, it wasn't, but it's important to be gracious to one's hostess. I learned that from your show."

I started for the door, not particularly fast. She let me get all the way to the knob before she finally said, "Perhaps . . . perhaps we got off on the wrong foot. I-I apologize about yesterday. I assure you it won't happen again. Sit down. Please."

I sat down, round one mine.

She treated me to her frozen smile. It was starting to bring to mind Nicholson in *Batman*. "People have always misunderstood me," she stated. "I've never cared about which fork they used for their salad. Simple, human consideration is what matters to me. Respect for your neighbor. Saying 'please' and 'thank you' and 'excuse me.' No one does anymore. It's all 'Me first' now. They cut each other off on the highway. They give each other the finger. They urinate in the street. They gather in sports arenas for the express purpose of chanting obscenities at visiting players."

"In New York we chant them at the home team as well. We like to think of everyone as the enemy."

The blue eyes flicked over me suspiciously. "I understand you brought some form of animal with you."

"Using the term loosely."

"My brothers were extremely vague about it. It's not vicious or something, is it?"

"I'll have to tell her that one—she can use a good laugh."

Mavis pursed her lips and frowned at me. "You've no notebook? No tape recorder?"

"Not to worry. If anything memorable is said, I'll remember it. Chances are I'll have said it."

Her eyes flashed at me. "Are you always this unpleasant, Mr. Hoag?"

"Generally. And it's Hoagy."

"Well, I am not impressed by your attitude, Hoagy," she said imperially.

I tugged at my ear. "My mother used to say that. Still does, come to think of it."

"Are you close to your parents?"

"I make sure I call them at least once every decade."

She stood up and moved over to the window and looked outside at the gardens. The peacocks were strutting around near one of the tulip borders. She watched them. "You may as well know this about me from the start—I never learned how to suffer weak willies or fools or mediocrity gladly. Or how to hold my tongue. I stand up for what I believe in, and what I believe in is doing one's best and tolerating nothing less. If I were a man, I'd be held in high esteem. Since I'm a woman, I'm called a bitch." She turned away from the window and faced me. "I respect talent. From what everyone says, you have it. Lord knows you don't get by on your charm. A lot of men can't work for a strong woman. Can you?"

"I'm here, am I not?"

She nodded, satisfied, and went back to the desk and sat down behind it. "James Madison was married in this room in 1794 to Dolly Payne Todd. This was a parlor in those days. They were all here to drink Madeira wine and dance the minuet and pay their respects to the Glazes. Washington, Jefferson, Monroe. My family's history is Virginia's history. The Glazes settled this valley, sat on the House of Burgesses, served in the Continental Congress. And this house is history, as well. John Ariss, the most important architect of the Virginia Palladian style, designed and built it in 1756. Jefferson himself designed the portico addition in 1767 to improve the upstairs ventilation."

"You can document that?"

She stiffened. "Pardon me?"

"I understood that virtually no documentation of Jefferson's designs existed from prior to 1770. They were all obliterated when Shadwell, his birthplace in Albemarle County, burned to the ground."

"Ah." She raised her chin at me. "I assure you we rely on a more accurate form of history, Hoagy. *Oral* history. You seem . . . well versed in the revolutionary period."

"Not really."

"It was the most exciting time in our nation's history," she declared. "A time of boldness and daring and risk. Not like today. Today we're afraid of our own shadows. Afraid of salt, of caffeine, of good, red meat. Afraid of the air we breathe, the water we drink. *Afraid.* All we want now is a life *without* risk. Guarantees—as if there are any in life. Our forefathers knew otherwise. They're the ones who made America a great power. We're nothing but a bunch of neurotics now, weak willies who sit cowering before our television sets wondering why our influence in the world has dwindled." She sat back in her chair, made a steeple of her fingers. "I suppose that is why *Oh, Shenandoah* remains so popular with readers. It evokes that boldness Americans like to believe we still have. And why there is so much interest in *Sweet Land of Liberty.*"

"Tell me what happens."

She moistened her lips. "Vangie marries John Raymond, Hoagy," she revealed. "De Cheverier dies at his hand. It is Raymond who lives. Flourishes at Jefferson's side. Helps author the Articles of Confederation. Becomes a great leader. Only Vangie doesn't love him, Hoagy. Not in her heart. She is miserable. She cries herself to sleep at night for the memory of Guy De Cheverier. In 1785, Raymond is posted to London as an aide to John Adams. She goes along at his side. She detests London. Despondent and lonely, she carries on a flirtation with a handsome young stableboy. Still, she remains true to Raymond. Until he is named minister to France two years later. It is in France, during the time of its own revolution, that Vangie's passion is rekindled beyond her ability to control it. It is in France that she meets Napoleon. She has a passionate love affair with him, Hoagy. An affair that must end when Raymond is recalled to America. She is devastated. Upon their return to Shenandoah, he becomes governor of Virginia. When Jefferson is elected president in 1800, he names Raymond secretary of state. And then, Hoagy, as the war of 1812 beckons, mother intended that John Raymond, husband of Evangeline Grace, himself be elected president of the United States. A truly magnificent story, is it not?"

"It is. How detailed are her notes?"

"Not very," she confessed.

"I understand you also have some ideas of your own."

"They are *not* my own," she insisted. "They are Mother's. Mother speaks to me."

"Want to tell me what she says?"

"That Vangie should have an illegitimate child with Napoleon," she replied firmly. "A beautiful girl."

"Good idea," I said.

"Do you really think so?" she asked, pleased.

"I do. She could arrive in America as a young woman toward the end of the story. Cause her mother no end of problems."

"Excellent, Hoagy," Mavis exclaimed. "You impress me right off. You *breathe* narrative."

"Yeah, I'm full of it. What else?"

She hesitated. "There's a certain . . . perspective that is missing. I feel—that is, Mother and I both feel—*Oh, Shenandoah* and *Sweet Land of Liberty* are but a small section of a much larger, more *cosmic* canvas."

"Cosmic?"

"Evangeline Grace is not merely a figure of the American Revolution, Hoagy. She is a woman of the ages, one who has led many lives. She was Cleopatra and Lucrezia Borgia and Anne Boleyn. She was Joan of Arc. Fictionalized, of course—"

"Of course."

"And before all of this, before she led these many fascinating lives, Vangie came here from far, far away."

"How far away?"

"Venus, before the greenhouse effect poisoned its atmosphere several million years ago and made it uninhabitable."

"So you're saying . . . ," I said slowly, "that Evangeline Grace, the heroine of *Oh, Shenandoah,* is actually an alien?"

Mavis nodded. "And that I intend—that is, Mother intends —to reveal this now, in *Sweet Land.* The entire story. It is vital. I insist upon it."

No wonder the lunch-pail writers had quit on her. The wonder was how they'd kept this giddy little literary morsel under their hats. Their silence must have cost the Glaze brothers plenty.

Mavis leaned forward now, anxious for my reaction. She was just like every other celebrity I'd ever met. Armor on the outside, tender, mortal ego underneath.

I waited her out. I sat back and took off grandfather's Rolex and rubbed at a scratch on its crystal. I put it back on, checked the time, and calculated what it would be in Greece, in Fiji, in Kokomo, Indiana. And then, with just a hint of awe in my voice, I finally said, "It's my turn to be impressed, Mavis. I didn't realize you had such a rich, bold imagination."

"Mother," she countered. "Not me. Mother."

I shook my head. "No, Mavis. Alma Glaze would never dare dream this big. This isn't Alma talking. This is your own voice crying to be heard. This is the you that no one knows. The primitive you. The sensual you. People fear you. They think you're some sort of tight-lipped martinet. They're wrong. I see that now. You're someone who has poetry inside her."

She gulped. The woman positively gulped. "Do you . . . do you really think so?" she asked breathlessly.

"I do."

"My brothers think I am mad."

"Naturally. They're businessmen. Earthbound, so to speak. You can't expect them to comprehend you."

"But *you* do?"

"I do."

"And you agree that this belongs in *Sweet Land*?"

"May I speak frankly, Mavis?"

"Please. Hold nothing back."

"I think it's powerful stuff. Too powerful. I see *Sweet Land* as a traditional, old-fashioned American vehicle—a Schwinn one-speed with foot brakes. Strap a jet engine onto it and you'll only total it."

"But—"

"This is another book, Mavis. Your own book. Not your mother's. *Yours.* And you will write a book, a book even bigger than *Oh, Shenandoah.* I believe that. And I think you do, too, deep down inside. But *Sweet Land,* I think you have to leave it be. This book is hers." Mavis said nothing. "Vangie and Napoleon. What an idea." And just think of the casting possibilities —Hoffman, Pacino, Michael J. Fox . . . "What a child they'll have."

"A girl," she insisted. "It's a girl."

"Perfect."

Mavis tapped the gleaming surface of the writing table impatiently with her fingernail. "I don't know . . ."

"I do," I said. "Trust me. I'm on your side."

She let out a short, humorless laugh. "That would be a first. It has been me against everyone else for as long as I can remember."

"No longer. You have me now."

She gave me her steely stare. I met it. Then she turned away and took a deep breath and let it out slowly. "You'll be taking over the writing?"

I nodded. "Just leave everything to me."

"What shall I be doing in the meantime?"

"Thinking about your own book. Let those ideas percolate. Let yourself go. We'll go over what I'm doing chapter by chapter. I'll be around if you need me."

Again with the stare, a bit more wide-eyed now. This was new for her—being bossed. She wasn't sure how to respond. "Very well," she finally declared airily. "I place myself in your hands."

"You won't be sorry."

She gave me her frozen smile. "When you get to know me better, Hoagy, and you shall, you will learn something about me."

"And what's that, Mavis?"

"I am never sorry."

• • •

Frederick and Edward were waiting for us in the east-wing peacock parlor wearing matching gray flannel suits and apprehensive expressions. Frederick was chain-smoking. A man and woman I didn't know were also in there. All four of them looked up at us when we came in. Mavis's eyes went directly to the man's and flickered a message his way. He then turned to the brothers and relayed it. They both exhaled with relief and came toward me with their hands out, beaming.

"So nice to see you again, Hoagy," exclaimed Frederick.

"Glad everything seems to have worked out," added Edward. "Thrilled. May I introduce you to Charlotte Neene, Mave's treasured assistant?"

Charlotte was a thin, anemic-looking little woman in her thirties, complexion sallow, short brown hair lank, dress drab. She wore no makeup or lipstick or jewelry. Her hand was bony and gelid. "Mr. Hoag," she murmured, careful not to make eye contact.

"Miss Neene," I said. "Would that be your red LeMans out there in the courtyard?"

"Why, yes," she replied, chewing nervously on her lower lip. She had pointy, rather feral little teeth. Her lip was pulpy from being chewed on. "Why do you ask?"

"I've been thinking of getting one. How does it handle?"

"Okay, I suppose," she replied vaguely.

"Glad to hear it."

"And this fine gentleman," interjected Frederick, with more than a hint of derision in his voice, "is Mave's husband, Lord Lonsdale."

"*Richard* Lonsdale, Hoagy," Richard said heartily, after he'd shot Frederick a quick, dirty look. "Do ignore the title bit. Freddy's just having you on. Welcome, and so forth. Damned decent of you to make it down."

Richard went at the ruddy English country-squire bit a little much for me, though I must admit it doesn't take much to be too much for me. He had the clipped, regimental voice, the brush mustache, the robust vigor. He had the tweed Norfolk jacket, the leather-trimmed moleskin trousers, the wool shirt, the ascot. He didn't completely pull off the ascot, but then no one has since Orson Welles died. His hair and mustache were salt-and-pepper. His shaggy brows were coal black and in constant motion. He had an involuntary blinking twitch that kept them squirming around on his forehead like two water bugs pinned to a mat. Evidently his drinking didn't subdue it, and he did drink. The red-rimmed eyes and burst capillaries in his nose said so. He was a big-chested man, so big he looked as if he were holding his breath all the time. But he wasn't tall. His legs were unusually short. His hands were big and hairy. They were also bandaged.

"What happened to your hands?" I asked.

"Tripped in the courtyard last night after I'd put the car away," he replied, twitching at me. "Those bricks get damned slippery. Fell flat and scraped them both raw. Stupid, really."

Edward leaned in toward him and softly inquired if perhaps Mavis would like a sherry before lunch. Richard glanced at her. She raised her chin a quarter of an inch.

Richard immediately flashed his large white teeth at me. "Sherry, Hoagy? To celebrate your undertaking?"

I said that would be fine and watched him fill a set of cordial glasses from a cut-glass decanter, marveling at the fine, civilized heights to which the Glazes had elevated sibling loathing. It was a subtle business, really, but it was undeniable— Mavis and her brothers never actually spoke to each other, or even made eye contact. They communicated only through Richard. He was their go-between, their envoy. He kept the peace. Or perhaps "truce" was a better word for it. Whatever, they had it down so pat they must have been existing this way for years.

Mercy breezed in the door from school as Richard was handing out the glasses. She sang out, "Hello, all," and started up the stairs.

"You're just in time to help us celebrate, Mercy," Mavis called after her. "Come."

She did, though Richard didn't fill another glass for her. I got my own special hello and smile. I could almost feel Mavis's eyes boring into the back of my head. We raised our glasses.

"Hoagy and I," began Mavis, "it is my great pleasure to announce, have arrived at a creative meeting of the minds. . . ."

"And here, ladies and gentlemen," Mercy cracked brightly, "we go for the ninth time."

"Mercy, either hold your tongue or leave this room at once," snapped Mavis.

"Now, Mave . . . ," said Richard consolingly.

"Quiet, Richard!" she ordered. Mercy started out of the room. "Mercy, *stay!*" There was no need for the lady to have dogs around. She had her family.

Mercy stayed, her eyes twinkling with amusement. Richard stood there twitching. Everyone else seemed quite used to this.

"Let us drink to *Sweet Land of Liberty*," continued Mavis. "And to Mother."

"To Mother," toasted Frederick.

"Mother," toasted Edward.

We drank. It wasn't very good sherry. It tasted like children's cough syrup. When mine was gone, I turned to Charlotte and said, "Do we throw our glasses into the fireplace now?"

"Why, no," she replied, a bit goggle-eyed. Whimsy obviously wasn't her forte. Or maybe I was just losing my touch. She excused herself and scurried off to the kitchen.

"Best of luck to you, Hoagy," said Edward genially.

"You'll need it," added Frederick under his breath. "And if there's anything you need—information, advice, a horse whip —just let us know." He went over to refill his glass.

Edward lingered. "I certainly do envy you, Hoagy," he said wistfully.

"You wouldn't if you knew me better."

"I would. You do something creative. I always wanted to.

As a young man, I even dreamt of following in Mother's footsteps. But it was never meant to be. No talent—of any kind. I've come to accept it. One of the last stages of maturity, I suppose, is coming to grips with one's own lack of uniqueness."

"Writing is the least amount of fun you can have with your clothes on. You're really a lot better off practicing law."

He shook his head. "No, I'm not, Hoagy. Believe me."

The dining table was set for seven.

Mavis, high priestess of American home entertaining, immediately took charge of the seating. "Richard, you're at that end, I'm at the other. Let's see, that leaves us with an odd man out."

"That would be me," I said.

"Charlotte, you will sit on Richard's left." Mavis gripped her assistant by the shoulders and gave her a firm shove in the right direction. "And next to you . . . no, that's no good. We'll have two men sitting next to each other. You'll have to sit between my brothers, Charlotte, with Hoagy and Mercy across from you. Yes, I believe so. No, wait . . ."

"I appear to be fouling up the seating somewhat," I suggested to Mercy.

"No, you're just giving her an excuse," she murmured.

"To do what?" I asked.

"Move me to a different chair. Mother won't allow me to sit in the same chair for very long for fear I'll get comfortable. She thinks comfortable people are soft people."

Mercy seemed to accept this with good grace. I found myself thinking how sorry I was she had Mavis for a mother.

The lady was still playing musical chairs. I started for the kitchen.

"Wait, Hoagy," she commanded. "Where are you going?"

"I want to tell Fern to start churning," I replied, smacking my lips. I could practically taste that homemade licorice ice cream.

"Churning? Churning what?"

"She's not in there," Charlotte informed me. "She went to the old house for a second."

I went to the old house after Fern. I had my priorities. I found her in the entrance salon. She was lying there on the floor at the bottom of the stairs. Her neck was at a very funny angle. At least I thought it was funny. She thought it was funny, too. She was grinning up at me. She hadn't lost her jolly sense of humor. Just her life.

Chapter Five

Polk Four was so clean you could eat off him.

There wasn't a wrinkle in his crisp khaki uniform. There wasn't a smudge on his wide-brimmed trooper's hat. His black leather holster gleamed. His square-toed blucher oxfords gleamed. He gleamed. Polk was in his late twenties and stood several inches over six feet and didn't slouch. He had the trim athletic build and flat stomach of a high school basketball star. His hair was blond and neatly combed, his eyes sincere and alert and wide apart over high cheekbones, a thin, straight nose, and strong, honest jaw. He had no blemishes on his face. I doubted he'd ever had any, or ever suffered from excess stomach acid or insomnia or the heartbreak of psoriasis. I hated him on sight.

He got there in ten minutes in his shiny-gray, sheriff's-department Ford, a deputy trailing behind him in another just like it. He took charge right away. There was nothing youthful or indecisive about Polk Four. He was the sheriff of Augusta County. The deputy kept himself busy taking photographs of Fern's body. The paramedics came, but there wasn't much for them to do except stand around. The body couldn't be moved until a doctor looked her over and signed the death certificate.

We all waited for him in the old parlor. Mavis was exceptionally still and composed. If there were tears in her, she would not allow them out now. Mercy wept openly into one of my white linen handkerchiefs.

The brothers had sharply contrasting reactions. Frederick was in total command—it was he who had called Polk Four and herded us into the parlor. Edward was unconsolable.

He rocked back and forth in his chair, sobbing and moaning. "I keep thinking of the night Mother died, Fred," he cried. "I was at Fern's when I got the news, remember? She was the one who actually told me."

"Let's not go into that, Ed," Frederick said sharply. "Come on, now."

"She was a rock, Fred, is all I meant."

"That she was." Frederick patted his brother gently on the shoulder. "That she was."

Richard had gotten himself a large brandy and sat there sipping it and furtively trying to make eye contact with Charlotte, who sat in a corner wringing her hands, her own eyes firmly fastened to the floor.

The doctor arrived in half an hour. He was weary and elderly. He examined Fern where she lay. Cause of death: broken neck. Then Fern O'Baugh was lifted onto a stretcher—it took three strong men to do that—and wheeled out.

Polk joined us in the parlor. "My deepest condolences, Mavis," he said, hat in hand. "It's a terrible loss. Just terrible."

"Thank you, Polk," she said softly.

"She was a real fine old lady," Polk went on. "Almost like another mother to Mercy." He looked over at her, coloring slightly. "Hi, Mercy."

"Hello, Polk," she said, sniffling.

"She was family, Polk," declared Mavis. "Family."

"Speaking of which . . ."

"We'll be handling the funeral arrangements," Frederick informed him.

"Fine, sir," Polk said. "We'll need some additional information for the certificate. Date and place of birth, social security number, parents' names . . ."

"Of course, Polk," Frederick said, lighting a cigarette. "Whatever you need."

Richard got up and started out of the room with his empty brandy glass.

"Sit, Richard," commanded Mavis.

He stopped. The muscles in his jaw tightened. "I merely wished to—"

"I *know* what you merely wished. Sit!"

He drew himself up, steaming. But he didn't erupt. He submitted. Sat back down, twitching.

"What do you think happened, Sheriff?" I asked.

Polk's clear blue eyes took me in for the first time. "We haven't met, sir."

"He's Stewart Hoag, the author, Polk," said Mercy. "Going to be living here for a while."

Polk Four looked me over, measuring me unsurely. I guess he didn't meet many fizzled literary icons. "Welcome to the Shenandoah Valley, Mr. Hoag," he said, "though I suppose this isn't what you'd consider a nice hello. She fell, in answer to your question. Those stairs are quite steep and narrow. That's how they built them in the old days. If you're not real careful on your way down, it's easy to take a tumble. Fern was a big lady. She tumbled hard."

"The guides always have to warn the tourists to watch their step," pointed out Charlotte.

"She must have gone up and down them a million times," I reasoned.

"That's true," Polk agreed with a reassuring smile. "But accidents do happen."

"Oh, Polk, must you be so banal?" demanded Mercy.

He reddened. "I realize you folks are upset. I'll not intrude on your privacy any longer."

"Thank you for everything, Polk," said Mavis. "And you're not intruding. You've been most kind. Hasn't he, Mercy?"

"Yes, Polk. You're always *most* kind," Mercy said hotly.

He walked out, singed at the ears. I followed him.

The ambulance and the doctor were gone. Polk's deputy was lingering.

"Any chance Fern's fall was something other than an accident, Sheriff?" I asked him.

Polk stopped and stood there looking at me with his hands on his hips. "Such as?"

"Something other than an accident," I repeated.

He frowned and scratched his chin. He had the closest shave I'd ever seen. It looked as if his whiskers had been surgically removed. "You mean like was she pushed or something? Everyone here loved Fern, Mr. Hoag. She was a fine old lady. And this is a fine old family. Mavis, her brothers, Mercy, they're not that sort of people."

"We're all that sort of people, Sheriff."

He narrowed his eyes at me. "You have some mighty strange ideas, Mr. Hoag. Where are you from?"

"New York City."

He nodded, as if this told him all he needed to know. Everyone from New York was crazy. Not like here, where the valley's biggest luminary wanted to turn her lead character into an alien. "You'll find things are a little different here, Mr. Hoag. This is a county where justice still has the upper hand. Fern O'Baugh's death was an accident, plain and simple. Take my word for it." He started for his cruiser, stopped. "I hope you won't be upsetting these good people."

"I wouldn't think of it, Sheriff."

"Good." He squared his shoulders, not that they needed squaring. "Mercy . . . she's a spirited lady, like her mother."

"She is."

"She and I . . ."

"I wouldn't think of that either, Sheriff."

He tipped his big trooper's hat to me. "Good day, Mr. Hoag."

"See you later, pardner."

He stuck his chin out at me. "Don't call me pardner." Then he got in his car and drove away, his deputy on his tail.

The man was right. Fern's death gave every appearance of being an accidental fall. Except to me. She'd told me Sterling Sloan was murdered. She'd told me she knew something about it. And now she was dead. That's how it looked to me.

I took the driveway around back to my guest quarters. Lulu was out cold in her easy chair, paddling her paws in the air, whimpering. Bad dream. I roused her. She woke with a start. Grudgingly, she followed me back to the old house. It was empty now. Everyone had gone back to the east wing.

We went up the stairs. They were steep. Creaky, too. There was a short central hallway on the second floor. Two bedrooms were open for public view, both of them furnished with lovely old canopy beds, washstands, wardrobe cupboards. One was the master bedroom, the other the room that had been Vangie's in the movie. There was a definite air of familiarity to it. The brocaded-silk bedcover upon which lay Vangie's most trusted confidante—Miss Penelope, her porcelain doll. The mirrored dressing table where Vangie sat each night combing out her wild mane of red hair. The vast double-doored wardrobe from which she chose her most tempting outfits. There was also a definite air of weirdness. Because Vangie wasn't a real character out of history. Vangie was fiction. And this was a movie set.

The room next to Vangie's was locked. So was another door across the hall. I stood there in the hallway, wondering what exactly Fern was doing up here in those seconds before she died. She was about to serve lunch next door. Why had she come up here?

Lulu was sniffing the floor at the top of the stairs. There was a carved banister post on either side of the top step, painted white to go with the hallway decor. Lulu looked up at me when I approached. When she did, I noticed she had white particles stuck to her wet black nose. I knelt beside her and wiped them off.

The particles were tiny flecks of white paint.

There were more of them on the floor at the base of each banister post. I ran a finger along one of them. The wood was hard and smooth with several coats of glossy paint over it. Except about three inches from the floor, where a set of thin grooves had been made in the paint. All the way around. On both posts. Fern hadn't been pushed. Nothing so crude as that. Someone had tied a trip wire across the top of the stairs after she'd gone up. She was easy prey—blind as a bat without her glasses. They'd lain in wait for her to go down—and down she went. Then they'd removed the wire and returned to the house. It could have been anyone in the family. Anyone could have slipped out for a minute while we were having our sherry. That's all it would have taken. One of them had shut her up. Made sure she'd never tell what she knew about Sterling Sloan. What was it she'd seen? What had been covered up? And how could it possibly matter now, fifty years later?

But it did matter. That much I knew for damned sure.

Mercy and Charlotte were in the kitchen getting our belated lunch together.

"I managed to drop a paper clip in my typewriter," I said. "Need a piece of wire to get it out."

"You'll have to ask Roy for it," said Mercy as she took a tray of food into the dining room. "I have no idea where you'd—"

"Bottom drawer there under the toaster, Hoagy," broke in Charlotte. "With the tools."

There was a flashlight in there, a pair of pliers, a hammer, screwdrivers, twine. There was also a spool of wire and a pair of cutters. I cut myself a length of wire.

"What's in those closed rooms upstairs in the old house?" I asked Charlotte.

She took a pitcher of iced tea out of the refrigerator. "They keep the vacuums and cleaning supplies in the room next to Vangie's. That used to be the sitting room. There's still a door connecting them. They moved the big wardrobe in front of it so the tourists would stop asking if they could go in there. The other room is a bathroom, from when the family still lived up there."

"I was wondering what Fern was doing up there."

"Getting something, I suppose," Charlotte said, chewing on her lower lip.

"Makes sense," I agreed. "Only she was empty-handed when I found her. Odd, don't you think?"

She looked at me strangely. Clearly, she thought I was being morbid and weird. "I can't imagine what difference it makes," she said brusquely. Then she sped out with the tea.

I put the wire and cutters back in the drawer and closed it. I turned to find Frederick standing there before me. I was getting good at telling the brothers apart now—as long as Frederick had a cigarette in his hand.

"I wonder," he said, "If you could drop by my office later this afternoon. We have business."

Frederick Glaze, investment counselor, did his business in Staunton on the top floor of the Marquis Building, a three-story, turreted, red-brick Romanesque on Beverley Street. I took the stairs. I was by myself. Lulu had shown more interest in her chair than a trip to town.

His offices were large, bright and hi-tech. No cobbler's shop, this. Modular cubicles filled with modular young brokers working the phones and the terminals. The place smelled of money. His own private office was located in the round turret, and the past. He had an old rolltop desk in there, and a pair of worn leather armchairs and no computer. There was also an old freestanding steel safe, the kind that fall out windows and flatten people on the street below in cartoons. His windows offered a panoramic view of the business district and the Victorian houses climbing up the steep hills beyond it.

Frederick's jacket was off. The sleeves of his white broadcloth shirt were turned back to reveal a silver wristwatch on one wrist and an ID bracelet on the other. He seemed profoundly weary under his smooth, genteel exterior. "Thank you for coming, Hoagy. Sit down, please. Ed won't be joining us. This Fern thing hit him pretty hard. Ed, Fern, and me . . . we all grew up together. We were classmates. Friends."

"I didn't realize that."

He coughed huskily, drank from a glass of water at his elbow. "When you get to be my age, you get used to losing your friends. But you don't get to liking it. You keep wishing you'd treated them better."

"Did she confide in you?"

He raised his eyebrows. "Confide in me?"

"Personal things. Doubts, fears."

"She had none. Fern O'Baugh was the happiest soul I ever met. Why do you ask?"

"Just curious."

He got up and went over to the safe. "Mavis certainly seems taken with you. She even seems willing to keep her queer notions out of Mother's sequel just because you said she should." He spun the tumbler on the safe and began to work the combination from memory. "I take my hat off to you, sir. You do indeed work miracles."

"Everyone ought to be good at something."

He opened the safe door wide, reached inside, and pulled out a loose-leaf, three-ring notebook and a legal document. He closed the safe and carried these back to his desk. He held on to the document. The notebook he handed over to me.

"Your copy of Mother's notes for *Sweet Land of Liberty*," he explained. "In her own hand, but quite legible. You'll find a lot in there to do with plot and character, and not a lot to do with the sights and sounds. We've the resources of the Staunton Historical Society should you need anything checked out. Girls at Mary Baldwin would be only too happy to help out. Just turn them loose. No sense you getting bogged down, I mean. Speed is of the essence at this point."

"I understand."

He lit a cigarette and sat back in his chair. "Mother's notes are in the form of a diary. As it happens, she was keeping it while *Oh, Shenandoah* was being filmed out at the estate. A lot of what you're going to be reading is her impressions of what was going on around her. How she felt the actors were doing, bits of gossip, things like that."

I found myself leaning forward. "Oh?"

"You may find it interesting reading. Not that it has anything to do with this project. It's more of a literary artifact, really. We plan to publish it as an introduction to the special golden-anniversary edition. You'll find the notes for *Sweet Land* scattered throughout. Fairly complete, except for the ending."

"The ending?"

"We have no idea how Mother intended to end the book," he confessed. "She evidently didn't like what she'd done because she tore it out. All we know is that John Raymond is elected president." He chuckled uneasily. "We don't know what is supposed to happen after that."

"Not to worry. Endings are easy. It's beginnings that are hard."

"Fine," he said. "We leave it to your capable hands. I simply didn't want to think you were missing something."

"I generally am, but it's okay. I'm used to it."

"The notebook is yours for the duration of the assignment. Please guard it with your life." Frederick buzzed his secretary, then picked up the document he'd pulled from the safe and examined it. "Anything else I can do for you while you're down here?" he asked.

"What did you have in mind?"

"Brokerage assistance. Investment opportunities. We're putting together some very exciting tax shelters."

"I usually shelter my earnings in the nearest cash register."

"Suit yourself. Never hurts to ask." He buzzed his secretary again, impatiently. "I'd like you to sign this Hoagy," he said, passing me the document. "It states that I have delivered to you on this day a copy of Mother's notebook, and that you will not reveal its contents to anyone without the prior written consent of the estate. To do so will constitute a breach of contract and leave you liable for a suit. Understood?"

I said it was.

He smiled. "Just a formality, really. Something Ed drew up. You know how lawyers are."

There was a quick tapping at the door. A heavy, plain-faced young woman with curly black hair came trudging in.

"Ah, here you are, dear," said Frederick brightly. "Come on over here beside me, Melinda. I need you to notarize this."

She waited next to him obediently, stamp in hand, while I read over the document and signed it. When I looked up, I noticed there was something odd about the way she was standing. Her entire body seemed frozen there. She was staring straight ahead, stone faced, deathly pale.

Frederick Glaze's right hand was on the desk before him. His left was clamped around Melinda's ample right buttock like a barnacle.

He had a blissful, elfin smile on his face. He looked like a beatific little boy. It was the happiest I'd seen anyone look in a long time.

They picked me up the second I hit the sidewalk with Alma's diary. There were two of them. One had a flattop crew cut, the other a ponytail. It was nice, I reflected, to see ponytails staging a comeback. They both wore flannel shirts and jeans. They both looked as if they ate meat three times a day, not necessarily cooked.

Now I knew why Lulu hadn't wanted to come with me.

They stayed a steady two storefronts behind me as I made

my way down Beverley Street. When I paused to window-shop, they paused to window-shop. They weren't particularly cool or professional about it. Maybe they just didn't care if I spotted them.

A sharp, cold wind was cutting into the soft spring air. Big gray clouds were blowing across the valley from the Blue Ridge Mountains. Winter wasn't gone after all. I turned up my collar and moved on down the block. They moved on down with me. I was loitering at the window of a bookstore, weighing my options and not liking them, when I spotted Charlotte inside there browsing. My lucky day. I went in.

She was over in paperback fiction with her nose buried in a copy of my second novel, the one with the cover that belonged on something by Sidney Sheldon. Both of my novels were well represented. There's no telling where you'll find exceptional little bookstores.

"In case you're wondering," I said to her, "the big sex scene is on page seventy-four, such as it is."

She clapped the book shut, blushing. "I-I came in for some stationery," she blurted out, hurriedly returning the book to the rack. "I was just sort of curious . . ."

I retrieved the book from the rack and handed it to her. "My treat."

"Oh, no, I couldn't," she said, her eyes darting nervously for the floor, for anywhere.

"I insist. Feel free to take it home and not enjoy it. Of course, I do expect something in return."

She frowned at me, suspicious. "Such as?"

There were some Mary Baldwin sweatshirts and bookbags over in the next aisle. I picked out a canvas portfolio with a zipper and slid Alma's diary inside it and tucked it under Charlotte's arm. "Would you take that back to the estate for me?"

"Oh, I'd be happy to," she said, relieved.

We went outside together after I paid. My two tails were waiting patiently for me beside a brass memorial plaque stuck in the sidewalk to mark the spot where Alma Glaze had been run over. Their arms were crossed, their eyes fastened on me. They really didn't care if I spotted them.

"How's the iced tea in that cafe across the street?" I asked Charlotte.

"Real good. They make it from scratch."

"Care to join me for a glass?"

She thought it over. "Well, only if you'll let me pay for both of us. So we'll be even." She tried to smile, but it never quite caught up to her eyes. "Okay?"

"It's a deal."

The Beverley Cafe was deep and narrow and dark. Hard wooden booths were set against the walls. We took one. A fat little kid was buying a candy bar at the cash register. Two old men in work clothes were having pie and coffee and muttering to each other. Otherwise it was empty.

Charlotte had put a drab coat on over her drab dress. She kept it on. Shifted uncomfortably there in the booth. Chewed on her lower lip. She seemed grateful when the sulky waitress shuffled over to us and said, "Hey, Charlotte."

"Hey, Luanne. Iced tea for two, please."

Luanne looked me over, lingered for an introduction, didn't get one, sighed, and moved slowly off.

"Were you and Fern close, Charlotte?" I asked.

"Not really. She was a meddlesome old thing. Always pestering me to change my hair and stand up straight. I guess she meant well, but I wasn't looking for another mother."

I glanced out the window at the street. No sign of my friends. "And you and Mavis?"

"What about us?"

"How long have you been working for her?"

"Two years."

"Like her?"

Charlotte clasped her hands primly on the table before her. "I despise Mavis Glaze more than I ever thought it was possible to despise another human being," she replied calmly.

Luanne came back with our iced tea. Charlotte dumped

three spoonfuls of sugar in hers before she took a sip. "You don't know about Mavis and my father, do you?"

I tasted my tea. It was already sweetened. Plenty sweetened. "What about them?"

"I may as well tell you myself, since you'll be hearing it before long anyway. There've always been two fine old families that ran things in the valley. Owned the land. Owned the LaFoons. One was the Glazes, the other the Neenes. Franklin Neene was my father, and the end of the line. I'm an only child and the family money is long gone. About the only thing left was the name—my father was judge of the Staunton Circuit Court, and a fine, respected man. Honest. Fair. Gentle. Sensitive. Too sensitive for his own good, really. When Mother died four years ago of ovarian cancer, he had a real problem bouncing back from it emotionally. He . . . He began to drink. I did my best to take care of him. Quit my job over at the high school—I was a secretary in the administration office. Kept house for him, watched over him. But he got worse and worse. Pulled away from his friends and his activities, resisted any kind of help. He was never drunk on the bench. Never. He was much too conscientious for that. He just sat in his room alone and drank, night after night. Until one night he suddenly jumped in his car and drove off. I didn't even hear him leave. He showed up at a local restaurant, the Golden Stirrup, drunk out of his mind. Rammed a couple of cars in the parking lot. Made quite a scene. Got himself hauled into jail." Charlotte drank some of her tea, gripping the glass tightly with her short, stubby fingers. "Mavis heard about it, of course, and she happens to be head of Virginians Against Drunk Driving."

"So I've heard."

"Well, she decided his behavior was unbecoming to a public servant of a judge's stature and launched a campaign to get him thrown off the bench. She urged people to write letters to the governor. She made it into a big story in the newspapers. And she wouldn't let go. She hounded him and hounded him. The poor man was ill. Everyone knew that. There were decent, humane ways it could have been handled. Medical leave, early retirement—something to save him his dignity. But she'd have none of that. She wanted his scalp. You see, Mavis always hated that there was another family name in the valley that rivaled her own. And this was her big chance to make sure there no longer would be. She forced him to resign in disgrace. He had no other choice. Two mornings later I found him inside his car in the garage, the garage door closed and the engine running. It was suicide, and Mavis Glaze drove him to it." Charlotte took a deep breath and let it out slowly. "We had a big old house here in town, heavily mortgaged, and not much else. I sold it and rented an apartment. And came to work for her."

"How can you stand to?"

"I need the job," she replied simply. "Besides, if you live in a small town, you get used to hating people and not being able to do anything about it, except leave. I can't. This is my home. I've never lived anywhere else. I'm too old to start over now, and too much of a coward."

"How do you feel about the rest of the family?"

She glanced furtively around the cafe, turned back to me with a conspiratorial gleam in her eye. "Well, Frederick's got a real problem keeping his filthy hands to himself," she said in a hushed voice.

"I noticed."

"I try not to be alone in a room with him if I can help it. He's never actually attacked anyone, as far as I know. But he did get in some trouble when he was younger. They say he made phone calls."

"Phone calls?"

"Dirty ones. You know, to women. They all knew it was him. Polk Two had to go out and talk to him about it. They were going to press charges if he didn't quit it." She shook her head in amazement. "He and Edward couldn't be more different. Edward's such a fine, considerate man. He always makes a point of asking me how I'm doing, and he listens to what I say. A lot of people never listen."

"Odd that neither of them ever married."

"Edward was once. A long time ago, to a French girl he met in Washington. He doesn't like to talk about it. I think she left him for another man."

"And Richard?"

She swallowed and looked away. "What about him?"

"He's in love with you, isn't he?"

"Who told you?" she demanded angrily. "Did he tell you?"

"He didn't have to."

She gave her lower lip a workout. "He thinks he is. Don't ask me why. Maybe because Mavis strips him of his self-esteem. Of course, he lets her do it. He never pushes back. Maybe that's what it's all about. Maybe he needs to feel . . . manly or something. I don't know. I've never encouraged him. If anything, I've discouraged him, y'know?"

I nodded. Trying to run a guy down with your car was certainly my idea of discouragement.

"But he keeps pestering me," she went on. "I've never had a married man pursue me this way before. Actually, I've never had any man pursue me this way. I don't know what to do."

"Do you love him?"

"I don't know. It's not as if we've ever . . . I mean, he and I haven't . . . I do know he drinks too much. He's not a very happy man."

"Who among us is?"

"He's actually offered to divorce her. He wants to take me home to England with him. He says he's about to come into money of his own over there. Lots of it."

"Oh?"

"Family money of some kind."

"I see. Does Mavis know about any of this?"

Her eyes widened. "You wouldn't . . . ?"

"She won't hear about it from me."

She smiled gratefully. She looked somewhat vulpine when

she smiled. "I assume she doesn't know. If she did, she'd fire me in a second, figuring I'd somehow engineered the whole thing to get back at her. Believe me, I don't have revenge in mind. I just want to do my job. I guess the smart thing to do would be to find a new one." She finished her iced tea and reached for the check. I let her have it. A deal's a deal. "Still, I sometimes wonder if it would serve her right."

"If what would?"

She showed me her pointy little teeth. "If I wrecked Mavis Glaze's proper, perfect, civilized little kingdom for her."

They were lounging against my rental car in the public lot around the corner, jeans riding low on their hips, trying to look tough. And succeeding. No one else was around. Unless you count Gordie, who watched over us from the giant VADD billboard by the hardware store next door. There was a black-and-white photo of him looking as if he were about to cry. And underneath: *If people didn't drive drunk, he wouldn't still be waiting for Mommy and Daddy to come home.*

"Hey, mister," the crew cut said, grinning at me crookedly. "Y'all help us out?"

"Be happy to," I replied, unlocking the car and tossing my jacket inside. Good tailoring is hard to find. It's a sin to waste it. "What did you have in mind?"

"Couple of bucks for something to eat?" suggested the ponytail.

"Okay," I agreed. "Provided you fellows do a stranger a kind turn yourself someday."

"We'll sure try," the crewcut promised, enjoying this. He was certainly enjoying it more than I was.

I took my wallet out of my trousers. Before I could open it he knocked it from my hands to the pavement. I looked down at it, then up at him, then over at the ponytail. "I have to hand it to you fellows—you've got real panache."

They stared at me blankly, waiting. There was a script to

follow, and they expected me to follow it. They also didn't know the meaning of the word *panache.*

I looked back down at the wallet and sighed. "Okay, here goes . . . You want to pick that up?"

The crew cut scratched his stubbly chin and thought it over. "You go ahead and do it."

"Okay. But just so you know for the future—this is not my idea of a kind turn."

I bent down for my wallet, bracing myself for the first one. It was a punch to my right kidney from the ponytail. It made my insides feel as if they'd exploded. I crumpled to my knees, gasping, and got a work boot to the shoulder, another to the neck, and then, as I pitched over onto my side, one smack in my bread basket. That one put me into the fetal position, fighting for breath. I hate getting hit. It hurts a lot. Besides, it really shouldn't be part of my job description. I wondered if Bill Novak and Linda Bird Francke ever got stomped. Probably not.

They patted me down roughly. Finding no notebook on me, they began searching the car, cursing to each other impatiently while I lay there, helpless.

"Shit, where is it?" growled crew cut when they came up empty.

"Musta passed it to the lady."

"Shit." Frustrated, crew cut kicked me again—this time behind my right ear.

This time things started spinning around. Then they went black.

Lulu was standing over me, sniffing at my face. I tried to say her name. Nothing would come out. My hand reached for her but she pulled away from me.

I opened my eyes. I was trying to pet Polk Four, who was crouched over me on the pavement sniffing at my breath to see if I was drunk. He'd already decided I was crazy. His sheriff's vehicle idled there behind him in the lot, radio squawking.

"You okay, Mr. Hoag?" he asked, brow furrowed with concern.

My stomach ached and my shoulder, neck, and head throbbed. But I could breathe okay. No broken ribs. "Fine. Just banged my head on a steel-toed boot."

"How many of them were there?"

"Four. Two to a man."

He handed me my car keys and wallet. They had taken my cash.

"What did they get?" he asked.

"Fifty, sixty bucks."

He shook his head, disgusted, and stood up and looked around, hands on his hips. He looked about eight feet tall standing there. "Heckuva thing, this happening in the middle of Staunton in broad daylight. Heckuva thing. You must not think too much of our little town now."

I sat up, groaning. "Oh, I wouldn't go that far, Sheriff."

"Drive you to the hospital? That's a nasty welt by your ear. Might have a concussion."

"I don't hear any bells, two and two is four, and my name used to be Stewart Hoag." I offered him my hand. "You could help me up."

"Fair enough." He gripped my hand and hoisted me up onto my feet. I think it was better for him than it was for me. "Feel well enough to follow me?"

"I don't know. Where are you going?"

"You should fill out a report. This'll be a Staunton City Police matter. Be happy to run you over there."

"Maybe some other time."

"It's the right thing to do," Polk Four said firmly. "You should do it."

I limped over to my car and dropped slowly in behind the wheel. My jacket lay on the passenger seat. The stupid clods had torn the lining out of it. "It was murder, Sheriff."

"I can imagine it was pretty painful," he said gently.

"Fern O'Baugh. It was murder."

He leaned in through the open window, rested his elbows on the door. "Now look, Mr. Hoag," he said patiently. "We've already been over this."

"I found some grooves in the banister posts at the top of the stairs. Flecks of paint on the floor. Somebody used a trip wire."

"Find the wire?" he asked skeptically.

"Well, no. But I did find some wire in the kitchen. Anyone could have gone in there and—"

"Listen to yourself, Mr. Hoag. You've got nothing. There's no telling how long those flecks of paint have been there, or how they got there either. Posts could have gotten bumped with a vacuum cleaner or a piece of furniture."

"It was a trip wire."

He bristled. He didn't like my stirring it up. Or maybe he just resented that I'd tried to pet his head. "I warned you about this once already, Mr. Hoag. I care about these people. I won't stand for you upsetting them. Understand?"

"Fully. You don't want to step on any fine old corns."

"Now that's uncalled for, mister!" he snapped. "I don't deserve that! No way!" He stopped and paused a moment to collect himself. "You've been knocked around some. You're not yourself."

"No, I am. That's the depressing part."

"Be careful driving back to Shenandoah, okay?"

"Will do, pardner."

"And don't call me pardner!"

He got back in his car and waited there, fuming. I edged the Nova out of the lot and started for the outskirts of town. He peeled off with a screech in the other direction.

I headed back to Shenandoah, wondering. How was it that Polk Four had happened along? Was he keeping an eye on me? Why? Who had hired the clods to get Alma's diary from me? One of the more enterprising supermarket tabloids? A trashy television newsmagazine? It didn't matter. Not really. What mattered was that whoever it was had good information. They knew I'd be picking up the diary at Frederick's office, and they knew when. They had very good information. They had inside information.

Chapter Six

Mavis Glaze liked to patrol her realm twice daily on a hot-pink dirt bike, I guess to remind all of the birds and the bees just exactly who was in charge. She was zipping across the front pasture when I pulled the Nova through the gate. The sight of her perched regally atop her motorcycle, back stiff, nose high, smile frozen, gave a whole new meaning to the words *bitch on wheels*.

Roy, the talkative old gardener, waved her down when she got to the ash-lined drive. He pointed to the outer wall over by the souvenir stand, where he'd left a shovel and wheelbarrow. She started over there with him. When she saw me, she indicated she wanted me to follow them. I did. Who was I to let her down?

The two of them had their heads together by the wall. Roy was kneeling on the ground, one knobby hand scratching fretfully at some fresh soil there.

"Roy seems to feel some form of animal life is getting in under the wall at night," Mavis informed me. Her biker outfit consisted of a trim white cotton jumpsuit and belted suede jacket, with a flowered scarf over her head. "A fox, or perhaps a coon."

Roy gave me his blank stare, worked the chaw of tobacco in his cheek.

"Not a matter we can afford to take lightly," Mavis added. "It's after the peacocks, you see."

"What will you do?" I asked.

"We prefer not to put down traps," she replied. "One of them might wander into it. Roy will have to hunt it down and shoot it."

He got to his feet and leaned over and murmured something to her, his lips barely moving.

She nodded. "Your dog," she said to me. "Keep it on a leash after dark, for its own safety."

"Thanks for the warning, Roy," I said. In response he spat some tobacco juice at my feet. Maybe it was just his way of saying you're welcome.

Mavis didn't care for it one bit. She turned her hard blue pinpoints on him and breathed fire. "Roy, I have told you innumerable times that if you *must* partake of that *disgusting* habit to please have the courtesy not to expectorate in my presence! Since I obviously have *not* made myself understood, perhaps docking you one day's pay will make my point clear. I will *not* be spat at! Do you understand!"

Roy bowed his head and nodded penitently.

"See that you do!" She turned her back on him and marched briskly toward her motorcycle. I followed. "There was a delivery for you about an hour ago," she said to me over her shoulder. "I had him leave it outside your room."

"Thank you."

She stopped and looked me over. "You look terribly pale. You're not ill, are you?"

"Nothing a short single malt and a half dozen tall ice packs can't handle."

"Excuse me?"

"Don't mind me."

She hesitated. "I've been thinking about the book. *My* book. I can't think about anything else, really. I'm just so alive with ideas and sensations. I-I feel like an exposed nerve. Is it that way for you? When you write, I mean."

"On my good days."

"They're coming so fast I can barely keep up. It's thrilling. I can't wait to tell you about them."

"And I can't wait to hear them, Mavis. In the meantime, write them down in a notebook as they occur to you."

"That's just what Mother did. She even kept a notepad by her bed at night. Father would tease her about it." Briefly, her face softened at the memory. Then it abruptly hardened again. She climbed on her little pink motorcycle.

"Nice little machine," I observed.

"It was a Christmas present from Richard."

"I'd have thought a horse would be more your style— strong, proud, classical." I also couldn't help thinking if she had a horse to kick, she'd do it less to people.

"I never go near them. I was thrown by one as a girl. Rather badly—I broke my collarbone."

"I'd have thought you'd climb right back up."

"People often say that to me, mistakenly. It's not that I am afraid. Fear doesn't enter into it."

"What does?"

"A horse failed me, Hoagy. Failure is a habit. I don't believe in giving in to it." She started up the motor and revved it. "I'm terribly upset about Fern. Such a loyal, dependable friend. Irreplaceable, as well. I've spent the entire afternoon on the phone with a host of agencies trying to find someone who can take over for her. They've checked Southampton, Palm Beach, Pasadena. No one seems available anywhere right now. I can't imagine why." She let out a long sigh. Then she turned the tiniest bit schoolgirlish on me. "Actually, that's not true. I *can*. I don't know how to lie to you. I wonder why. Perhaps because you're not afraid of me."

"Why should I be afraid of you?"

"The truth," she confessed, "is that I am not considered a desirable employer. I am too hard on people."

A car came zipping up the drive from the gate. Charlotte in her red LeMans. She stopped beside us and rolled down her window and handed me the zippered canvas portfolio with Alma's diary in it. Before I could thank her she'd floored it and was off for the house.

"Interesting woman," I observed. "I understand her father—"

"Franklin Neene was a weakling," Mavis snapped.

"Still, you must have felt pretty awful about what happened."

"Why should I? I didn't tell him to climb into his car and shut the garage door. I didn't tell him to give up. That was his decision. His *cowardice.* Only a coward quits on life."

"It's true, you know."

She gave me her frozen smile. "I'm glad we see things—"

"You *are* too hard on people."

Her eyes flashed at me. "I can't help being who I am. I've tried to be easygoing, accommodating. Someone who has lots of friends to laugh with, confide in. Someone who isn't so . . . isolated . . ." She looked away uncomfortably. "It's not in my nature. A person must be true to his or her nature. I simply cannot tolerate weakness. There's no place for it in my life— with one notable exception, of course. We all have our flaws. Richard happens to be mine. I'm afraid we can't all be lucky in love."

"Careful. You'll spoil what few illusions I have left."

"Maybe the reason you're not afraid of me," she suggested, "is that you don't give a damn."

"Maybe the reason I'm not afraid of you is that I *do.*"

She narrowed her eyes at me challengingly. "You puzzle me, Hoagy. I'd like to get to the bottom of you."

"Careful, I'm semispoken for."

"I meant," she said sharply, "I'd like to figure out what makes you tick."

"Feel free. And let me know if you do—it would be nice to know myself after all these years."

The sky was becoming dark and threatening now, the air raw. Rain wasn't far off.

Mavis looked up at the clouds and shivered. "I never learned how to cook. At Mother's insistence—she feared I'd be made a slave to some man. Thank goodness Charlotte volunteered to make little Gordie dinner tonight."

"Will she tuck him into bed, too?"

"Gordie is a very, very lucky boy," she pointed out.

"I'm sure he reminds himself of that on a daily basis." I tugged at my ear. "I happen to know a gifted, mature woman who has managed several prominent British estates. Hasn't got a weak bone in her body. Also happens to be quite discreet." As well as a born ferret for inside information, and just what I needed right now. "If my friend Pamela's available, you couldn't do any better."

Mavis pursed her lips. "I know Richard would adore having a fellow countrywoman. . . . She's good, you say?"

"She's the best."

"I'd need references."

"She'd have them."

"Could she start right away? Time is of the essence. I'm expecting a thousand guests here for my VADD costume ball the night of the golden-anniversary premiere. The Quayles are flying in. Senator and Mrs. Robb. The Kissingers, the Buckleys. Patricia Kluge. Gore Vidal, Bill Blass, King Juan Carlos. Barbara Walters is taping a three-hour special for ABC. . . . I don't know what I'll do if—"

"Shall I call Pam?"

"I'd love for you to call her." She placed her long fingers on my arm and left them there. "And thank you, Hoagy," she said warmly. Or what was warmly for her.

"All part of the service," I assured her, glancing down at her fingers. She removed them, coloring.

I only hoped Pam wouldn't mind standing in for someone who had just been murdered.

It was the Jag that was waiting for me outside the door of my guest cottage, the red 1958 XK150 drophead Merilee and I had bought when we were together, and which was hers now. It is a rare beauty, every inch of it factory original. Seeing it sitting there in the courtyard with its top down, sixty-spoke wire wheels gleaming, almost made me forget I'd been used as a soccer ball that afternoon. There was an engraved Tiffany note card on the tan leather driver's seat: *I wouldn't want you to forget me, darling.*

I couldn't forget her if I wanted to, and I didn't want to.

A few fat raindrops were starting to fall. Quickly, I put the top up and went inside. Next door, Gordie's TV was blaring. There was, I was pleased to note, no sign of his goddamned cat.

Lulu growled at me.

Sat there in her chair and growled at me as if I were a stranger who'd barged into the wrong room.

"Excuse me, miss," I said. "I don't mean to intrude, but I happen to live here. At least I did the last time I looked."

She stopped growling. Now she was just glowering at me.

I went over and sat on the arm of the chair and patted her. Or tried to. She pulled away from me, as if I'd sprayed my hand with some kind of doggy repellent.

"For your information," I pointed out, "Hoagy could use a little sympathy. Possibly a lick on the face."

No response.

"Lassie would have been right there by my side," I said. "Chased those two off. Or at the very least raced over to Polk's office and barked. 'Hoagy's in trouble! Hoagy's in trouble!'"

She continued to glower at me from under her beret.

"Are you feeling all right?" I grabbed her nose. Cold and wet. "Want to go back to New York or something?"

She hopped down and waddled over to her bowl. She wanted her dinner or something.

I gave it to her. She ate mechanically, like a middle-aged husband chewing on his wife's pot roast for the thousandth time. I watched her, concerned. She wasn't herself. She seemed very far away to me. I couldn't imagine why.

I made a fire in the small fireplace and put some ice in a towel and laid it against the throbbing welt on the side of my head. I was pouring myself a Macallan when I heard it. Softly at first. Then louder.

Meowing.

I ignored it. I sat and enjoyed the fire and my single malt and ignored it. It got louder. And then she began to yowl, loud enough to be heard across the valley. Certainly loud enough for Roy to hear her. Roy and his shotgun.

Disgusted, I went to the front door and opened it. Sadie sat there in the doorway in the rain, all bright-eyed and perky and wet. She'd brought me a token of her affection. A dead mouse. At least, I think it was dead. I didn't look too close. I told her to go away and take her friend with her. I closed the door. She promptly started yowling again. I threw it open. Now she was hanging from the screen door by all fours, eye to eye with me. I went out there and yanked her from the screen and set her down on the ground. She immediately leapt up onto my right shoulder, scampered around the back of my neck, down the other shoulder, and into the crook of my left arm, where she nestled moistly and began making small, comfortable motor-boat noises. At least someone seemed happy to see me.

"Tell you what," I said to her grudgingly. "If you'll shut up, I'll bring you out something. But just this once. Never again." I put her down. "Wait out here. And don't ever bring me a ro-dent again."

Lulu was still eating and still giving me the cold shoulder. I spooned the leftover mackerel from her can into a saucer and took it back out to Sadie. The rain was really coming down now. Not that she was complaining. She was waiting just as I asked her to, quietly getting wetter and wetter. I sighed and held the door open. She came right in. The mouse she left on the doorstep. Lulu eyed her from her bowl but didn't seem to mind. Whatever was bothering her it wasn't Sadie. I put the saucer down inside the door and Sadie went for it, starved.

I sat back down before the fire with the telephone. I talked the rental agency into hauling away their Nova and a florist into delivering a dozen long-stems to the farm in Connecticut. I tracked down Pam through her brother in Croydon. She was being a woman of leisure at a residential hotel in Bournemouth, and bored stiff. She'd be at Shenandoah as soon as the airline schedules allowed.

I fed the fire and my whiskey glass. I put on a Garner tape and let the little elf and the rain have their way for a while. Then I opened up the notebook. Alma Glaze had kept her diary on unlined paper. Her writing had a tendency to go uphill as she got to the right edge of the page. No curlicues or flourishes. Her handwriting was small, tight, and no-nonsense. Just like the text. Just like the woman.

Chapter Seven

June 9

I sit in the gazebo, gazing out at the North Lawn, trying to stay out of everyone's way. They have begun their filming today. The very last scene, the duel, is being filmed first. I'm told they do everything out of sequence in Hollywood. How can they? How can the actors know what to feel if the preceding scene has not yet been filmed? Curious. The lawn is filled with their modern equipment—cameras, lights, trucks, trailers. Amidst all of it stand the duelists, Errol Flynn and Sterling Sloan, in their costumes and powdered wigs.

Mr. Flynn cuts such a tall, dashing figure as De Cheverier. He is an utterly charming, devilish man. Last evening he kissed my hand and pronounced me "the loveliest writer I've ever laid eyes on." He is so full of life, so eager to embrace its challenges. . . . Mr. Sloan is in many ways his opposite. He is a small man, five feet six at most. He must stand on a platform to see eye to eye with the strapping Flynn. He has such tiny hands that the costumer told me he must wear boy's gloves. His forehead is unusually high, his skin fair, his mouth delicate, hair a lovely ginger color. But that voice! So rich and baritone! Were it not *for that he would seem too small and frail to project John Raymond's inner strength. Sloan is a very quiet man. There is an air of deep suffering about him, of dark inner torment.*

Laurel Barrett is an exquisite, fine-boned creature. She has the loveliest, purest white skin I have ever seen. However, she is very arrogant and high-strung. When I told her how pleased I was she had been chosen to play Evangeline, she said, "I can well imagine you would be." I gather she is not well liked by the cast and crew. Certainly she makes no attempt to be cordial. There seems to be more than a little marital strain between her and Mr. Sloan. Or perhaps I simply do not understand performers.

Mr. Wyler, the director, certainly seems to. Willy is very much in charge. He asked the gentlemen to perform one small part of the duel scene over and over again this morning. They did so without question. I suppose they are used to this, since so much of moviemaking seems to be mindless, painstaking repetition. . . . Happily, Mr. Goldwyn has returned to Hollywood for the time being. What a vulgar, horrid snake! What a total figment of his own imagination! And what does he actually do? His sole interest here seemed to be in trying to bed any living, breathing woman he could get his hands on. Briefly, he even pursued the "dahlink" widowed author of "Old" Shenandoah, as he insists upon calling it. We were not amused.

June 10

The children are in heaven. They consider this entire enterprise their personal playground. The twins are enamored of the cameras and lights and of the men who handle them. Particularly Edward, who, with the typical verve of a man with one entire year of college under his belt, has pronounced himself bound for a career in the theatrical arts. He is terribly underfoot, I'm afraid. . . . Little Mavis has taken to worshiping Mr. Flynn with every ounce of her ten years. She follows him about and constantly seeks to dominate his attentions. He's been quite charming about it. Her main competition is Miss Barrett, who appears to be terribly smitten by him. I can only hope the filming will not be highlighted by a real duel between these two gentlemen.

Mr. Flynn has liquor on his breath at nine in the morning. Still, he is a perfect professional and the crew adore him. They do not care for the moody aloofness of Sloan and Barrett, whom they have dubbed Himself and Herself. Mr. Niven is most ingratiating. Miss Barrymore intelligent and convivial. I believe she and I shall become friends.

Seeing my characters come to life this way, I cannot help but think of their continuing on after Oh, Shenandoah. *Of Evangeline's going forth to live the joys and the sorrows of this sweet land of liberty. John Raymond must win the duel. For it is he, a statesman, a man of peace, who is destined for greatness in the new land. De Cheverier, the eternal rebel, is a man of war. He is a flame, burning brightly in Evangeline's heart, but his time has now passed.*

And on it went. Alma's notes for *Sweet Land* were, in fact, rather sparse. There was little here that Mavis hadn't already told me. Mostly, there was gossip. Pretty good stuff, though, if you're interested in that sort of thing. It so happened I was.

June 14

Everyone is talking about how Mr. Niven and Linda Darnell are sleeping together. Neither of them has bothered to be discreet about it. I do not understand these people.

My poor Frederick is hopelessly in love with Helene Bray, the fast young actress who plays Evangeline's best friend, Abigail. Helene curses like a sailor and flirts with most of the young men on the set. She also happens to be sleeping with Rex Ransom, the handsome young actor who plays James Madison. I don't have the heart to tell Frederick. . . . Edward has the acting bug now. But he's so enthusiastic and genuine that he's

*actually managed to befriend Himself, the moody Mr. Sloan,
who has consented to discuss his craft with Edward in his free
time. Quite an unexpected privilege.*

*Little Fernie O'Baugh, the daughter of that fellow who fixes
cars in town, looks simply lovely in her costume as Evangeline's
sister, Lavinia. . . . I wonder if perhaps Mavis is spending too
much time around Mr. Flynn. He made the oddest, crudest re-
mark today about how much he enjoyed having her sit in his
lap. I do believe I will start keeping her away from him.*

June 25

*Willy drove Miss Barrett to utter hysterics this morning.
They were filming the scene where Donald Crisp, the fine actor
who plays her father, tells Vangie he despises De Cheverier and
would never countenance their marriage. Willy wanted Miss
Barrett to break down in response and was not satisfied with
what she was giving him. He made her film it over and over
and over again, tormenting her, driving the poor woman to
such a state of frenzied exhaustion that she genuinely was
breaking down. She was not acting. Only then was he satisfied.
It did not seem to bother him in the least that she then had to be
given a sedative and put to bed. Mr. Sloan got into a violent
quarrel with Willy because of it. I thought the two would come
to blows. An aide had to separate them. Mr. Sloan then refused
to come out of his trailer after lunch. He said he had a severe
headache. Willy instructed the crew to pound on the trailer
with hammers, creating such an unbearable amount of noise
within that he simply had to emerge. The shooting went surprisingly smoothly after that. . . . Actors are children. Willy is
their father.*

*I must say I am appalled at how casual they all are about
altering my dialogue. Mr. Sherwood was most faithful in his
script. Not so Willy and the performers. They keep changing a
word here, a phrase there, and in the process destroying its
authenticity. When I sell the film rights to* Sweet Land of Lib-

erty, *I will make sure they cannot do this. It shall be in the
contract.*

June 29

*Whispers about Mr. Flynn and Miss Barrett. They have
filmed several love scenes together, and the passion they are
generating appears to be quite genuine. She has been seen coming out of his trailer. Such a lovely creature. How could she?
And with her own husband right here! I do not understand
these people.*

July 12

*Quite a scare today. Little Mavis didn't turn up for lunch
and no one seemed to know where she was. Toward late afternoon she was found across the road in the Appleby pasture,
which they've rented for the battle scenes. The little fool had
taken off on a horse and had a nasty spill. Dr. Toriello rushed
her to the hospital, where it was discovered she had broken her
collarbone. She's in a great deal of pain, but she'll live. I must
remember to thank Mr. Sloan. The crew said it was he who
found her.*

July 16

*The rains came again today, washing away all of Willy's
best-laid plans. He is under increasing pressure from Mr. Goldwyn to finish on time. The strain is beginning to show on him.*

*The bad weather did give me an opportunity to lunch with
Miss Barrymore. She is a lovely person, hardworking and professional and very proud of the fine theatrical tradition of the
Drews and the Barrymores. She is deeply concerned about her
dear brother John, whom she calls Jake, a darling boy but so
troubled by drink and demons. She believes he will soon die.
She has noticed the same sickness in a member of this cast. I
assumed she meant Mr. Flynn, but she meant Mr. Sloan, who,*

*like John Barrymore, achieved greatness in his portrayal of
Hamlet. Ethel believes certain men are born to play the Sweet
Prince, and that these men are also born to be destroyed young
by the poisoned cup just as he was. . . . If Mr. Sloan drinks he
hides it well. I have never noticed him intoxicated.*

July 27

*Newsreel cameramen came today to fan the flames of pub-
licity. Went away with the impression that everything was going
well. Nothing could be further from the truth.*

*The love affair between Mr. Flynn and Miss Barrett is quite
evident now. So is the effect her brazen infidelity is having on
Mr. Sloan. He is pale and drawn and complains of constant
migraines. Frequently, he is unable to leave his trailer. The doctor has been attending him. Miss Barrett dismisses his condition
as a display of martyrdom and refuses to yield to it. This has
resulted in a frightfully juvenile battle of wills. If he will not
come out of his trailer to do a scene, then she will not come out
of hers. This afternoon they kept the crew waiting for hours
before they would appear. Everyone, I must say, seemed quite
unconcerned about it. Stars will be stars, or some such thing.
. . . Willy's reaction was the most surprising. While he is upset
at the delays, he actually seems pleased that Miss Barrett is
involved with both men, for it mirrors my story and consequently makes the scenes among them all the more genuine. I
told Miss Barrymore I thought this was rather inhuman of him.
She said it was always a mistake to think of a director as a
human being.*

*Mr. Niven told me it is best not to take sides in such mat-
ters. Most of the crew have taken Miss Barrett's, partly because
they adore Mr. Flynn, partly because Himself, when he does
emerge from his trailer, is so snappish and unpleasant. There is
something about that man I don't like. My Edward believes he
is a genius and terribly misunderstood. Edward thinks Miss*

Barrett is a witch. Actually, he used a stronger word than that. College man.

August 10

Mercifully, they finish today. A party is planned in town tonight. I suppose I shall have to go.

Something rather strange happened this morning. They had been shooting the last bedroom scene upstairs in my old room, the scene in which John Raymond bursts in on Vangie while she is dressing to demand once and for all whether she loves him or De Cheverier. Her sister, Lavinia, little Fern O'Baugh, happens to be in the room at the time, as is Bessie, Vangie's wise old personal maid. Pearl Blue plays Bessie and is a dear. It being rather cramped and narrow up there, I stayed out of the way during filming. When they were done, I went up to see Fern. I was at the top of the stairs when I heard a scream, and then Fern came flying out of the sitting room, her face white, her wig cockeyed. The poor child practically knocked me over in her haste to get down the stairs. I wondered, naturally, what had happened. When I went in there, I found only Pearl and the makeup girl, Cookie Jahr, finishing up. I asked them what on earth had frightened Fern so. They had no idea. They said she had been chatting gaily away when suddenly, without warning, she had screamed and run out of the room. Mystified, I went next door into the bedroom. The crew had cleared out. However, I did find Mr. Sloan in there with one other—

That was it. Alma's notebook ended here. The rest had been torn out.

Chapter Eight

Why had Fern O'Baugh screamed?

What had she seen? Whatever it was, someone had made damned sure there'd never be anything on paper about it. Alma Glaze hadn't changed her mind about how to end *Sweet Land of Liberty,* as Frederick had advised me. I knew better. She, or someone else, had torn out those last pages of her diary because of what they had to say about Sterling Sloan, and how he died. But what? Who had been there in Vangie's room with him? What had been going on? How was I going to find out? Fern had told me time was running out. She'd mentioned the golden-anniversary celebration. Did a survivor from the cast or crew know something? Cookie Jahr, the makeup girl? No telling. I only knew that something had been covered up just like Fern said. And that somebody wanted it to stay that way. Real bad.

I put the notebook down and yawned and knuckled my eyes. It was past one. The rain had let up. The fire was just a glow of coals. Lulu was asleep in her chair, Sadie in the kindling box. Across the courtyard, the east wing was dark. The Glazes were asleep, too.

I carried Sadie next door. Gordie's light was on. So was his TV. He was fast asleep before it on the love seat in his Washington Redskins knit pj's. I turned off the TV and picked him up off the sofa. He didn't weigh much. I carried him up the spiral staircase to his room and got him into the bed without waking him. Or so I thought.

I was reaching for his bedroom light when he opened his eyes. "Had me a looth tooth, Hoagy. Bottom tooth."

"Oh, yeah?"

"Fell out. Kept it though." He sure did. He had it clutched right there in his clammy little hand.

"That's swell, Gordie. Real nice."

"There a tooth fairy here?" he asked gravely.

"I seriously doubt it."

Out came the lower lip. He rolled over and faced the wall, crestfallen.

Don't look at me that way. I never claimed I was good with kids. Just that I don't like them. "Uh . . . actually, I'm pretty sure there *is* one, Gordie. Has to be one. I mean, this is the planet earth, isn't it?"

He turned back to me, brightening considerably. "Hoagy?"

"Yeah, Gordie?"

"G'night, Hoagy."

I turned out his light. "Good night, Gordie."

I slipped across the courtyard and into the east wing, which was left unlocked at night for Gordie's sake. I closed the kitchen door softly behind me. It was dark in there, except for a light over the stove, and quiet aside from the hum of the refrigerator and the growl of my stomach. Charlotte's meat loaf at supper tasted as if it had been made from remnants of the Berlin Wall. As sandwich makings, however, it might do. I found its remains in the fridge, cut a slab, and slathered two pieces of bread with mayo and ketchup and Fern's homemade pickle relish. I took a bite. Not terrible. I opened a beer and drank from it. I went into Fern's bedroom off the kitchen and turned on the light.

It was a small, narrow room. Single bed with rock-maple headboard and woven white cotton spread. Matching maple dresser and nightstand. *Oh, Shenandoah* memorabilia crowded the walls. Autographed photos of a fifteen-year-old Fern, costumed and bewigged, standing on the set with Sloan, with Barrett, with Flynn. Framed pages from her shooting script. A review from the local paper that singled out her fresh beauty and fine performance. It had been the high point of her life. I wondered, as I ate my sandwich, if it had been on her mind as she tumbled headlong down that stairway.

There was a paperback copy of a Jackie Collins novel on the nightstand next to an old-fashioned windup alarm clock. One drawer, shallow, containing two pairs of eyeglasses, a prescription bottle of high blood pressure pills with her doctor's name on it, two rolls of pennies, a small tin of Bag Balm antiseptic ointment, and a snub-nosed, .38-caliber Smith & Wesson Chief Special, loaded. There were no personal papers of any kind. None in any of the dresser drawers either.

I found them on the top shelf of her closet in a shoebox, a big fat wad of them wrapped in tissue paper and bound up in rubber bands. Love letters, all of them written by the same strong hand on plain white stationery and dated during June and July of the year the movie had been made: *Fern, my darling, I cannot eat or sleep for the pain and longing of thee. I cry out in the night for your touch* . . . And so on. Each letter was signed *Thine Sweet Prince.* No other name. He wrote her poetry, too, with no apologies to either Emily Dickinson or Hallmark:

> *O beauty, whose name be Fern*
> *She who comes to me whilst I sleep*
> *It is for her lips, pouting blossom, I yearn*
> *And for her pure, pure heart I weep.*

There were dozens more of them. I wrapped them back up and pocketed them and put the shoebox back up on the top shelf of the closet. I turned around to discover Mercy standing there in the bedroom doorway, blond hair tousled, blinking from the light. She wore a sleeveless white cotton nightshirt and nothing over it. The material wasn't quite sheer but it wasn't exactly flannel either. I could see the curve of her hips beneath it, the ripe fullness of her breasts and thighs. On her feet she wore a pair of fuzzy slippers fashioned to look like giant bear paws.

"What are you doing in here?" she wondered, yawning.

"Got hungry," I replied. "Wandered in and started looking at all of Fern's pictures. Sorry if I woke you."

She ventured into the room a few steps. "Fern was so proud of that," she said softly, gazing at the wall. She turned to me and swallowed. She didn't seem quite as confident as she usually did. She glanced at the bed, hesitated. She sat down on it, hands folded in her lap. "You didn't. Wake me, I mean. I've been tossing and turning."

"Thinking about her?"

"More about Polk, to tell you the truth."

"What about him?"

She shrugged her shoulders. Her bare arms were smooth and strong. I offered her my beer. She reached for it and took a small sip.

"Kind of hard on him, aren't you?" I suggested.

"Maybe I am," she conceded. "There's just something so solemn and perfect about him that sometimes I can't help myself, y'know? I mean, there's no trace of the man after he leaves the room—he's odorless, colorless, tasteless . . ."

"He's a politician," I pointed out. "To the bone."

She helped herself to more of my beer. "I really do like him. He's kind and fair. It's just that mother *loves* him, and I feel like she's pushing me into it. I'm used to that. Mother has never given me much freedom. Most of the time that's okay. I know she wants what's best for me. But this . . ." She trailed off, stabbed at the braided rug with her giant slipper. "Sometimes I think I'd like to buy a ticket to somewhere, anywhere, and just go and not tell a soul. And never come back." She looked up at me. "I know what you're going to say—never is an awfully long time."

"No, that's a little Manilowish for me."

"All I've ever done is go to school. There are so many places I still want to go, so many things I want to experience. I can't even begin to think about settling down and marrying Polk. I mean, how can I know if I even want to stay here until I've been somewhere else first?"

"You can't," I replied. "I took a year off when I got out of school. Bummed my way through Europe. Scribbled in a notebook. It was something I needed to do before I settled down."

"And were you glad you did it?"

"I don't know yet. I still haven't settled down."

She looked at me seriously. "How come you seem to understand me and no one else here does?"

I left that one alone, very aware of her there on the bed. Her soft young mouth, the smell of her. She smelled like baby powder. Merilee smelled like Crabtree & Evelyn avocado-oil soap, though I can't imagine what made me think of that just now. "My parents didn't understand me either," I said. "Still don't."

"Does that bother you?"

"Only if I think about it."

"Fern sort of did," Mercy said. "But she never did have the nerve to leave here. Do things on her own."

"How about your uncles?"

"My uncle Edward has traveled a lot. But he's a guarded sort of person. He and I have never found it easy to talk to one another. It's easier to talk to Uncle Frederick, only he still treats me like I'm a little girl."

"He mentioned that someone at your school might be willing to track down period detail for me."

"How about me?"

"You?"

"I'd love to help you. It would be an honor, really. I'm really good at library work. Just let me know what you need and I'll find it for you. Okay?"

She stuck out her hand. We were in the process of shaking on it when Mavis appeared in the doorway wearing a blue silk robe, her tight copper ponytail brushed loose. She didn't like any of it—her daughter sitting there on the bed in her see-through nightshirt. The empty bottle of beer. The two of us holding hands. She didn't like it one bit. She turned her icy blue eyes on me, jaw clenched under her permanent smile. "You're fired!" she snapped. "Get out!"

"But nothing is going on, Mother!" protested Mercy.

"I came in for a snack, Mavis," I exclaimed. "I'm afraid I woke Mercy and she—"

"We were just *talking*," insisted Mercy.

"Go upstairs, Mercy!" Mavis ordered.

"But Mother, nothing was—"

"Go upstairs!"

Mercy rolled her eyes and got up. "We were just talking, Mother." Then she padded out the door.

Mavis watched her go, her arms crossed. Then she turned back to me. "I hate you for this."

"Mavis . . ."

"I feel betrayed. I feel violated. I feel used. You are no longer welcome here. I expect you to be gone by morning."

"Mavis, I assure you it was entirely innocent—"

"Don't insult me any more than you already have."

"She just needed someone to talk to. It happens. However, if you insist, I'll be out in the morning." I started for the door. She stepped aside so I could pass. "Naturally, you have my word I'll divulge none of the contents of your mother's diary. And I'll try to set aside the fact you've insulted me, though I'm not sure I can."

"I've insulted *you?"* she cried. "How?"

"By not believing in me. By thinking I'd ever do something sleazy. Something to hurt you."

She lowered her eyes, unclenched her jaw. She went over to the bed and yanked on the spread until it was good and taut. She sat down on it. "Perhaps I . . ."

"Perhaps you did."

"You . . ." She cleared her throat. "You read Mother's diary?"

"I did. I'd like to take a look at the original."

"It's in the safe in Mother's library."

"May I see it?"

Mavis frowned. "Right now?"

We took the covered arcade, her slippers clacking on the bricks. There was an electronic security panel at the back door. She entered a numerical code to disarm it. Then we went in, and she turned on the lights in the library. The safe was hidden behind a hinged section of raised paneling next to the fireplace.

"Father installed it," she informed me. "He had it done in the early thirties, when the local banks began to fail. Including the one he himself ran." She spun the tumbler once, then began to work the combination. "There's no money in it now, of course."

"Who else knows the combination?"

"My brothers."

"Not Richard?"

"Richard is not privy to private family matters."

The safe clicked open. She reached inside, pulled out a worn old leather-bound writing tablet and handed it to me. Blobs of red wax remained where it had been sealed shut. I opened it to the end. Alma's writing left off where my copy did —just before she identified who was in Vangie's room with Sloan. There was nothing but blank pages after that. I held the first blank up to the light to see if any impression from her pen had been left on it. It hadn't. I examined the gummed binding. Slivers from the pages that had been ripped out remained stuck in it. Several pages. I closed it and looked at the traces of sealing wax.

"This seal was unbroken when you opened the vault on *Geraldo*?" I asked.

"It was," Mavis replied.

"So these pages were torn out fifty years ago? There's no way it could have been done after that?"

"Not that I can imagine." She looked at me, puzzled. "Why do you ask?"

"Could someone other than your mother have done it?"

"I seriously doubt it. None of us knew the notebook existed at all. Not until after she'd died and her will was read. She'd told no one she was working on it."

"Not a soul?"

Mavis mulled this over. "Her lawyer must have known. He had to. He drew up the codicil to her will. Yes, Polk LaFoon knew. Old Polk One. He's long dead, of course."

"Why did she insist on the fifty-year delay?"

"Mother was not a haphazard or arbitrary person. Whatever she did she did for a reason."

"And what was that reason?" I pressed.

"I can't say."

"Can't or won't?"

"Can't. I honestly don't know, Hoagy. None of us do." She took the notebook from me, put it back in the safe, and closed it. "Nor do I understand what you are getting at."

"I'm getting at this, Mavis. Those pages were torn out because they revealed what made Fern O'Baugh scream. Fern knew something. Whatever it was got her killed. She was murdered."

Mavis's eyes widened in shock. "Fern *fell.*"

"She had help."

"But Polk Four said she—"

"Polk Four doesn't agree with me. In fact, he thinks I'm nuts."

"And why shouldn't I?" she demanded.

"No reason. Except for the fact that I'm not. Did Fern ever say anything to you about what she saw?"

"Not a word. I did wonder about it myself when I read the diary."

"Any ideas?"

"I know she worshiped Laurel Barrett. Possibly she found Sloan in there embracing another woman. Evidently a great deal of that sort of thing went on. I wouldn't know myself. I was only a child then."

"But would that send her fleeing down the stairs?" I wondered aloud. "Screaming hysterically?"

Mavis sat in the chair behind her mother's writing table. "I've figured it out, you know. It's been bothering me. It's why I was awake at this hour, heard you and Mercy."

"Figured what out, Mavis?"

She reddened. "Why I can't lie to you," she replied, going schoolgirlish on me again. "I think it's because you see inside me. No one else can. Richard . . . he sees only my strength, not my vulnerability. But you do. I don't know why, but you do. I sensed it the very first time we met. I-I apologize about before, Hoagy. About not trusting you. I do trust you. And I don't think you're crazy."

"Thank you, Mavis."

"Only, answer me this, Hoagy—why would someone want to kill poor Fern now, all these years later?"

"Fern believed that Sloan's death was covered up," I said. "She'd decided to stir up the waters. Someone didn't want her to."

"Why?"

"I haven't figured that part out yet. Tell me something, Mavis. Did Fern have a boyfriend at the time the movie was being made? An admirer? Some guy who carried a torch for her? Was there anybody like that?"

She thought this over. "There was someone."

"Who?"

"He was a few years older than Fern, and already engaged to another girl, whom he eventually married."

"Who was it, Mavis?"

"It was Franklin Neene," she replied. "Charlotte's father."

Lulu was no longer asleep in her easy chair. She was sitting just inside the door, scowling at me.

Richard had taken the chair. Also a glass of my single malt. He sat there waiting for me, comfy as can be. He and his gold-inlaid Browning twelve-gauge, which was pointed right at me.

Chapter Nine

"Handsome little piece you've got there, Richard," I observed.

"Isn't it, though?" he agreed, draining his scotch. His navy-blue cashmere robe had fallen open to reveal his bare, exceptionally simian legs. The barrel of the Browning was resting on one of them, setting it on a course due south of my equator. "A Christmas present from my Mave," he added thickly.

"Would it happen to be loaded?"

"Yes, it would, lad," he replied, shaggy eyebrows squirming.

"Can I talk you into pointing it, say, somewhere else . . . ?"

"I'm afraid you can't, lad. Sorry."

"Quite all right. Pour you another?"

He held his empty glass out to me. "Damned gentlemanly of you."

He'd gone through about half of my Macallan. I poured us

both some, then sat on the love seat. We drank. The Browning never left me.

"You're messing with trouble, lad," he said.

"I generally am, in spite of myself."

"Sniffing about my henhouse in the wee hours. My women tiptoeing up and down the stairs, their little hearts aflutter. Bad business this, a young rooster about."

"Your description is most flattering," I said, my eyes on the shotgun, "but I assure you I—"

"Can't tolerate it. Won't. Expect you to stay out here at night."

"I got hungry."

"Then I expect you to starve." He puffed out his deep chest. "Got it?"

I said I did.

"Excellent. Knew we'd understand each other. Now that I've spoken my mind we can relax and enjoy your fine whiskey." He stood the gun on the floor against the sofa and sipped his drink. "Do you hunt, lad?"

"No, I'm too good a shot. I might actually hit something."

"But that's the sport of it."

"I've never considered murder a sport."

He twitched at me. "I've not yet made up my mind about you—whether you're good for Mave or not, I mean. She's spoken of little else since you arrived."

"I do have that effect on some people."

"Still," he said, "I think you and I are more than a little alike."

"Oh?"

"Saw it about you from the start. Way you carry yourself. You're a gentleman, lad. We speak the same language. Live and die by the same code. It's in our blood. They haven't got it in theirs, you know. The brothers Glaze. That's why they've never understood me."

I got busy with my drink, wondering who else was going to open up to me tonight. Roy? One of the peacocks? I only wished Lulu would. She was still giving me the Greta Garbo from under the coffee table. Maybe she just needed more fiber in her diet.

"They've never shown me an ounce of respect," Richard went on. "Think I checked my balls at the altar. Think I've no proper job. Not true, any of it. Someone has to do what I do—make sure Mave is contented. Because if she's not, she makes bloody well sure no one else is. That's my job, twenty-four hours a day, seven days a week. Tricky as brain surgery."

"How long has it been since Mavis and her brothers have actually spoken to each other?"

He grinned at me from behind his mustache. "At least as long as I've been around, lad, and that's twenty-six years."

"Any particular reason?"

"It's the money. Of course it is. Alma gave Mave complete control of the family purse strings. The brothers, they're merely glorified bean counters. Resent it terribly. Despise Mave for it."

"They both have professions of their own," I said. "Why didn't they ever move on, start fresh? Why hang around here and torture themselves?"

"They can't help it, lad. They're pampered little babies, and Shenandoah, it's their mum's golden tit. Besides, this way they can try their damnedest to make Mave miserable. It's bats, all of it. Of course it is. Plenty here for everyone. But you know about families. . . ."

I tugged at my ear. "Yeah, I suppose I do."

"As do I. Why I came to North America as a young man. And why I've never been back. I'm second son, you see. Kenneth, my older brother, he got it all. The lordship. The property. Master of all he surveys. I got nothing. That's how it's done. Kenneth offered me a position. But I wasn't about to have that bastard ordering me about. The brothers Glaze, they like to ride me about it. They know it's a sore spot with me. Know it because it's their own damned sore spot as well, isn't it?" He chuckled to himself. "As it happens, I merely traded one chain of succession for another, but this one's tilted a bit more in my favor. I've a fine life here. A grand life." He sipped his whiskey.

"And yet you're willing to give it all up."

He narrowed his eyes at me over his glass. "Am I?"

"Charlotte seems to think so."

He smoothed his mustache, turned ultracasual on me. "What did Charlotte say? I mean, strictly out of curiosity . . ."

"That she's tried to discourage your advances."

"And?"

"And that you don't discourage easy."

He winked at me. I think. It might just have been his tic. "Man to man, she's nothing more to me than a bit of bed fluff."

"Not exactly the description of her that leaps to my mind."

"That's where you'd be wrong, lad. Take an older man's advice—it's the quiet ones are the best. They appreciate your attention. Do anything for you. Unfortunately, they also happen to be the toughest to catch. So I've been feeding her a bit of line about running off with her. But I've no intention of actually doing so. I'd never leave Mave. Never."

"Charlotte told me you were coming into money."

"That little bitch," he said tightly. He hesitated, then said, "I am. That's the truth. And perhaps I *have* thought about running off. Being my own man again. Being . . . needed. A man has to be needed by someone. Makes him feel alive. Mavis, she needs no one. Always has everything her way. Never gives an inch. Don't get me wrong, lad. I'm happy being with a woman who fights back. I'm just not happy being with one who wins *all* the time. . . . I've thought of running. Taking someone with me. Sure I have. But it's only idle fantasy. I know I'll never do it. That's what makes me different from other men."

"No, that's what makes you just like other men. Tell me, how much are they paying you?"

"Who?"

"Whichever sleazy tabloid you tipped off about me picking up Alma's diary yesterday."

"Whatever do you mean?" He sounded genuinely baffled.

"Fifty thousand? A hundred?"

He shook his head. "You're wrong, lad. Couldn't be more wrong. My brother, Ken, he's on his deathbed with cancer. Ken never married. When he dies, I inherit the title and all that comes with it."

"I see."

"It's the truth. I'm not in contact with the press. I'd never sell Mave out like that. Never." He drained his glass and reached for his Browning. Slowly, he got to his feet. "I've kept you up long enough."

"A word of advice?"

"By all means."

"I wouldn't keep stringing Charlotte along. Because if she decides to take you up on your offer, and then discovers you weren't serious, you'll need more than that Browning. You'll need a bazooka."

Lulu woke me in the night again.

She was crouched on the pillow next to my head, whimpering. When I asked her what she wanted, she jumped down off the bed and skittered over to the spiral staircase. Down she went . . . *hop-thump-thump* . . . *hop-thump-thump* . . .

She wanted me to let her out.

I started to, until I remembered Roy's warning. "Are you sure about this?" I asked her.

She was sure about this.

I got into my trench coat and aged pair of Timberlands. Then I dug her leash out of my Il Bisonte bag. She hates the leash. Considers it an affront to her dignity. But she'll usually submit to it if I insist. Not this time. She changed course on me the second she spotted it. Went back upstairs. Jumped up onto the bed with a grunt. She didn't want to go out now. At least not with me.

I went to the bottom of the stairs. "Lulu, I am getting a little tired of this moody, high-handed tyranny. You're starting to make me feel like a goddamned cat person. There happens to be a man with a gun out there. A man who has been ordered to shoot anything with four legs. If you want to go out, you go with me and go on a leash. Take it or leave it."

She took it. Most sourly.

The sky had cleared. The stars were brighter than I'd seen them since I was out on the Aegean. I stopped to get the flashlight from the Jag's glove box. Then I flicked it on and we set out. We walked alongside the historic service yard until we picked up the path that rimmed the great north lawn along where Raymond and De Cheverier fought their climactic duel. There was only a sliver of moon. It was black out there beyond the flashlight's beam, and silent except for the occasional rustling of night animals in the brush. I found myself thinking about the Glaze family as we walked. I thought about Mavis and how afraid she was underneath her armor. Afraid she wasn't as perfect as she expected everyone else to be. I thought about Mercy and how she was chaffing at the narrowness of the life Mavis had laid out for her. I thought about Frederick and Edward—their bitterness toward Mavis, their high-handedness toward Richard. I thought about all of them. And as I did, I began to feel that same sense of melancholy I always feel when I'm getting pulled into my celebrity's family troubles. Not that I ever want to. I don't. But I can't seem to help it. Hazard of the profession, at least it is for me. I'm not the answer man. I've never solved my own problems, let alone somebody else's. I'm no healer. But it's hard to tell somebody that when they're begging you to heal them. Especially when it has gone as far as murder.

I wondered if there was more to the rift between Mavis and her brothers than their mother's will. I wondered if something else had happened a long time ago—fifty years ago—to turn them against each other. I wondered.

A narrow path plunged into the woods just beyond the cemetery. We took it. We hadn't gone far when I started to hear a scuffling sound of some kind, steady and rhythmic. Then I saw the flicker of a lantern through the trees. We started through the brush toward it.

"That you, Roy?" I called out, so he wouldn't blow our heads off.

It wasn't. It was Gordie, hard at work in a small clearing digging a hole in the damp earth with a shovel. He still had his pj's on, with a pair of sneakers. He was covered with dirt. He worked so intently that he didn't even hear us coming.

"Hey, Gordie," I said. "What are you up to?"

He looked up in total panic at the sound of my voice and started to run. I grabbed him by the arm. "It's okay," I assured him as he squirmed in my grasp. "I'm not going to tell anybody. Just wondered."

He swallowed and took a deep breath, relaxing. "Nothing. Not doing nothing."

I released him and went over and checked out his hole. It was narrow, about three feet deep. "I'd say you're digging a tunnel." No response. "Where to?" Still no response. "Come on, you can trust me."

"Out," he confessed solemnly.

"Out where?"

"The other thide of the wall." He cocked his head toward the six-foot brick wall that was beyond the trees where we stood.

I nodded. I understood perfectly. I dug holes myself when I was his age. Straight down through the earth toward Europe —my sense of geography wasn't much. Only, I dug in daylight.

"Kind of late, isn't it?" I suggested.

He shook his head. "Betht time. You can be detected during daylight."

"Hard to argue with that," I admitted. "Well, I guess I'd better let you get back to it. Onward and downward."

He nodded and grimly resumed digging. Strange little guy. If he wasn't careful, he might grow up to be a writer.

"Hey, Hoagy," he called after me.

"Yeah, Gordie?"

He grinned. "Tooth fairy came."

"Yeah, I had a funny feeling he might."

"Only left me a quarter though. Got me a dollar before."

"I'm afraid they don't make anything like they used to, Gordie," I informed him. "Including fairies."

Lulu led me back through the woods, straining at her leash. She now seemed to have a firm idea of where she wanted to go and was anxious to get there. She led me across a muddy pasture in the direction of the souvenir building, then steered me past that to the exact spot in the outer wall where I'd seen Mavis and Roy conferring. The spot where the peacock predator was getting in.

About twenty feet short of the wall she pulled up abruptly, black nose quivering in the flashlight beam.

Roy was sitting there on a folding chair behind a tree, a shotgun in his lap, motionless. The consummate hunter.

"That you, Roy?" I called out, so he wouldn't blow our heads off.

He didn't respond. Not that he's a particularly verbal kind of guy, but he didn't so much as move. I started toward him. I was leading Lulu now. She wanted nothing to do with this.

There was a good reason why Roy wasn't moving. He was fast asleep on the job, breathing slowly and deeply like an old draft horse. There was a thermos at his feet. I opened it and smelled its contents. Equal parts coffee and bourbon.

Lulu moseyed over to the burrow under the wall and sniffed at it delicately. Then she snuffled at me, pronouncing herself ready to move on. We started back. We hadn't gone far when I heard an animal crashing through the brush alongside us. Lulu froze and let out a soft, low growl. It was met with an answering growl. Then she relaxed and whooped softly, tail thumping on the ground. And out of the brush it came, eyes glowing in the flashlight beam. It was a mutt, part terrier, part collie, male, with a dirty-gray muzzle and a busy stub of a tail. They greeted each other in the way dogs will do. Then Lulu yapped in a manner I can only describe as girlish and tumbled over onto her back, dabbing at him playfully with her paws while he sniffed at her in an extremely personal manner. I stood there holding the flashlight and watching them. My chest felt heavy, my knees weak. The signs had all been there, but I'd been too dumb to read them. They do say a father is always the last to know.

Lulu was in love.

"Your daughter has a boyfriend."

"How cute." She yawned. It was five in the morning.

"It is not cute, Merilee. He is a mongrel, a cur. He looks like a Butch or a Bowser. Definitely a Bowser. And who knows where the hell he comes from?"

"I'm sure he comes from a very fine—"

"He had his nose in her bum."

"And what did you do?"

"Chased him back under the wall, the no-good mutt. I *knew* something was up. She's been acting weird ever since we got here. I think this calls for prompt, decisive action, Merilee. I'm putting her on the first plane to New York tomorrow morning."

"Hoagy, she's a big girl now and there's not a thing you can do about it," she said lightly. "Face it, darling. Your little one hears the call of the wild."

"Then I'm getting her a pair of earmuffs—shearling."

"Hoagy?"

"Yes, Merilee?"

"Hello."

"Hello yourself. How's Elliot?"

"Mr. Hewlett, the cranky old farmer down the road, came and looked him over. Said he was all stopped up."

"Elliot or Mr. Hewlett?"

"Elliot, you ninny. So we rolled him over onto his back and—"

"Elliot or Mr. Hewlett?"

"*And* dumped two ounces of caster oil down his throat. He squealed in protest but—"

"Elliot or—"

"If you don't stop that, I'm going to hang up. . . . Anyway things seem to be moving along smartly once again. I was going to call you in the morning, actually. It seems your housekeeper there *is* on to something."

"Make that was."

"Oh, dear. Hoagy . . . are you okay?"

"Just dandy. What did your aged chums say?"

"There were some very hush-hush whispers around the lot about Sterling Sloan."

"What about him?"

"Apparently he was a rather serious morphine addict."

"Oh?"

"Hollywood drug of choice in those days, I'm told," she said. "Goldwyn made sure it stayed a deep, dark secret because of all the major drug scandals in the twenties. And it has pretty much stayed that way, actually. None of Sloan's biographers have gotten on to it."

"That's not too surprising. Most show-biz biographers would rather make up the dirt than dig for it."

"They also said Rex Ransom has been going around town for years bragging he knows something nasty. It seems he had the hotel room next door to Sloan's. And he was there when Sloan died."

"Excellent. I'll talk to him when he gets here. I'm dying to meet him anyway."

"Rex Ransom?" she said, surprised. "Whatever for?"

"It so happens, Miss Nash, that Rex Ransom was my very first hero."

"Your *hero*? Why on earth was he . . . Oh, wait, didn't he do one of those fifties kiddie serials on TV?"

"Not just any serial, Merilee. He was the Masked Avenger, he and his faithful steed, Neptune. When I was five, I had a

Masked Avenger mask, a lunch box, time-traveler ring. I walked like him. I hitched up my trousers like him . . ."

"And I'll bet you were cute as a bug's ear."

"That's not for me to say."

"I hope he doesn't let you down," she said vaguely.

"Why would he let me down?"

"Some things a little boy has to find out for himself."

"You've been a big help, Merilee. How can I repay you?"

"Well, I do have something in mind. . . ." She hesitated. "I-I had a nice chat on the phone with your parents last night."

"Why, what did they want?" I demanded.

"Don't shout at me. They didn't want anything. I called to wish your father a happy birthday. It was his seventieth yesterday, you know."

I left that one alone.

"They've been in Hobe Sound," she said.

"Naturally. It was winter."

"He sounded so sad, Hoagy."

"Price of brass must be down."

"That's not it at all. He *misses* you. You're his only child. He knows he made mistakes, tried to turn you into someone you're not. He understands that now. He doesn't know what else to say to you, except that he's sorry."

"This all sounds a lot more like your dialogue than his."

"You can repay me by calling him. It's been so many years since you have."

"What's your second choice?"

"He's an old man, Hoagy. He won't be around much longer."

"He'll never die," I assured her. "He'll simply stare death in the face and say, 'I am very, very disappointed in you.' "

"You have to settle this, Hoagy, or you'll be sorry for the rest of your life."

"I've prepared myself for that. Look, Merilee, I'm—"

"You're a grown man, and I can't make you call him if you don't want to, nor should I try to. Does that cover it?"

"Thank you for being so understanding. I knew there was a reason we were friends."

"Oh, is that what we are?" she asked sweetly.

"Good night, Merilee."

"Be kind to Lulu, darling. She needs you now more than ever. This is a grand adventure she's embarking on."

"So to speak."

"Hoagy?"

"Yes, Merilee?"

"She's a Virgo, Hoagy."

"Oh, God. I hate this."

The morning was bright. So was my left side. The bruises there had blossomed numerous eye-catching shades of yellow and purple. My head felt fine. Well, not fine but okay. I got up slowly, groaning, and made my way downstairs naked. I started my coffeemaker. I put down Lulu's breakfast. I threw open the sitting room curtains, the better to breathe in that fresh country air, only to find myself face-to-face with a pair of elderly ladies in pastel leisure ensembles. Stray tourists. One of them gaped at me, wide-eyed—the sight of me unclothed does have that effect on some women. The other one started fumbling for her camera.

A uniformed security guard came loping across the courtyard after them. "Area's off-limits, girls!" he called out. "Staff only. Follow me, please. Peacocks are this way."

Off they went, chattering excitedly. They're probably still talking about it. I know I am.

I showered. I dressed in the gray cheviot-wool suit while I sipped my coffee. Fern was being buried that morning. I hadn't known her for long, but I felt like going. I met up with Mavis, Mercy, and Charlotte in the courtyard. Mavis had on a severe navy-blue pin-striped pantsuit and was tense and quiet. Richard was backing the Mercedes out of the garage. He hopped out and opened the front passenger door for Mavis and closed it after her while Mercy and Charlotte got in back. There was room for me back there, too, but I didn't want to intrude. I was also anxious to get behind the wheel of the Jag again.

I was putting the top down when Charlotte got out and offered to take her own car so I could ride with the Glazes.

I thanked her but declined. "Why don't you ride with me?" I suggested. I did want to talk to her.

She turned me down. Mercy didn't.

"Do you mind?" she asked me shyly. She wore a jacket and skirt of matching black gabardine. She looked good in black. I have yet to meet a good-looking woman who doesn't. "I've always wanted to ride in an antique car."

"I prefer to think of it as a classic." I started it up. It kicked right over, began purring. "I don't mind a bit. Hop in."

"Okay with you, Father?" she asked Richard.

Richard wore shades against the bright morning. Sunshine can be somewhat rough on bloodshot eyes. "Fine, child," he replied unsteadily.

"Great." She climbed in next to me.

"Follow me, Hoagy," Richard said, with a lazy fly-boy salute that was straight out of *Dawn Patrol.*

"I shall."

He got in the Mercedes and was about to pull away when I heard the eruption. Mount St. Mavis. She immediately flung her door open and marched toward us, heels smacking sharply on the bricks.

"*What* do you think you are doing, Mercy?" she demanded.

"Riding to the funeral, Mother," Mercy replied mildly.

"Get in the family car at once!" Mavis ordered. "You will *not* ride to Fern's funeral in some flashy open sports car. This is the most preposterous, disrespectful thing I have ever—"

"Father said it was—"

"I said it was all right, Mave," Richard acknowledged from next to her, soothingly. "What's the harm?"

Mavis whirled on him, outraged. "How *dare* you interfere?"

"Interfere? Bloody hell, woman. She's my daughter."

"She's *my* daughter!"

Richard whipped off his sunglasses, twitching, red-faced. "She's *our* daughter!"

"She's *mine!*" cried Mavis, toe-to-toe with him, the cords in her neck standing out. "Shenandoah is mine. She is mine. *Mine.* And don't you forget it!"

"How can I forget it?" he snarled. "You never stop reminding me!"

Mavis faced Mercy again. "Get in the car, Mercy," she commanded, nostrils flaring.

"I'm riding with Hoagy," Mercy said defiantly.

"In the car, Mercy!" Mavis insisted.

"No!"

Mavis turned back to Richard, her chin raised, the better to look down her nose at him. "Are you happy now?" she demanded viciously. "You've turned her against me. Soured her. You've always wanted to. Are you happy now?"

"The only way I'd be happy, woman," he roared, "is if this were *your* funeral I was driving to!"

The slap caught him flat-footed. It was a hard, ringing blow and he took it full on the cheek. It knocked him back on his heels.

"That was a dreadful thing to say," Mavis whispered icily. She spun and marched back to the Mercedes.

Richard stood there for a second, stunned. Then he stormed after her. When she got in, he seized the car door and slammed it shut behind her with all of the strength his fury could muster.

Only Mavis wasn't all the way in. Her right foot was still sticking out when she saw Richard's hand on the door. She had only a split second to react. A split second to yank her foot inside the car. She just made it. Just missed having her ankle shattered by the heavy steel door. Just.

She stared at him through the window with her mouth open. She was genuinely frightened. I doubt she often was.

"Thought you were in, Mave," Richard growled in apology. "Sorry."

But he wasn't. She knew it and he knew she knew it. She glowered at him. He glowered back. Then he got in and they drove off.

"I don't understand them," Mercy said quietly after we'd tailed the Mercedes in silence for a few minutes.

"Don't even try," I said, enjoying the Jag's eagerness, the way it hugged the narrow country road. "You can never understand what goes on between two people. It doesn't matter whether you're related to them or not."

"But they hate each other."

"Seem to."

"So why don't they get divorced?"

"Could be they're happy this way," I offered.

"I don't believe that."

"Could be that facing the alternative—a life alone—is even worse than what they have now. Plenty of couples are like them. They complain. They fight. They make each other utterly miserable for forty or fifty years. I don't know why. All I know is if your parents wanted to get a divorce, they would. If people genuinely want out of a relationship, they get out."

"I don't understand you either," she said softly.

I glanced over at her. She was gazing at me. She looked more like an adult dressed this way. Or maybe I just wanted to think she did. Her eyes were a child's, utterly without guile. They caught and held mine a moment. Until I remembered the road. "What about me?" I asked.

"Why you never smile."

"That's a funny thing to ask someone who's on his way to a funeral."

"Why don't you?" she pressed.

"I smile all the time. It just doesn't show on the outside."

"Are you smiling right now?"

"Grinning my ass off."

"Hoagy?"

"Yes?"

"I like your car."

"So do I. Only it's my ex-wife's."

"You're divorced?"

"Somewhat."

"Because you wanted out?"

"Because one of us did."

There was no church service. Just a brief graveside cere-mony. Frederick and Edward met up with us at the cemetery, each of them clutching a single long-stemmed red rose. Two dozen or so townspeople were there, too, most of them aged. It was a small cemetery set on a hill overlooking green pastures and a river that sparkled in the morning sunlight. It was a nice place to be buried, if you have to be buried.

Mavis wouldn't stand next to Richard during the cere-mony. She stayed on the other side of the grave from him. Occasionally, they shot quick, poisonous glances across Fern's coffin at each other.

The brothers stood close together, their faces grim masks. After the coffin had been lowered into the ground they tossed their roses onto it. They left together.

I drove back to Shenandoah alone and changed into my work clothes. I always wear the same chamois shirt, jeans, and tattered pair of mukluks when I write. I do this because I wore them when I was writing the first novel. Ballplayers have their superstitions. So do writers. We're no more in control of our awe-inspiring gifts than they are.

I made a fresh pot of coffee and sat down before my Olym-pia with a cup. Alma's diary, my copy of *Oh, Shenandoah,* my sharpened pencils, and my blank sheets of paper were arrayed before me. I was all ready to go. Except for Lulu. She always dozes under my chair with her head on my foot when I work. This morning she wouldn't budge from her chair. She was act-ing shy and insecure now, as if she needed some kind of reas-surance from me. Why hadn't we gotten a male? I asked my-self. I went over to her and sat with her there in my lap for a while. I said a few things I won't bother to go into here. Then I went back to the typewriter. A few minutes later she ambled over and plopped down under me and rubbed my mukluk with her head. Then she went to sleep, still my girl.

He was a kind and decent man. Everyone spoke of his wisdom and his uncommon good sense. Truly, John Raymond was a man to admire. He was not, however, a man to love. And this was a sad thing, Evangeline reflected as she gazed across the dining table at him. For she had given this man her body and the past ten years of her life. And now she was miserable.

The work went quickly. Whenever I got stuck for a period detail such as an article of clothing or an eating utensil, I jotted it down on a list for Mercy. Occasionally, I found myself glancing up when I heard a noise outside, thinking it might be Sadie. Not that I wanted it to be Sadie. I just thought it might be, that's all.

I knocked off at lunchtime and went inside. Gordie was in the kitchen chewing on a peanut butter and jelly sandwich, his baseball and mitt next to him on the table. Charlotte, still dressed for the funeral, was pouring him a glass of milk.

"Hey, Hoagy," he said brightly. "Wanna play catch?"

"Maybe later, Gordie," I said.

"When?" he wondered.

"Gordie, why don't you go finish your lunch in your room," Charlotte broke in. "Hoagy is very busy."

The lower lip started to come out.

"Before dinner, Gordie," I promised hastily. "Okay?"

"Okay!" He snatched up his mitt and darted for the back door.

"Hey, Gordie," I called after him. "Take it slow."

He grinned, then slammed the door behind him.

Charlotte was puzzled.

"That's what McQueen said to people in *Bullitt* instead of good-bye," I explained.

She nodded, still puzzled. She obviously thought less of

me now. It happens. I joined her at the counter and made myself a sandwich. The jelly was Fern's. Black plum.

"He sure does like you," she observed.

"Go ahead, rub it in."

"Hasn't said but five words to me," she confessed. " 'I-want-a-Big-Mac.' "

Couldn't blame the little guy. I wanted one myself after I'd tasted her meat loaf. "So take him out for one."

"And if Mavis needs me while I'm gone?"

"Wouldn't she understand, under the circumstances?"

She stared at me.

"Of course not," I said. "How silly of me."

"I don't suppose I could talk *you* into taking him out."

"Sorry. Midget human life-forms are not my specialty."

"He's lonely. He needs a man."

"There's always Richard."

"He needs a *man.*"

"You may be selling Richard short. I know you're selling me long." I poured myself some milk. "So, how are you at handwriting analysis?"

She frowned at me. "Handwriting analysis?"

I dropped Fern's bundle of love letters down on the counter. "I understand your father and Fern were romantically involved before he married your mother."

"It's true, they were." Curious, she picked up the letters and leafed through them, chewing on her lower lip. "If you're asking me would I recognize my father's handwriting . . . the answer is yes. And this isn't it." She handed them back to me.

"They're from a long time ago," I pointed out. "People's handwriting changes over the years. You might not recognize it at first glance."

"I *do* recognize it."

"You do?"

She nodded.

"Well, whose is it?"

She showed me her pointy little teeth. "You help me, I'll help you."

"All right, all right. I'll take the midget to McDonald's."

"Thanks, I knew I could count on you," she said, a triumphant glint in her eyes.

And then she told me who Fern's Sweet Prince was.

Chapter Ten

A herd of tour buses was grazing outside the souvenir building. Hundreds of *Oh, Shenandoah* faithfuls sat at the picnic tables intently stuffing their faces on box lunches while they waited their turn to tour the old house. A number of them looked up hopefully at me as I eased the Jag past them down toward the front gate. I didn't cut a terrible figure. I had my navy blazer of soft flannel on over a turtleneck of yellow cashmere and pleated, gray houndstooth trousers. My plaid touring cap from Bates was on my head, Lulu's beret on hers. Still, it was Mavis Glaze they were hoping to catch a glimpse of, not the first major new literary voice of the eighties, and friend. Disappointed, they went back to cramming with both hands.

Edward Glaze had his law office in Barristers' Row, a choice little colony of 150-year-old carriage houses nestled across a courtyard from the domed Augusta County Courthouse in downtown Staunton. His reception area was small and neat, his secretary black, crisply dressed, efficient. He came right out to greet me when she buzzed him.

"Hoagy, I was so pleased you called," he said warmly, shaking my hand. "Lovely ceremony this morning, wasn't it?"

"It was."

"I've asked my cook to prepare us lunch at my house. We can walk. That be all right?"

"More than all right."

Edward strode briskly. He was in good shape for a man his age. Lulu trailed a few feet behind us, large black nose to the sidewalk. The town was hopping. Workers were stringing banners across Beverley Street. Shopkeepers were hanging colonial-style carriage lamps and hand-lettered wooden signs outside their stores. An ABC News crew was shooting background footage for the Barbara Walters special. The townspeople all seemed to know Edward and like him. They smiled and waved. He did the same.

"Hell, you ought to run for mayor," I teased.

He laughed softly. "Oh, no, that's much more Fred's style. I'm afraid I'm not particularly adept socially. It takes me a while to get comfortable around people."

"You're doing fine."

"Thank you," he said, coloring slightly. "I've been wanting to get to know you better, actually. Ask you about your work. Writers are such fascinating people, it's been my experience."

"I guess we've had different experiences." I tugged at my ear. "But feel free to ask."

The business district ended at Coalter Street. We turned there and started up a steep hill.

"They call this Gospel Hill," he informed me as we climbed, "due to the religious meetings held here in the late 1790s at Samson Eagon's blacksmith shop."

Soon we were among gracious Victorian and Greek Revival mansions set well back from the road behind blossoming magnolias and sourwoods.

"Not a terrible town," I observed. "Gorgeous, in fact."

"We try. We recently got the business district named to the

National Historic Register. Quite an effort, but well worth it, I think."

Edward lived down the block from Woodrow Wilson's birthplace in a turn-of-the-century Georgian-style home of red brick. Fluted columns supported the ornate white frontispiece. An ornate fanlight topped the front door. It was a handsome place, though not unique. There was another next door exactly like it.

The entry hall was dark and cool and smelled of lemon oil. There was an ornate oak hatstand with a beveled mirror inside the door. I left my hat on it. Lulu held on to hers. Double doors led into a masculine front parlor lined with bookcases and furnished with matching leather wing-back chairs and a chesterfield sofa.

Edward went over to a butler's table next to the fireplace. "Sherry?"

"As long as it isn't the same brand Mavis serves."

He filled two glasses, smiling. "It isn't."

We carried them into the octagon-shaped dining room. It was sunny and airy. The French doors were opened to the garden, which was fragrant and ablaze with perennials. The dining table was a twin-pedestaled mahogany George the Third, set for two. A vase of tulips sat in its center.

"Lovely home," I observed.

"Thank you. It's somewhat large for one person, but I bought it a number of years ago for a good price and I've never regretted it. The garden, in fact, keeps me sane." He gazed out at it lovingly. "I spend most of my free time digging around back there."

"Where does your brother live?"

"Fred has a home of his own."

"The one next door?"

"Why, yes. How did you know?"

"Wild guess."

A uniformed black woman brought us our lunch. Veal

marsala, boiled new potatoes, string beans. It was excellent. Sancerre wasn't terrible either.

I pulled Fern's love letters out of my pocket while we ate, placed them on the table before him.

Edward frowned, dabbed at his mouth with his napkin, and reached for them. It took him a moment to recognize them. He turned bright red when he did. "Lord, these are dreadful. I was all of eighteen at the time—the last of the great romantics." He laughed to himself sadly. Then his eyes began to fill with tears. "I can't believe Fernie saved them all these years. Dear, dear Fernie."

"Mind telling me about it?"

"Not at all—there really isn't that much to tell, Hoagy. We read poetry together in the tall grass and dreamt of running off to Greenwich Village and becoming great, starving writers. It was all so . . . *romantic.* And terribly tragic."

"Why so tragic?"

"Mother didn't approve of Fern," he replied. "Thought she was too common for her young college man. After all, Fern's father worked on our *car.* So Fernie and I overdramatized it, as we did everything. It was playacting. Kid stuff." He smiled faintly and sipped his wine. "Besides, Fern already had a serious beau, Frankie Neene. Frankie was a blustering, cocky kid then, a football player. Used to take her for rides in his car and make love to her. She told me all the lurid details. Told me he promised to marry her, too. He never intended to, though. He married a proper Mary Baldwin girl. Broke Fern's heart."

"I understand he committed suicide."

Edward's face darkened. "Yes. He was a broken man. Terrible business." He shook his head. "When I was your age, Hoagy, I wanted to lead three or four lives. Now that I've been around nearly seventy years, and seen what life does to people, I've come to realize that once is plenty."

"In her diary, your mother mentions that you got to be somewhat friendly with Sterling Sloan during the filming."

"As much as anyone could," he acknowledged. "Sterling

was a strange, lost soul, a man who lived only for truth and beauty—the two things in shortest supply in this world. He was the saddest man I've ever known, and one of the most fascinating. Please stop me if I start to bore you. . . ."

"You won't."

"It rained the night before they were all due to arrive from Hollywood," he recalled. "The convoy of trucks, the specially chartered train, the hundreds and hundreds of production people—an invasion. In the middle of the night the doorbell woke me. Someone at the door. I heard our caretaker answering it. Heard voices. Then the doorbell started ringing again. I got up and went downstairs to see what was going on. No one else stirred—I was the light sleeper of the family. The caretaker said it was someone who claimed to be with the movie. He'd told the fellow to come back in the morning with everyone else, but he refused to go. I opened the door to find this thoroughly bedraggled-looking vagabond in a moth-eaten black cape seated out there in the rain on top of an ancient steamer trunk. He was soaking wet and unshaven and smelled more than a little of cow manure. He apologized for the late hour, explained as how he'd hitchhiked his way on a farmer's truck to be with the movie, and alas, had nowhere to stay and no money. He was unusually polite and well-spoken. 'What do you do?' I asked him. 'I drink,' he replied. 'I mean,' I said, 'who are you?' 'Oh, I am not any sort of person at all,' he replied. 'I am an actor.' A down-and-out one hoping for a bit role, I supposed. Still, he was shivering from the wet and had nowhere to go, so I let him in. It wasn't until he'd removed his hat and cape that I realized who he was. 'Why, you're Sterling Sloan!' I exclaimed. 'Someone has to be,' he replied in that cryptic, disembodied way he had. 'Unfortunately, I am that one.' I told him the cast would be staying at the Hotel Woodrow Wilson in town, and that I'd be happy to drive him there. But he was so pale and chilled I offered him a brandy first. His hand shook so badly half of it dribbled right down his chin. He hadn't eaten for days. I made him a sandwich, and he devoured it and drank several more brandies. He began to get some color in his cheeks. He told me I was a rare and kind young soul. Then he stretched out on the sofa in the parlor and fell instantly asleep. From then on, he attached himself to me. He seemed to like being around me. I have no idea why. Naturally, I was thrilled and pestered him for advice about acting. He told me to get proper classical training in Britain, learn to carry a spear, and play toothless old men and blushing young girls. He was quite generous—he even offered to write me letters of introduction to several theater companies over there. He was very offhanded about his fame. Had no use for the trappings of stardom, no star presence at all off camera, not like Miss Barrett or Flynn. You *knew* they were stars. Not Sterling. He came to life only when he was in front of the camera. The rest of the time, he almost wasn't there. He was so very quiet and remote. He spent long hours just stretched out on the daybed in his trailer, reading. And sometimes he really *wasn't* there. By that I mean he seemed disoriented, not totally sure where he was or what role he was playing. . . . He and his wife weren't at all close. He'd arrived from London, she from Hollywood. I felt he was a deeply lonely man. And then those headaches of his kept him in great pain for hours at a time."

Edward's cook came in and cleared the table. She left us a pot of coffee and a plate of cookies. Edward poured the coffee.

"Would you happen to know if he used morphine?"

"Not that I ever saw," Edward replied, nibbling on a cookie.

"Was there a doctor on the set?"

"There was. He arrived with the production team from Hollywood. Dr. Toriello. An older fellow with dirty fingernails and hair growing out of his ears. He spent a lot of time with Miss Darnell. I was told she suffered from severe menstrual cramps and refused to work when she had them."

"Sounds like a Dr. Feelgood," I suggested.

He frowned. "A what?"

"The studios always kept some borderline quack around

to make the little green men go away. They still do. Did he spend time around Sloan?"

"Yes, he often looked in on him for his headaches." Edward's eyes widened. "Why, do you think he was . . . ?"

"I'm afraid so."

Edward shook his head sadly. "Morphine. It's for pain, isn't it?"

"It is."

"It was her, Laurel Barrett. She was so angelic, so delicately beautiful. Yet she was the dirtiest, rottenest tramp imaginable, Hoagy. God, how she tortured him. It was as if she took delight in punishing him for his love. She and Flynn—the two of them would go into his trailer in the middle of the day to have sex. Everyone knew. It was disgraceful." He lowered his voice. "She even made a play for me."

"Did you . . . ?"

"I was tempted. Lord, was I tempted. She was one of the most gorgeous women in the world. But Sterling was my friend." He sighed longingly. "I must confess I still wonder sometimes when I'm lying in my bed alone at night. I wonder what I missed out on." Abruptly, he reached for his coffee. "Drugs? Who could blame the poor man?"

"The night before she died, Fern told me she believed he was murdered."

"And you believe she was murdered, as well. Yes, I know all about your theory. Mavis phoned me first thing this morning. I was shocked, truly. It's been so many years since she'd phoned. I almost didn't recognize her voice."

"And my theory?"

"I'm skeptical, frankly."

"So is Polk Four," I admitted.

"Yes, I know. I spoke with him as soon as I got off the phone with Mave. I wanted to have the facts of the case. Lawyers, by nature, have an aversion to surprises." He sipped his coffee. "I've been curious about Mother's diary myself. Why those pages were torn out. Why Fern screamed."

"Did Fern ever say anything to you about it?"

"Not a word. The entire incident came as news to me."

"Do you have any idea who was there in Vangie's room with Sloan?"

"None."

"You said his wife was sleeping around on him."

"Gleefully."

"Was he doing the same?"

"There weren't any whispers," he replied. "As I mentioned, Sterling kept to himself most of the time. He certainly said nothing to me about anyone." Edward got up and went over to the French doors. "One thing you should bear in mind about Fern, Hoagy, is that she was always inclined to exaggerate. The fact is Sterling died of a ruptured aneurysm. The warning signs were all there. He had been complaining of blinding headaches. He acted strangely, he was frequently drowsy. The medical experts later agreed that these symptoms indicated the leakage in his brain had already begun. He looked particularly pale and drawn that last day of filming. He was so weak he was barely able to finish. That very night he was stricken in his suite at the Woodrow Wilson."

"Who else was there?"

"She was—Laurel. And Dr. Toriello arrived almost immediately. He was staying in the hotel. He sent for an ambulance at once, but Sterling died before it arrived."

"Did any other doctor besides Toriello see him?"

"I imagine so. Someone local had to sign the death certificate. Toriello was licensed out of state."

"Were the police called?"

"Of course. The sheriff got there right away."

"Not the Staunton city police?"

Edward smiled. "Town was a lot smaller then. There was no city police force."

"I see. Who was the sheriff?"

"Polk Two," he replied. "Polk Four's granddad. Fine man. Only just gave up his senate seat in Richmond last year. Represented us there quite proudly for the past forty-five years. His legs are bothering him—he's eighty-seven, after all. But he's still sharp as a tack, old Polk Two."

"How would I get in touch with him?"

"If you wish to be gracious, you go through Polk Four and get his blessing. He's very protective of the old fellow."

"And if I don't?"

Edward stared at me for a moment, then turned and looked out the door at his garden. Stiffly he said, "He's in the book."

Polk Two lived on a small farm out off Route 11 on the way to Harrisonburg. The road to it wound back through lush, fragrant farmland and through time. A colony of Mennonites lived there. I passed a couple of their black, horse-drawn carriages clopping slowly along, and a farm where four women in bonnets, long dresses, and sneakers were planting vegetables in a garden. They waved as I passed. I waved back and fleetingly, wished I lived there with them.

A big silver Lincoln Town Car was parked out in front of the white, wood-framed farmhouse, which was badly in need of paint and a new roof. The broad wraparound front porch had a serious case of dry rot. There was a bank barn and grain silo out behind the house, a poultry house, hilly pasturage. All of it looked neglected.

I left the Jag behind the Lincoln and rang the doorbell and waited. And waited some more. Finally, I heard heavy footsteps inside and a cough.

"Sorry to keep you waiting, son," Polk Two said cheerfully as he opened the door. "It's my legs—they've pure gone to hell on me."

He was a tall, beefy man and he still had the lawman's air of authority even if he did have to walk with two canes. His coloring was fair. His full head of white hair was still streaked with blond. His eyes were blue and twinkly behind the heavy, black-framed glasses, his loose, saggy skin so pale as to be almost translucent. I could see the blue veins on the backs of his hands as they clutched the canes, trembling slightly. He wore a white button-down shirt, black knit tie, a heavy gray wool sack suit, and hearing aids in both ears. He smelled like witch hazel and Ben-Gay.

"Come on in, son," he said. "Come on. Your dog, too, if she wants."

She didn't. She likes porches.

He moved slowly, waddling like a large, heavy penguin. Wheezing, he led me into a small parlor that hadn't been painted or aired out since V.J. Day. The air was heavy with cigarette smoke and dust and heat. Portable electric heaters were going strong in each corner. It must have been ninety in there.

"Too warm for you?" he asked.

"No, it's fine," I replied as I felt the perspiration beginning to run down my neck. "Cozy."

A radio was on, tuned to the police band. He waddled over to it and turned it off. "Can't get too warm when you get to be my age, you know," he observed. He chuckled. "I have to turn up the thermostat another degree every birthday. In three more years I'll be able to bake bread in here."

A captain's chair piled with cushions was set before a table. A large-type edition of *Reader's Digest* lay open on the table along with the phone and a carton of cigarettes.

Polk Two plopped *slooooowly* down in the chair. "Have a seat, son," he commanded, indicating an easy chair. "That one used to be mine. Most comfortable one in the house. I just can't get up out of it anymore."

I took off my cap and sat. "Nice place you have here, Mr. LaFoon."

He turned up his hearing aids. "Thanks. Been in the family a long time. And make it Polk Two, Mr. Hoag."

"If you'll make it Hoagy."

"As in Carmichael?" he asked, turning them up some more.

"As in the cheese steak."

He nodded. "Always like his songs. 'Stardust,' 'Georgia on My Mind'—you could hum 'em. Yessir." He lit a cigarette and looked around. "It'll all be Polk Four's when I pass on, if he wants it. Needs work, of course. Haven't done much to it since the wife died in '72. But the land's good. Twenty-five acres of it. My boy, Polk Three, he's retired down in Florida with his wife. I'm all alone here. But it suits me, except for this habit I got of not being able to shut up when I trap some poor fellow here like you." He chuckled. "Polk Four, he looks in on me regular as clockwork. He's a good boy. I just wish he'd take a drink of whiskey or a dip into a cute little blonde once in a while. A man needs to let off a little steam now and again, or he'll blow." He glanced at me sharply. "I phoned him after you called. He said he'd try to make it over."

"It sure is nice how everyone in the valley talks to everyone else."

"He said you were trouble." The old man looked me over with a practiced eye. "Don't know. You look to me like about as much trouble as a tub of warm grits. Take off your jacket, son. You'll sweat right through the material and stain it. Now what can I do for you? Something about this sequel to Alma's book, you said?"

I stripped off my jacket. "Yes. The publisher wants me to write an introduction recalling the sensation it caused when it first came out. The making of the movie, Sterling Sloan's death . . ."

He puffed on his cigarette. "Ah, that business."

"I understand you were there on the scene when he died."

"I was."

"I wondered if you could share some of your recollections with me."

"Newspapers covered the hell out of it." He moistened his thin lips. "You ought to go on over to the *News Leader* and go through their old issues. They give you any trouble, tell 'em I sent you. They'll treat you right."

"I'm not interested in what was reported," I said. "I'm interested in what *happened.*"

He grinned at me. "Well, whatever you are you aren't dumb." He coughed, a deep, rumbling cough. "Okay. Sure. It's the recent things I can't remember, you know. Like what I had for dinner last night. But fifty years ago I can remember just fine. . . . Pork chops, mashed potatoes, and okra—that's what I was eating at my desk the evening I got the call. Sent over from Joe's Cafe across the street. They're out of business now. Joe got himself killed in Korea. No wait, that was Joe Junior. Joe had a coronary and dropped dead."

"The phone call . . . ?"

"Something about the movie folk over at the Woodrow Wilson," he continued. "Quite some hotel in those days, it was. Fanciest place within fifty miles. Fine dining room, ballroom, orchestra. I headed on over there, none too happy about it. Those movie fellas, they'd been making my life miserable ever since they got here. I had no complaint with the performers. Or with all them boys and girls from the fan magazines and newsreels neither. They behaved themselves. It was the damned film crew, dozens of healthy young roughnecks with money in their pockets. Whole bunch were like sailors on leave, drinking, chasing local gals, getting in brawls with the local fellows over 'em. I was sick of the whole lot, even if they did bring money into the town. But I'd had no trouble with the actors, like I said. Until that evening. . . . The manager and house detective, fella called Lou Holt, met me right at the front door, all agitated, and said there was an emergency up in the Sloan-Barrett suite. Quite some suite it was, too. Living room. Two bedrooms. Very first thing I noticed when I got there was the beds in both rooms were mussed. Odd for a man and wife, I thought. What I mean is, I don't believe the two of 'em slept together." He coughed. "I don't know if that's the sort of recollection you're interested in . . ."

"Go right ahead."

"Miss Barrett was standing there in some kind of flimsy

dressing gown, without any makeup on. Or slippers. I remember she looked like a frail young girl standing there like that. She was a pretty thing, but no meat on her. Had the whitest little feet I've ever seen, like a baby girl's. Seems they'd been dressing for some big party being thrown that night down in the ballroom to celebrate finishing up the filming. Seems he, Mr. Sloan that is, got himself a blinding headache while he was dressing. She had sent a bellhop out for some aspirins, but by the time he got up there with 'em the fella had collapsed."

"Where was he?"

"On the sofa, unconscious. The doctor from the movie company, Dr. Toriello, was with him. Ambulance was on its way. But it was pretty obvious he wasn't going to make it. He was breathing with great difficulty, huge gasps. Died just a minute or two after I got there."

"Was anyone else in the room?"

Polk Two stubbed out his cigarette, thought it over. "The bellhop was still hanging around."

"What was his name?"

"Don't recall. Just some scrawny kid. I got rid of him."

"Anyone else?"

"One other fellow came in, some sort of take-charge right-hand man of Mr. Goldwyn's. Melnick. No, Melnitz. Seward Melnitz. One of those high-strung types, kept trying to boss me around. Telling me not to say a word to the press, not to let nobody in. Treated me like I was retarded or something."

"He was probably just used to dealing with producers. No other witnesses?"

"If there were, they were gone by the time I got there."

"I see. What happened then?"

"Well, since Toriello was from California, I had to get a local man up to sign the certificate of death. It was Doc Landis I called. Discreet, professional man. He got right over, came to the same diagnosis as Toriello—that some kind of bubble had burst in Sloan's brain. After that the body was—"

"How?"

"Excuse me, son?"

"How did he arrive at his diagnosis?"

"Ah. Well, he asked Toriello a lot of questions. Don't recall what they were. I do remember they talked about Sloan's blood pressure. . . ."

"What about it?"

"It dropped dramatically after he collapsed, Toriello said. Apparently that told them something. And they discussed Sloan's symptoms of the previous few days. His headaches, way he'd been behaving . . ."

"Did you get the feeling Landis thought Toriello was negligent?"

"No, sir," replied Polk Two firmly. "Not at all."

"Did he examine the body?"

"His eyeballs. He looked at Sloan's eyeballs. Don't ask me why."

"To see if a pupil had dilated," I said. "A brain aneurysm would compress the optic nerve of one eye, possibly both. Was there an autopsy?"

"No, sir, there wasn't."

"Why not?"

"No reason to. The man died of natural causes. Medical men were satisfied."

"How long had you been sheriff at the time?"

"Three, four years."

"You'd been to a lot of death scenes, filed a lot of reports."

"My share of 'em," he acknowledged. "Yessir."

"Did you get any sense that something funny was going on in that hotel room?"

He frowned. "Funny? I'm not following you, son."

"That it wasn't what they said it was."

Polk Two reached for his cigarettes and lit one. I'm still not following you, son," he said, a little chillier this time.

"Sloan's headaches, drowsiness, disorientation . . . And the collapse itself—loss of consciousness, severe drop in blood pressure, difficulty in breathing—all of it could point to an entirely different cause of death."

"And what's that?" he asked.

"Sloan was heavy into morphine. I think he died of an overdose."

Polk Two didn't react much. Just looked at the ash on his cigarette and tapped it carefully into an ashtray and took a puff and blew out the smoke. His blue eyes gave away nothing. "Doctors said it was an aneurysm," he said quietly.

"Of course they did. Sloan was a major star. Ugly things like drug overdoses had a way of being prettied up for people like him. Is that what happened, Polk?"

Polk Two shook his head. "No offense, son, but I genuinely don't know what the hell you're talking about."

"Was there a cover-up, Polk?"

"There was no such thing!" he fired back angrily. "I didn't run this county that way. Or my district when I sat in Richmond. And I don't like you coming here to my home and suggesting I did!"

"I'm trying to get at the truth."

"You *got* the truth, boy. The man died there on the sofa from an aneurysm. I don't know how I can make it any plainer."

"Okay," I said, backing off. "What happened then?"

"Body was removed to Hamrick's funeral parlor over on Frederick Street. He was cremated there next day."

"Quick, wasn't it?"

He shrugged. "There was a certain desire on everyone's part to get it over with. Town was so damned full of reporters, radio people, newsreel cameras—a real carnivallike atmosphere. Pretty ghoulish, you ask me. Miss Barrett, she took the ashes home to England for burial. Funeral service was held over there a few days later."

I took my linen handkerchief out of my pocket and mopped my forehead and neck with it. "I understand your father was Alma Glaze's lawyer."

He scratched his chin. "That's right."

"Shortly before her death she had him draw up a codicil to her will that sealed her notes for *Sweet Land of Liberty* for fifty years. Any idea why she did it?"

"Daddy said she was getting pressured by Goldwyn. He wanted her to hurry up and write it so he could get himself another movie. She didn't like the idea of being rushed, particularly by him. She detested the man."

"Isn't fifty years a little excessive?"

Polk Two chuckled. "Not if you knew Alma. That woman, she was *ornery*. Mavis is a pure pleasure compared to her mammy. It was about control, son. Alma was showing Goldwyn she was boss, not him, and she was rubbing his nose in it for good measure. That man simply was not going to make more millions off of her creation. Not as long as she was around, and not in the event of her death, either."

"In the event of her death—meaning she expected to die?"

"We all expect to die, son."

"But she was a relatively young woman. It seems like an extreme form of insurance to take, unless of course she had reason to believe she would die soon. Was she ill?"

"Not in the least. You had to know her. It was just Alma being Alma, sticking it to that Hollywood fella."

"She was run over soon after that on Beverley Street."

"That's right. Just after the movie came out. Biggest money-maker in history, you know, until all those damned spaceship movies come along." He coughed and shifted in his chair with no little effort. "It happened on a Saturday night, about eight o'clock."

"Any idea what she was doing in town?"

"Kids said she told 'em she had some business to do. The three of them were home alone when it happened."

"She was meeting someone on business at that hour?"

"I never did buy that myself," he confessed. "I figured maybe she had herself a fella in town. Didn't much matter. She was dead was all that mattered. Run down while she crossed the street. Some fool ran the traffic light."

"You never found out who?"

He got defensive. "I made some progress. Had the make and color of the car from a witness. A car matching it turned up ditched on the outskirts of town next morning, blood on the fender, seats and floorboard reeking of cheap whiskey. Had been reported stolen from an old lady's driveway an hour or so before Alma was hit. I figured it was a couple of local boys having themselves a toot before they headed off to the Pacific to get their poor dumb asses shot off. I followed up. Had my eye on a particular pair of young hotheads, but they'd gone overseas by the time I got on to 'em. And they never made it back. So I reckon justice was done, in its own way."

"There must have been a lot of pressure on you to catch them."

"There was indeed. Alma was an institution here."

"Any chance her death was something other than an accident?"

He peered at me intently from behind his heavy glasses. Then he chuckled and shook his head in amazement. "Son, you're not interested in the truth one bit. You're looking to spin wild yarns for the funny papers."

"I'm looking to figure out why Fern O'Baugh died the other day."

"Fell down a flight of stairs, I heard," he said mildly.

"Yeah. Lots of accidents seem to happen in this place."

"It's a place like any other," he said, grinning. "A little nicer, if you ask me."

A car pulled up outside, and someone got out. Lulu started barking from the porch. She has a mighty big bark for someone with no legs.

"That'll be Polk Four, I reckon." Polk Two lifted the window shade and glanced outside. "Making friends with your pup. Always has been good with animals. Yessir, that boy's just naturally likable."

"So I'm told." I got to my feet. "I won't keep you any longer, sir."

He started to struggle up out of his chair.

"Don't trouble yourself," I insisted. "Thank you for your time."

"My pleasure, son," he said, easing back down. "Helped fill the day. Retirement's a lousy deal. Better off if you die young."

"I'll do my best." I went outside, closed the front door, and stood there on the porch inhaling the fresh air and watching Lulu and Polk Four. I counted to ten before I hurried back inside.

The old man was on the phone. He panicked when he saw me, slammed it down, red-faced.

"Sorry," I said. "Forgot my hat." I plucked my cap off the arm of the easy chair and grinned at him. "Like I said, it sure is nice how everyone in the valley talks to everyone else."

Polk Four was scratching Lulu's tummy out on the thick grass by the mailbox. She was on her back, tongue lolling out of the side of her mouth. She'd fallen for him. What can I say—she happened to be vulnerable right now.

When Polk Four saw me, he stood to his full height and smoothed the wrinkles in his khaki trousers—not that there were any. "Pretty car," he said, gazing at the Jag.

"It is," I agreed.

"Yours?"

"My ex-wife's."

"So you're divorced?"

"We are but we aren't."

He frowned, puzzled. "What does that mean exactly?"

"It means we're both mad as hatters," I replied. "Why do you ask?"

He adjusted his trooper's hat. "I'm just trying to figure out why you're attempting to ruin my life."

"I wasn't aware that's what I was doing, Sheriff."

"Mercy called me first thing this morning," he revealed darkly.

"Oh?"

"Said she had something very important to tell me." He narrowed his alert blue eyes at me. "Any idea what it was?"

I tugged at my ear. "None."

"She's decided to go to Europe for a year when she graduates in June. She said she wants to experience life on her own."

"No kidding."

"No kidding." He clenched and unclenched his jaw. "She said it was your idea."

"I wouldn't go that far, Sheriff. I simply told her that's what I did when I was her age."

He crossed his arms. "I don't appreciate this at all, Mr. Hoag, you filling her head with crazy ideas."

"Not so crazy. She's kind of sheltered."

"She's kind of impressionable is what she is," he argued. "She's also kind of terrific, and I intend to marry her."

"I'm sure that's what she has in mind, too, Sheriff. She just wants to kick up her heels a little first. It'll be for the best," I assured him. "This way she won't wonder."

"Wonder what?"

"If she missed out on anything. She'd only end up taking it out on you."

"What makes you such an expert on the subject?" he demanded testily.

"You want advice on marriage, talk to a man whose own turned to shit."

"I wasn't asking for your advice," he said crossly.

"My mistake. Sorry."

He crouched back down and patted Lulu's soft, white underbelly. Out came her tongue again. "Sometimes Mercy . . . she gives me the feeling she thinks I'm a real clod."

I left that one alone.

"Has she said anything to you?" he pressed.

"She said she likes you."

He brightened. "She did?"

I suddenly felt as if I were back in junior high school. I hated junior high school. "Only she feels like you're being forced on her by her mother. It's got to be her own choice. Don't crowd her. Let her come around to it in her own time."

He mulled this over. "Think I should loosen up on the reins a little, huh?"

"If that's how you want to put it. But you'll do better if you start thinking of her as a woman and not an Appaloosa."

He shook his head at me, disgusted. "I really don't get you, Mr. Hoag. Bothering her. Bothering my granddad. Pestering everybody in town with your weird ideas about Fern O'Baugh being murdered—"

"She wasn't the only one, Sheriff. Alma Glaze was murdered, too." I glanced up at the house. Polk Two was watching us through the window. "Why she was, I'm still not sure. Something to do with Sterling Sloan's death—which was not caused by any brain aneurysm. That was just a cover-up."

"Uh-huh. Is there anything else?" Polk Four asked with exaggerated patience.

"Franklin Neene's suicide."

"What about it?"

"Maybe it wasn't. Suicide, I mean."

Polk Four stayed calm. Dangerously calm. "I have to tell you, Mr. Hoag," he said very quietly, "I've had just about as much of you as I can stand." He came up close to me now. I felt his breath on my face. It smelled of Tic-Tacs. "I'm not ordinarily one to get tough. You can ask anybody. But I sure do feel like taking off this badge and gun and punching you in the mouth."

"I'm real sorry to hear you say that, Sheriff. Because if you do, we'll have to fight, and one of us will end up in the hospital, and it won't be you."

"What I *am* going to do," he promised, "is advise Mavis you're a public nuisance and ought to be put on a plane back to New York."

"Mavis happens to need me," I reminded him. "As long as she does, I'm not going anywhere. Sorry."

"Not as sorry as I am."

"What is it going to take for you to realize that I'm not doing this for laughs, Sheriff?" I demanded. "You happen to be sitting on one of the biggest scandals in motion picture history. Bigger than Thomas Ince. Bigger than William Desmond Taylor. Bigger than Fatty Arbuckle. Well, maybe not bigger than Fatty Arbuckle, but *big*. People have been *murdered*. I realize these are your folks down here, your family, your friends. Their lives may be ruined. I can't help that. And neither can you. You have a choice to make. You can put your money where my mouth is or you can stand by and watch. Only, if you do, you'll be the one who is ruined. Because I will get to the bottom of this, and when I do, it will go very, very public, believe me."

He took a deep breath. Slowly, he let it out. "Why are you doing this?"

"Fern asked me to. It was her last request. You're supposed to honor those."

"Okay, fair enough. You've said your piece. Now I'll say mine: Number one, I think you're full of crap. I think you smell a buck and you don't care who gets hurt. Number two, I'll be watching you. You bother anybody in Augusta County, I'll be on you. You exceed the speed limit by one-half mile per hour, I'll be on you. You so much as smile at a girl under the age of eighteen or smoke in a no-smoking—"

"I don't smoke."

"Or step on a crack in the damned sidewalk, I'll be on you! Got it!"

"Got it, pardner."

"And *don't* call me pardner!"

Polk Four didn't wave good-bye when he went tearing off in his big sedan. He didn't smile or tip his big broad-brimmed trooper's hat either. I don't think he liked me anymore.

I drove slowly back through the Mennonite farms toward Route 11, wondering.

Say Sloan *had* died of an overdose—why had Alma been killed? Had she found out about the cover-up? Threatened to expose it? Was Goldwyn possibly behind her death? If not him, who? Why was Fern killed? Whom could she hurt now, all these years later? How much did Polk Two know that he wouldn't tell me? Did Polk Four know anything, or had he been shielded from all of it?

I was thinking about these things when I got to a stop sign. It was a rural intersection, nothing but farmland in all four directions. A four-wheel-drive Ford pickup came to a stop directly across from me, all styled up with racing stripes and fog lamps and chrome roll bar and tires so huge you'd need a pole vault to reach the seat. I'd seen a lot just like it since I'd arrived in the valley. They seemed to hold great appeal for cretins aged seven to seventy. I didn't pay too much attention to this one.

Not until I noticed the two men riding in it. The driver had a crew cut. The other man had a ponytail. And an over-under shotgun aimed out his window right at me. He pulled the trigger.

Chapter Eleven

I dove down onto Lulu just as the Jag's windshield exploded, showering me with broken glass. I stayed down, eyes squinched shut, breath sucked in, heart racing. He wasn't through—one more shot boomed out in the country quiet. This one hit nothing. Then they took off for the hills with a screech.

I sat up at once, pellets of broken glass tumbling down the back of my neck. Lulu climbed down onto the floor under the glove box and cowered there, shaking. I assured her I could handle it.

Then I went after them.

I can't explain why. I had no idea what I'd do if I actually caught up with them. Die, maybe. All I knew was I had to do it. I tend not to be totally rational when I've been kicked in the head and shot at.

They were heading toward the Shenandoah Mountains and the West Virginia state line, moving fast but not that fast. Maybe they didn't know I was after them yet. The narrow farm road dipped and darted through the undulating pastures. No other cars were on it.

Merilee kept the Jag perfectly tuned. It responded at once as I tore my way through the gears, the wind biting at my face through the empty windshield. My eyes started to tear. I fumbled in the glove box for my aviator shades. Lulu glowered up at me, not liking this one bit. She had enough on her plate already.

The road started getting curvy right about when I got close enough for him to spot me in his rearview mirror. I could tell when he did—he speeded up. I did, too. His partner turned around. The cab's rear window slid open and the muzzle of his shotgun poked out. He took one wild shot at me, then another. Ignore those high-speed gunfights you see on TV—you can't get off any kind of a shot when you're bouncing down a country road at sixty miles an hour. Still, it crossed my mind that he might get lucky. So I floored it and cozied in right under the truck's upraised tail, the Jag's nose almost touching its *Keep on Truckin'* mud flaps. He was up so high on those stupid tires he couldn't get a clear shot down at me now even if he tried— the tailgate was shielding me. I was okay there. Unless they decided to hit the brakes.

Lulu let out a low moan. Again, I assured her I could handle it. There was no one to assure me I could handle it.

Faster. Seventy . . . eighty . . . veering past a Mennonite horse and buggy on a blind curve. Edging back over just before getting splattered by an oncoming car. Climbing hard into the mountains now, road twisting, narrowing. Signs shooting past . . . Head Waters—Elev. 2,925 Ft . . . Bullpasture Mountain—Elev. 3,240 Ft . . . Climbing up among pines now, swollen spring rivers roaring past. Climbing, curves blind, road a narrow ribbon hugging the side of the mountain. No shoulder. No rail. Only a sheer drop. And down, down, down . . . Jack Mountain—Elev. 4,378 Ft . . . The entire Shenandoah Valley laid out far below us now. I had no time to admire the view. I was too busy pushing him on. Faster . . .

We crested. Briefly, the road flattened out. Then we were descending. Flying down the twisting road, tires screaming, the Jag hugging the pavement like a panther. Twice he fishtailed, but held the big truck in check. We were playing a dangerous game of chicken now. I could stop at any time, turn around. I had his license number. But I didn't want to. I wanted to make him go faster.

He took his eyes off the road. Must have, because he didn't ever even try to hit the brakes. One moment he was flying down that twisting road. Next moment he was still flying, only there was no road under him. Only sky, his wheels spinning in the air.

I had just an instant to react. No time to weigh my options, to arrive at a sound, measured plan of action. There was only the Jag and the road that was no longer right in front of me. My brain shut down. My body took over. Feet rammed the brakes and clutch. Hands drove the wheel hard left. I spun out, wildly out of control. Skidded to a stop on the very edge of the road, facing uphill, stalled. I sat there like that for a moment, too dazed to move. Then the thought processes returned, and I jumped out to look.

The truck had touched down at the base of the mountain three thousand feet below, its wheels up, still spinning. A puff of gray smoke wafted lazily up from it, like from a campfire. It looked kind of peaceful. Until it blew. I saw it before I heard it. Saw the tongue of angry orange flame, the hunks of twisted steel flying off in every direction. I heard the explosion a second later. And for many seconds after that. It echoed across the entire valley, like a clap of thunder.

Lulu squirmed in between my feet and nuzzled my leg. I reached down and rubbed her ears. I got the battered silver flask of Macallan from the glove box and drank deeply from it. I stood there for a while taking in the panoramic view of the valley. I had time to admire it now.

And to wonder just whom Polk Two had been on the phone with when I'd gone back inside for my cap.

.   .   .

Pamela, housekeeper nonpareil, was waiting patiently outside the airline terminal in a sweater and skirt of matching bottle-green cashmere and knobby brown oxfords, her raincoat folded over her arm, two old leather suitcases beside her on the pavement. Pam's in her early sixties, plump and silver haired, and owns the loveliest complexion I've ever seen. Also the most unflappable disposition. I got to know her in Surrey a couple of years back when I was ghosting the life story of Tristam Scarr, the British rock star. Maybe you read it. Or about it. It got a little messy.

She smiled cheerily and waved when I pulled up at the curb and hopped out. "Yes, yes, it's so lovely to see you again, Hoagy."

I kissed her cheek. "Glad you could make it, Pam."

"Nonsense, dear. I'm thrilled you called—my life has gotten so appallingly dull of late. All of that new money buying up the country estates and trying so desperately hard to act the part. You simply would not believe how stuffy they are. Poor dears don't realize that the ruling class are, and always have been, utterly bats."

I grabbed her bags. "In that case you should find your new employer a refreshing throwback."

"Excellent."

"Though something of a challenge," I cautioned.

"Even better," she assured me. "Keeps one alert. You will tutor me, of course."

"Of course. What are friends for?"

One suitcase fit in the trunk, the other behind Pam's seat. Lulu wriggled around in her lap when she got in, happy to see her. Lulu is generally happy to see someone who has fed her kippers and eggs and will likely do so again.

"And hello to you as well, Miss Lulu," Pam cooed at her, getting her nose licked. "I see she hasn't changed her eating habits."

"No such luck."

"In the pink otherwise?"

"That," I replied, "is a long story—and not a particularly pleasant one." I found a spare pair of Merilee's sunglasses in the glove box and handed them to her. "You'll be wanting these."

Pam figured out why as soon as I eased away from the curb and picked up speed. "My Lord, you've lost your windscreen."

"Call me crazy, but I like the taste of bugs in my mouth."

She raised an eyebrow at me. "So it has turned into one of those, has it?"

I filled her in as we worked our way through the outskirts of Charlottesville to the highway. She listened intently, Lulu dozing in her lap.

When I was done, she said, "Sterling Sloan. My lord. Such a lovely, lovely man. I saw his *Hamlet* when I was a girl. He was so gifted and handsome. So tragic. I wept when he died. Every schoolgirl in Britain did. To think he was a drug addict. How sad. How very, very sad."

"I have an ulterior motive in bringing you in on this, Pam."

"I'm terribly flattered, dear boy. But how many times must I tell you? I'm much too old for you."

I grinned. I do know how. "Actually, I wondered if you could—"

"Quietly pick up what information I can from the staff and locals?" she inquired. "Of course. I'll get started first thing in the morning."

I glanced over at her. "How is it you always know what needs doing before anyone says so?"

"Because, dear boy, unlike so many others who make the claim, I am a professional. You've not said a word about Merilee. How is she?"

"Fine. We've entered into a state of peaceful non-coexistence."

"Meaning *you're* not ready to settle down again."

"No, we're equally qualmish about it."

"Why?" she demanded.

"It failed before. And there's no reason to think it won't again."

"Rubbish. When you fall off a horse you must get back on."

A bolt of electricity shot through me. *When you fall off a horse you must get back on . . .*

"Is something wrong, Hoagy?"

"Nothing . . . Meanwhile, I'm here and she's home and everyone's somewhat happy."

"More rubbish." Pam sniffed. "That's no home. One needs children to make a home."

"Pam . . ."

"I hate to see two such bright, lovely young people go without—"

"Pam, this car does have a reverse gear," I pointed out. "And they do have flights back to—"

"Very well. I'll shut up."

"Thank you. I knew you'd get the idea. Now I think we'd better start your tutoring . . ."

Mavis was a little tied up. There was her powwow with the ad hoc committee of Stauntonians coordinating the golden-anniversary festivities. Another with the media person handling the gala screening for the studio that was rereleasing the movie. There was her casual, reflective stroll through the grounds of Shenandoah with Barbara Walters and her camera crew. Still, Pamela swung into action just as soon as she got her chance.

We sat in the peacock parlor. Richard poured the bad sherry, he and Mavis circling each other warily. His cheek was still red from her slap. Her eyes made a point of avoiding his. She was giving him the same treatment she gave her brothers now. Serious punishment.

"We shall get along quite well, madam," Pam declared

briskly, "provided you bear in mind a few vital facts about me."

Mavis gave her the regal glare. "Facts? What sort of facts?" she demanded stiffly.

"For starters, I have no use for mediocrity," Pam replied brusquely. "Never have."

"I assure you that is fine with me, Pamela," Mavis said, pleased. "As it happens, I myself am—"

"I speak my mind," Pam broke in. "You'll not find me the shy, retiring type. I believe a great estate needs a firm hand. Some employers cannot accept that, in which case I have little use for them. Not that you'll find me an impertinent woman. I abhor rudeness."

Mavis nodded eagerly. "Absolutely, Pamela. I myself—"

"Then we shall get along just grandly, madam. It's a lovely, lovely home. You're blessed to have it. The American Revolution is such a fascinating period, don't you think? Of course, being a Brit, I myself see it from a somewhat different vantage point. . . ."

"As do I, dear lady," Richard chimed in, helping himself to more sherry. Both of his cheeks had a rosy flush now.

"Yes, of course you do, Pamela," Mavis acknowledged readily. "And we must discuss that. I'll look forward to it. Would you care to see the old house now?" she asked her, a bit shyly.

"I would consider it a privilege, madam," Pam replied.

The kitchen door swung open just then and little Gordie wandered in, a cookie in one fist and a batch of comic books in the other.

Mavis whirled on him. "Yes, what is it, Gordon?" she demanded, pouncing on him as if he were a field hand who'd stumbled in, manure caked on his clumsy boots.

"Nothin', ma'am," Gordie cried, shrinking from her. He looked around at everyone, wide-eyed. He relaxed a little when he saw me there. "Hey, Hoagy," he said uncertainly.

"Hey, Gordie."

"Well, as long as you're here, you may as well say hello to Pamela," Mavis told him. "Our new housekeeper."

"Yes, yes, and what a sincere pleasure it is." Pam knelt with a refined grunt and placed her hands on Gordie's narrow shoulders. "And how are you?"

Gordie withdrew from her, a turtle retreating inside his shell. He didn't respond.

"I said, 'How are you?' " Pam repeated, a bit louder. "Are you well?"

"Of course he is," said Mavis. "He's a very happy boy. Aren't you, Gordon?"

Gordie still didn't respond.

"Now run along outside," Mavis commanded.

He did, relieved to get out of there. The two women started out on their tour. Richard started to join them.

Mavis stopped him. "Richard, you're terribly underfoot. Go watch a ball game on television or something."

He made straight for the sherry decanter, twitching.

As they strolled out, I heard Pamela say, "The odd thing is, I can't help but feel I've been here before. You'll think it silly of me, but I happen to believe each of us leads a number of different lives through the ages . . ."

And then I was left alone there with Richard. Defiantly, he downed his third sherry, clutching the delicate cordial glass tightly in his big, hairy hand. "One of these days, Hoagy . . . ," he growled between his teeth. He squeezed the glass tighter. It shattered in his hand. Blood began to stream down his fingers. He paid it no attention. "One of these days."

I started for my quarters. Before I could reach the back door, Charlotte appeared from her office to block my path. "Aren't you forgetting something, Hoagy?" she asked sweetly.

"Oh, God, I hate this."

"Boy, I never thaw nobody throw a ball like you can, Hoagy."

"It is a somewhat awesome sight."

We were seated in the McDonald's parking lot outside

Staunton near Highway 64, where the newer, uglier sprawl was. Gordie wanted to eat in the Jag so we were eating in the Jag. Sadie was playing with a wad of paper at my feet. Lulu was curled on the floor at Gordie's feet, which he kept swinging up and down, up and down. He was a bundle of energy, squirming, waving his fingers, which were drenched with oily pink dressing from his Big Mac.

"You ever play in the majorth, Hoagy?" he asked.

"Yes, I did," I replied, trying to keep my eyes off his fingers. The sight of them was making me nauseous. Or maybe my own Big Mac was doing that. "Ever heard of Jim Palmer?"

"Uh-huh."

"I pitched for the Orioles at the same time he did. He threw harder than I did, but I looked better in my underwear."

"Did ya really pitch for them?"

"No."

"You shouldn't lie to people, Hoagy."

"You're right. Sorry." I stuffed the soggy remains of my hamburger back in the bag. Lulu sniffed at it disdainfully. "I did throw the javelin."

Gordie sucked on his Coke through a straw. "What'th a javelin?"

"A kind of spear. They throw it in the Olympics."

"Were you in the Olympicth? And don't lie."

"No, but I was once the third-best javelin thrower in the entire Ivy League."

"That the truth?"

"No one would lie about that."

"What'th the Ivy League?"

"It's a group of very expensive Northeastern colleges known for their academic reputations, their hard women, and their soft track stars—try not to drip Secret Sauce all over the upholstery, will you, big guy?"

"Thorry."

Sadie was chewing on my shoelaces now. I kicked at her. She thought I was playing and began to swat at them. I

THE WOMAN WHO

grabbed her and put her down next to Lulu, who promptly
scrambled over the gearshift knob and into my lap with her
head stuck through the steering wheel, which would be fine
until I needed to turn it. I was starting to understand why they
invented station wagons. Also baby-sitters.

"Tooth fairy came back, Hoagy," Gordie informed me happily. "Left me three more quarterth."

"Yeah, I had a feeling he would."

"Do I gotta go, Hoagy?"

"Go where?"

"The VADD cothtume ball. Mavith ith makin' me go, on
account of I'm an object, um, object . . ."

"Object lesson?"

"Yeah. Do I gotta?"

"Whatever she says, Gordie. She's your mom, now."

"I hate her."

"Don't hate her. She's not a bad person. Just sort of diffi-
cult."

"You got parentsth?"

"Somewhat."

"What'th that mean?"

"It means we don't get along."

"Why?"

"They don't approve of me. And I don't approve of them."

"Why?"

I sighed. "How come you ask so many questions?"

"How long ya gonna be here, Hoagy?" he asked, waving
his greasy fingers.

"A few more weeks."

"Then where will you go?"

"I don't know. My ex-wife lives on a farm in Connecticut."

"Where do you and Lulu live?"

"Manhattan. A fifth-floor walk-up on West Ninety-third
Street."

"I'd rather live on the farm with her."

"Go ahead, rub it in. Are you done eating?"

"Uh-huh."

I seized him by his left wrist and wiped his hand clean with a napkin. Then I did his other one and stuffed the sopping napkin in the bag and wiped off my own hands. I got out and hurled the whole mess in the trash. I needed a shower now.

"Your wife got animalth?" Gordie asked when I got back in.

"Ex-wife. Couple of horses, some chickens, a pig."

"You be goin' there when you leave here?"

"Like I said, I don't know."

"Can me and Thaydie come, too? If you do, I mean. You don't have to thay yeth or no now. Think it over."

"Okay."

"Okay we can go or okay you'll think it over?"

"I'll think it over."

"Hoagy?"

"What?"

"I want another Big Mac."

"You'll get sick."

"Will not."

"*I'll* get sick. I'll buy you an ice cream cone on the way home instead."

He brightened. "Okay!"

I moved Sadie to his lap and Lulu to the floor under him. Then I started up the Jag and pulled away.

"My favorite'th chocolate," he confided.

"Mine's licorice."

"Ugh."

"You ever had it?" I demanded.

"No."

"Then don't say 'ugh.' You'll love it."

"Will not."

"You like Steve McQueen don't you?"

"Yeth . . ."

"It so happens licorice was his favorite flavor, too."

"How do you know?" he asked suspiciously.

"I just do."

"That another lie?"

"No, it's a supposition."

"What'th that?"

"You're too young to know."

Gordie asked if Sadie could spend the night with me. He was deathly afraid Pam would come into his room and find the kitten and send her off to the pound to be gassed. I assured him Pam was a very nice person and would do no such thing, but I couldn't convince him. So Sadie was parked on the love seat, asleep, when I came downstairs with Lulu at four A.M. for her nightly walk on the wild side.

She led me toward that same hole under the wall over by the souvenir shop. The shop loomed about fifty feet ahead of us in the beam of my flashlight when I heard the shotgun blast.

I pulled Lulu close to me on her leash and called out, "That you, Roy?" so he wouldn't blow our heads off.

It was. He stood near the hole, inspecting it by the light of his Coleman lantern, shotgun tucked under his arm.

"Evening, Roy," I said.

He peered at me, then back down at the hole.

"Have any luck?" I asked him.

He spat and reloaded. Then he sat back down in his chair behind the tree to wait for the return of the first great love of Lulu's life.

"Nice talking to you, Roy. Let's do lunch, okay?"

Lulu and I started back toward the house. Bowser intercepted us about halfway there, his stubby tail wagging furiously as he and Lulu greeted each other. I stood there wondering what the hell to do about him. Roy was sure to nail him when he made his way back out. His only chance was to hide out until daylight, then slip out after Roy had gone off watch. Only hide out where?

Lulu was gazing up at me imploringly now. She knew where. I sighed, and we three headed for home.

Bowser attacked the remains in Lulu's mackerel bowl when we got there—that'll give you an idea just how downscale he was. She watched him from her chair, tail thumping contentedly. When he'd had his fill, he stretched out on the floor next to her and licked his chops. He had no tags or collar, and more than a little gray in his muzzle. An older man. A breaker of young, innocent hearts. He probably had six or eight Lulus scattered around the neighborhood, waiting in vain for him to come home at night. But there was nothing I could do about it. Merilee was right. Lulu was a big girl now.

"I'll be turning in now, kids," I announced. "Don't play the stereo too loud. And stay out of my Macallan."

I went up the narrow spiral staircase and climbed back into bed. It wasn't easy getting comfortable. I was used to Lulu being on my head, not downstairs with a stranger old enough to be her father. I was just getting settled in when I felt something under the covers down near my feet. Something alive. Hurriedly, I flicked on the light and tore back the covers. Sadie peered up at me, all perky and bright-eyed.

"What are you doing down there?" I demanded.

I grabbed her and was going to hurl her downstairs until I remembered Bowser, who might enjoy her for dessert. I put her down on the floor and climbed back into bed. She promptly jumped up there with me and stretched out on my chest, dabbing at me gently with her paws, the small motorboat noise coming from her throat. Grudgingly, I scratched her under the chin. She moved up a little more and buried her nose in my neck, purring. She wasn't Lulu. She was more like a vibrating heating pad. But she did smell like mackerel, and that was some small comfort. I fell asleep with her there.

Lulu and I saw Bowser off at dawn. It was a damp, foggy morning. The two of them frolicked in the wet grass like a pair of frisky pups. Roy's chair was still there by Bowser's hole. But Roy and his shotgun weren't. Bowser squeezed under the wall without looking back and arfed once from the other side. Lulu answered with a strange moan that sounded like the air being let out of a balloon. It was a sound I'd never heard come from her before. It occurred to me for one awful moment that she might actually be considering joining him. Leaving me. But she just snuffled and turned her back on the hole. The two of us returned to our quarters.

Lulu ate an unusually large breakfast, then drowsed contentedly on my foot while I wrote. Sadie spent her morning chasing a fly around up in the bedroom, her claws skittering across the wood floor. Ah, to be so easily entertained.

He was the handsomest boy Evangeline had ever laid eyes upon, this stableboy. And he was a boy. His cheeks barely knew the edge of a razor. His complexion was fair and pure, his hair golden, his eyes the blue of the peacocks back home at Shenandoah. Her beloved Shenandoah.

"Shall I assist you up, m'lady?" he inquired.

"Please," she said, offering him her hand.

"Here we are, m'lady," he said as he boosted her up onto the chestnut mare.

She gazed down at him, trembling from his touch, from the earthy smell of him. He was gazing up at her, frankly, longingly, unashamed.

"What is your name, boy?" she whispered, her heart pounding.

"Andrew, m'lady."

"Mine is Evangeline, Andrew. I wish for you to address me by it. For I am of Virginia, not England. And I am most certainly not a lady."

I took a lunch break a little before one. Pam was busy at the big round kitchen table reorganizing the household accounts, a plate of biscuits and a cup of tea at her elbow. Charlotte was on the phone in her office with a caterer.

"Getting settled in, Pam?" I asked.

"Quite nicely, dear boy," she replied cheerily. "It appears Fern had a filing system all her own. I have yet to fathom it, but once I have, I trust the operation will begin to make some form of sense. Fortunately, Charlotte is helping me prepare for the VADD Ball." Pam glanced over her shoulder at Charlotte's office, lowered her voice conspiratorially. "Are she and Richard . . . ?"

"He wants to, she's not so sure."

"Well, I shall help make the poor dear sure," Pam declared. "The man's a complete fraud."

"Oh?"

"Indeed. I discerned the faintest trace of commoner in his accent yesterday—not something one of you Yanks could detect. First thing this morning I rang up someone back home who knows of such matters. She assured me there is no title such as Richard described to you. No Kenneth Lonsdale, ill or otherwise. A fabrication, all of it. Oh, the man may be a second son. But certainly not one who is about to come into any family money in the near future."

"So that explains it," I mused aloud.

"Explains what, dear boy?"

"The snide little way the brothers have of calling him 'Lord' Lonsdale. It's all a pretension of his, and they know it. And like to rub it in."

Pamela sniffed. "I shall take it upon myself to inform Charlotte. I cannot allow her to get involved. She'll do herself no good. He's a miserable sort." She reached for a biscuit and nibbled on it. "Of course, what man wouldn't be—married to Mavis."

"What do you make of her?"

"She's a lonely woman," Pam replied. "I feel somewhat sorry for her, actually. But I can afford that luxury—I am not related to her. Speaking of which, her brother Frederick happens to owe everyone in town money."

"How do you know?"

"I've been ordering supplies for the ball. Each merchant has asked me who'd be signing the checks—because if it were Frederick, they said that they would have to have cash. They were quite apologetic about it, but also quite firm."

"Hmm. Interesting. Good work, Pam."

I heard footsteps on the stairs. Mercy came rushing in toting a knapsack full of books. She wore a plaid wool jumper over a pink cotton turtleneck, knee socks, and penny loafers. Her hair was in a ponytail. She looked good. Good and twelve.

She flushed slightly when she saw me there. "Oh, great, you're here," she exclaimed breathlessly. "I was going to have Pam give this to you." She handed me a manila envelope. "The historical details you wanted."

"Terrific. Thanks."

She flashed me a big smile. "Anything else you need just let me know—gotta run—I'm late for class—bye." She dashed out.

Pam raised an eyebrow at me.

"Something?" I asked.

"The girl gets positively saucer-eyed around you," she observed.

"I do have that effect on some people."

"You wouldn't be encouraging her just a bit, would you?"

"Now why would I want to do that?"

"Because she's young and lovely, and you're here and Merilee is in Connecticut."

"Makes perfect sense when you put it that way," I admitted. "Except that she's all but engaged to the redoubtable Polk LaFoon the Fourth, and I'm too nice a guy and he's in a lot better shape than I am. How are you getting on with Gordie?"

She frowned. "Not well. The child seems terrified of me, for some reason. Says next to nothing. All I've gotten out of him so far was something about the *tooth* fairy."

"And how generous he is?"

She peered up at me, amused. "You aren't becoming attached to him, are you?"

"Me? No chance. No use for him. None."

She shook her head sadly. "The poor little thing has been through so much. I can't help but feel this is not the ideal environment for him. He needs a home. He needs to feel he belongs. Here he seems to be somewhat in the way." Pam sipped her tea. "Mavis has been asking for you. She's read the pages you left her and wants to discuss them with you."

"Where is she?"

"On patrol somewhere in the northern portion of the estate. You, dear boy, are to find her."

I found her pink dirt bike before I found her.

It was lying in the brush alongside the dirt path that twisted through the woods out beyond the gazebo. The engine was running.

Mavis was lying another thirty feet or so up the path, facedown. Or I should say, what was left of her face was down. She'd been thrown—headfirst into the trunk of a tree. The tree won. Not much of a contest, really. She hadn't been wearing a helmet.

It wasn't a very civilized way to die. But I haven't come upon one yet that is.

Chapter Twelve

P olk Four pulled his car right out onto the lawn next to the trees. Two more sheriff's cars and an emergency medical services van were right behind him. So was a local news radio crew, until one of Polk's deputies chased them off.

Richard and Charlotte had been home with Pam. Frederick and Edward arrived from their offices within minutes. They brought Mercy with them from school. All of them stood there on the lawn in silence, gray faced.

Polk wouldn't let them anywhere near Mavis. He didn't want them to see her like that. He was polite, but firm. He handled it well, considering how upset he was himself.

"I told her a million times to wear a helmet," he said to me hoarsely, his blue eyes moist, as we stood over her body. "I told her it doesn't matter how slow you're going on these paths, you never know when you'll run into a stump or a rock or a—"

"Trip wire?"

He shot me an angry look and squared his jaw. "You already know I don't care for what you've got to say, Mr. Hoag. Right now is a particularly inappropriate time to—"

"Take a look, Sheriff."

His face reddened. He looked dangerous. "Get the heck away from me!" he snapped. "I mean it. Get away or I'll—"

"Take a look. That's all I ask. One look."

He hesitated. His shoulders relaxed a bit. Reluctantly he said, "Okay. One look."

I led him back up the path a ways to a slender, young redbud tree growing alongside it in the brush. A foot up from its base something had been wound tightly around its trunk, tight enough to cut through the bark, exposing the live green growth underneath.

Polk crouched next to me and examined the tree. "The bike probably did this when she lost control. So what?"

"The bike would have left a gash in one side of the tree, or broken it clean. It wouldn't have damaged the bark all the way around like that." I got to my feet. "Besides, there's another one just like it over here." I showed him the matching wound in a tree directly across the path. "A wire did this, Sheriff. A wire stretched across her path. It stopped the bike cold. She went flying. She was murdered—same way Fern was. They were both murdered. You know it and I know it."

Polk stared down at his shoes. He swallowed uneasily. The emergency people were lifting Mavis's covered body onto a stretcher now. He glanced at them, motioned for me to follow him. We moved farther down the path to the rough old wooden gazebo where, fifty years ago, Alma Glaze had sat writing in her diary.

He sat down heavily at the weathered pine table, removed his trooper's hat, and smoothed his short blond hair, not that it needed smoothing. "I was going to come out and talk to you today," he said quietly. "Seems a couple of boys in a Ford pickup got themselves toasted on their way down Jack Mountain yesterday. Stevie Tucker and Tommy Ray Holton. I went to high school with both of them. Been in and out of trouble for as long as I can remember—breaking and entering, receiving stolen property, aggravated assault. They never did any serious time, but they were no great loss to the community either." Polk cleared his throat. "A passerby believes he saw them a few minutes before it happened . . . being pursued by an antique red car."

"I prefer to think of it as a classic."

"They the two who roughed you up?"

I nodded. "Someone hired them to try and get Alma's diary that day. It's worth a lot of money. Yesterday they were just trying to get me. They took out my windshield with an over-under shotgun."

"That checks. We found one near the truck. Who were they working for, Mr. Hoag? Who hired them?"

"I don't know, Sheriff. But I do know who can tell us."

"Who?"

I tugged at my ear. "You won't like it."

"I don't like any of this," he assured me quietly.

"Your grandfather can. Polk Two knows."

Polk Four slumped and let out a weary sigh. "No."

"Yes."

A look of genuine anguish crossed his earnest, unlined face. "What is going on here, Mr. Hoag? What the devil is going on?"

"I told you—a cover-up is what's going on."

"I know you did," he acknowledged. "And I didn't listen to you. Too unimaginative. That's what Mercy says I am—unimaginative. Christ, poor Mercy . . ." He looked at me sharply. "I'm thinking that all of this has happened since *you* got here."

"I know. And I'm the one who found the bodies. I could have done in both of them, hid the trip wire, then yelled for help. I look good for it. Only why, Sheriff? I've no reason to want either of them dead."

"I was thinking that, too." He scratched his jaw thoughtfully. "Publicity for your book?"

"It doesn't need it—not that badly. If you're looking for likely candidates to do in Mavis, there are plenty. There's Richard, who's been wanting to run off with another woman. There's the other woman, Charlotte, who also happened to blame Mavis for her father's death. There's Frederick and Edward, cut out of their mother's estate, bitter, jealous. . . . It could have been any of them. They were all familiar with her patrol route. Only, why kill Fern, too? What's the connection?"

"Maybe there isn't one," Polk suggested.

"I doubt that. Fern knew something. And so, it would appear, did Mavis. This whole business is about what got covered up fifty years ago, during the filming of the movie. I'm certain of it. I just can't figure out *how.*"

He gazed out at the woods for a moment. Then he turned back to me, his face softening. "I'm sorry, H-Hoagy. About not listening to you before. Maybe Mavis would still be alive if I had. But I couldn't. I just couldn't. Nobody wants to believe that everyone they hold dear, everything they belong to, that all of it may have been built on something *wrong.*"

"I know, Sheriff. And I know this is tough for you. You grew up believing that as long as you respected your elders and kept your nails clean and your shoes shined that good things would happen to you. And so far they have—you've been lucky. I'm sorry your luck has changed. Truly sorry."

"Whatever needs doing, I'll do it," he declared. "My personal considerations must be set aside."

"Glad to hear it."

"Any ideas?"

I had several things he could check out that I couldn't. He said he'd get right on them. He was utterly determined now. He had set a goal for himself and he would not be knocked off course. This was, after all, a guy who made it through law school.

"By the way, Sheriff, I'd also put Mercy under twenty-four-hour guard."

He frowned. "Mercy? Why?"

"She's twenty-one, isn't she?"

"Two months ago. I gave her a pearl necklace, belonged to my grandmother."

"Shenandoah is hers now. She's sole heir. If this whole thing is about money, and it probably is, she now owns everything. That means . . ."

He nodded. "You're right," he said grimly.

I didn't have to tell him what it meant. I didn't have to tell him that Mercy's life was now in danger.

Chapter Thirteen

Mavis Glaze's death was front-page news across America. The television news crews stormed Staunton. So did *Entertainment Tonight, Time* and *Newsweek,* the major daily newspapers, *USA Today* and the tabloids. Within hours, reporters from all over were elbowing each other in the street for interviews with average townspersons. Barbara Walters landed an exclusive with Mavis's hairdresser, who wept on the air. Geraldo dug up a psychic who had foreseen that Mavis would die just as her mother had—in a vehicular accident, alone, wearing blue. Maury Povich, not to be outdone, found a Hollywood spiritualist who was convinced that Alma Glaze was haunting Shenandoah—how else to account for *two* accidental deaths at the estate in recent days?

Actually, that one made about as much sense as anything I had come up with so far.

Polk Four didn't breathe a word about the trip wire. Airing it in the press, the sheriff believed, would only turn Mavis's death into a bigger circus—and make her killer a lot warier.

Better, he reasoned, if he or she figured they'd gotten away with it. He kept the truth from the family, too, since it would only frighten them. And since the killer was very likely one of them. I was the only one who knew Mavis had been murdered. Not even his deputies knew. Not the pair posted at the Shenandoah front gate to keep out the press and the gawkers—tourist visitation was suspended until further notice. Not the one in the house, who was partly there to screen phone calls and mostly there to keep his eye on Mercy.

Mercy didn't leave the house for several days. None of the family did. They just sat in the peacock parlor, dazed. Richard drank brandy after brandy and twitched a lot. Frederick chain-smoked. Edward kept coughing and opening the window, and Frederick kept closing it. Mercy sat on the sofa with a box of Kleenex, sniffling. No one talked. It was kind of pathetic, the silence. They had held such bitter feelings toward Mavis, yet they seemed lost without her. She had defined their lives. Her will, her demands, had dictated how each of them functioned and interacted. Without her there they were like strangers, sitting around waiting for a bus. And a new master. I had a pretty good idea who that master would be, too, only he was reluctant. He wasn't a family member. Not yet, anyway. But when it became obvious they needed him, Polk Four did step forward. It was he who made the funeral arrangements. Charlotte worked the phone. Pam kept the place running and meals on the table.

Little Gordie made for kind of a sad footnote to the story. The kid had already lost his natural parents. Now he'd lost his adoptive mother, too. Strangely, he didn't seem upset or hurt by it. I guess it was impossible to hurt him now. To him, this was just business as usual. And that was the saddest thing of all.

There was much debate in the *Staunton Daily News Leader* over whether or not to cancel next week's golden-anniversary festivities, the gala screening, the VADD costume ball. Naturally, the film studio was eager to capitalize on Mavis's death. They weren't alone. The Virginia tourism people had a lot riding on the anniversary, as did the town fathers of Staunton. Still, no one wanted to look too crass, so they left it up to the Glazes. Polk Four had to pull them together and make them decide. They decided the celebration would go on. Mavis, they felt, would have wanted it that way. Everyone was glad. I know I was. This meant Rex Ransom would still be coming to town. It also meant I'd actually have the opportunity to see Henry Kissinger in a powdered wig, red velvet knee breeches, and white silk stockings.

The Major League Editor who was publishing *Sweet Land* kept calling me from New York, and I kept ducking her. I returned her fourth call. It would have been unprofessional not to.

"Exactly how far along are you?" she wondered anxiously. "Not that I'm trying to pressure you."

"Exactly two chapters into it," I replied.

"That's *all*?"

"I've only been here a few days," I pointed out.

"I know, I know. I just . . . I mean, we're all over the front page right now. Do you need help, Hoagy?"

"Generally."

"I mean, is there something I can do to help speed things up? Anything?"

"Do you really want to help?"

"Absolutely. You're our top priority. Just name it."

"You could stop calling me."

"Stop calling you?"

"Yes. Every minute I spend on the phone with you is a minute I'm not spending at the typewriter."

"You mean like right now?"

"I mean like right now."

Click. She was gone. Smart lady. There's even talk she'll be getting her own imprint when she turns twenty-five.

My involvement with *Sweet Land* was actually out in the open now. Sort of. They put out a bogus press release saying

Mavis had completed most of the manuscript herself before her fatal accident, and that I was being brought in to do a light polish. Hey, if you're looking for the truth, don't read the newspapers. And if you're looking for appreciation, become a licensed plumber—ghosting isn't for you.

I worked around the clock to the sounds of Garner and Gordie, who sat outside in the courtyard, tossing his ball against the wall for hours. I had no contact with the outside world, unless you count the telegram from Merilee: "I WANT YOU OUT OF THAT HORRIBLE PLACE RIGHT NOW, MISTER. STOP." To which I replied: "CAN'T. HAVING TOO MUCH GOOD, CLEAN FUN." Sadie was a frequent visitor, though unlike Lulu she kept climbing up on my desk and playing with the paper in my typewriter. I left my quarters only to eat and to take Lulu out for her midnight assignations with Bowser. Roy was keeping up his vigil by the wall. Mavis might be gone, but the precious Shenandoah peacocks were still in danger, or so he thought. If he thought. I had my doubts. Mostly, we caught him snoozing.

It was the morning of Mavis's funeral when Mercy knocked on my door, wearing a Mary Baldwin sweatshirt and jeans, face scrubbed, notepad in hand, composed, alert, all business. "I've looked into Vangie and John's marital vows, like you asked," she announced briskly.

"You really didn't have to do it now."

"I wanted to. It's keeping my mind off . . . other things, you know? I can come back later if you'd rather."

"No, no. Now is fine."

I gave her some coffee. She sat on the love seat with it, looked around at the room. It's entirely possible she'd never been in it before. She'd certainly never owned it before. Lulu sniffed at her, then turned her back on her and sat with a loud, disapproving grunt. Mercy watched this curiously.

"Don't mind her," I said. "She's just a little overprotective."

Mercy smiled. "She thinks I'm going to steal you from her?"

"From Merilee, actually."

Blushing, Mercy dove into her notes. "Okay, it seems the Anglican Church was the only officially recognized faith in the Virginia Colony," she reported. "And Anglican clergymen were the only ones empowered to perform marital vows. So I guess they would have had an Anglican wedding."

"Okay."

"What did people do who *weren't* Anglicans, I wonder?"

"Either pretend to get the faith or pretend to get married, I suppose."

She glanced through her notes, shaking her head. "Totally medieval. Do you know if you didn't attend an Anglican service at least once a month you could actually be fined? And if you . . . you . . ."

I heard a soft, plopping sound first. The sound of her tears falling onto the page. Then she hiccoughed once and her shoulders began to shake and then she was gone. I went to her. She hurled herself into my arms, heaved great sobs, held on tight. When she was done watering my shoulder, I gave her my linen handkerchief.

"Sorry," she said, sniffling, wiping her swollen eyes. "Didn't mean to . . ."

"It's okay. Nothing to be sorry about."

"I'm just not ready."

"For what?"

"Any of this. The estate, being in charge. I don't understand it. I don't understand anything." She buried her face in my chest. "I'm so *confused.*"

"You're growing up all at once. Sorry to be the one to break it to you."

"I'm just not ready," she repeated.

"You'll be fine. You've got your father, your uncles, Polk . . ."

She shook her head. "I'm breaking it off with Polk."

"Since when?"

"It's something I decided I have to do."

"I wouldn't. At least not right now."

"Why not?"

"Because you're under a lot of strain. It's not a good time to make this kind of decision. Besides, he's not such a bad guy, in his own way."

Her eyes shone as they searched my face. "You surprise me. I thought . . . I mean, I thought you'd kind of approve." She lowered her eyes shyly. "You left someone out. You said I had Father and my uncles and Polk. There's also you."

"I'm not worth much on the open market."

"You are. You're so, I don't know, *sure* of things."

"The only thing I'm sure of is that I'm not sure of anything. I'm merely good at pretending. Comes with being old."

"Not so old," Mercy said softly. She raised her face to mine, her young lips parted slightly.

I shook my head. "That'll make things even more confusing."

My intentions were good. At least I think they were. Unfortunately, my timing stank. Richard stormed in just then without knocking. Finding us like that on the love seat didn't make him too happy.

"I've been looking everywhere for you, Mercy!" he roared. "I see I was looking in the wrong room! Go inside and get dressed at once! The *minister* is here!"

"Yes, Father." She gave me back my handkerchief. "Thank you, Hoagy. For everything." Then she went out.

Richard waited until she'd closed the door behind her before he lunged at me, grabbing me by the throat with his big hairy hands. "I don't believe there's a word in the language vile enough to describe you!" he spat out. "Taking advantage of a grieving girl, her mother not even in her grave yet!"

"Believe what you want, Richard," I gasped, sucking for air. "But you're wrong. She needed a shoulder to cry on. She happens to be the tiniest bit upset at the moment."

Richard stared deeply into my eyes. Abruptly, he released me, ran his hands through his hair. He slumped wearily into the easy chair. He seemed older to me. Mavis's death had aged him. "Sorry, lad," he said hoarsely. "Awfully damned sorry. Didn't mean to . . . Just not myself."

"I can't imagine why," I panted, fingering my throat.

Mercy had gotten coffee. Daddy got a single malt.

"It's a bitch, this," he confessed, sipping it gratefully. "An honest-to-Christ bitch. Mave was a hard, hard woman, lad. At times, I hated her more than I ever believed a man could hate a woman. But I did love her as well. I don't believe I realized just how much until now. I've no one now," he added mournfully. "No one in this world who gives a good goddamned about me."

"There's Mercy."

"She has her own life ahead of her. Marriage, children . . ."

"There's your brother, Kenneth," I suggested.

That one he left alone.

"Too bad he can't make it over for the funeral," I pressed. "Being so ill, I mean."

He glanced at me sharply. "You know the truth, don't you?"

I nodded.

"One of the brothers tell you?"

That one I left alone.

"Ah, well." He chuckled softly to himself. "We all play a role of some kind. I've played mine, and damned well, I like to think. Mave's idea from the start, you know. To impress the great unwashed. Meant a lot to her, bringing a fine English gent home to America with her, rather than a postman's son from Derby. I refused to play along at first. Wounded my pride. But I did it—for her. Sorry I had you on before. Been playing at it so long it almost seems real. It's certainly so to Mercy. She still doesn't know who I really am. That's how Mave always wanted it."

"She won't hear about it from me."

"Thank you, lad. Damned gentlemanly of you." He

drained his whiskey. "I'm not coming into any money of my own, of course, other than whatever stipend Mercy gives me. I was having you on about that as well. Sorry."

"That's okay—I didn't entirely believe you. But I think Charlotte did."

He shifted uneasily in his chair. His face darkened. "Charlotte . . ."

"What are you going to do about her?"

"I honestly don't know, lad. What should I do?"

I sighed inwardly. I was getting tired of being the answer man. "Tell her the truth about yourself, for starters. If you don't, Pam will."

He grunted unhappily. "Dear, dear. And then?"

"Do I really look like Mary Worth to you?"

He stared at me, waiting.

I stared back at him. "Do you love Charlotte?"

"I don't know."

"Find out. See what happens now that you no longer have Mavis between you. See if a relationship grows."

He thought this over. "That's good advice, lad."

"It's true. I give excellent advice. I just don't take any of it myself."

There was a tapping at the door. Charlotte. She had on a black dress, drab, for the funeral.

"What are you doing out here, Richard?" she asked crossly. "You're needed inside."

"Sorry. Was on my way in."

She looked down at him. "You were not," she said gently. "You were sitting here jawing. Come along." She held her hand out to him, like she would to Gordie, if she cared for Gordie.

He reached up meekly and took it. "Yes, Charlotte."

Obediently, he followed her out. I watched him go. He needed this. He needed another woman to take charge of him. And Charlotte? I wondered about her. What was Charlotte capable of doing to get what she wanted? Did she figure in? How?

Mavis was buried that afternoon in the Glaze cemetery. It

was a brief affair, and private. Immediate family only. And Charlotte and Polk Four and me. I don't know why I was invited, but I was, so I went.

She was buried next to her mother and father, beneath a big family stone. Frederick's and Edward's names and birth date were inscribed on it next to hers. A blank space remained —to be filled in when they died. Neither of them took their eyes off that space once during the entire ceremony.

Chapter Fourteen

he *Oh, Shenandoah* golden-anniversary celebration was a truly major nonevent. Charter buses began pulling into Staunton shortly after dawn five days after the funeral, disgorging thousands of fans from all over America, most of them elderly ladies in pastel pantsuits who had seen the movie fifty times and knew every line, every detail, every morsel of gossip about the filming—or so they thought. The whole town gave itself over to the promotional frenzy. There were parades and banners and horse-drawn carriages and lots of people in Revolutionary War costumes. There were Vangie look-alike contests and movie memorabilia auctions and reenactments of battle scenes and panel discussions among self-proclaimed *Oh, Shenandoah* scholars. There were tours of historic homes and demonstrations of historic crafts and firearms. There were vendors selling peanuts and cotton candy. There were people, people everywhere, milling around the streets, stuffing their faces, taking pictures of each other, yelling, buying.

The Hollywood contingent began arriving later that afternoon. Most of them were billeted at The Shenandoan, a big new conference center built up on a hill on the outskirts of town. Such noted sons and daughters of the South as Chuck Heston, Ed McMahon, Shelley Winters, Gene Kelly, Roddy McDowall, Zsa Zsa Gabor, and Sonny Bono were on hand to pay tribute to Mavis Glaze's favorite charity and to get their faces on *Entertainment Tonight*. A number of them were granting interviews in the lobby when I got there. Sam Goldwyn, Jr., was on hand, attending to his father's interests. Cookie Jahr, the makeup girl who had been in the sitting room when Fern O'Baugh screamed fifty years before, was there. And so were Helene Bray and Rex Ransom, the two surviving *Oh, Shenandoah* cast members. Helene, the fast young actress who had played Vangie's friend Abigail was now the seventy-three-year-old proprietor of an art gallery in Carmel, California. She had short, severe white hair and a deep tan and wore a lot of heavy, jangly jewelry. She arrived in the company of a young, blond hunk of Eurotrash named Wulf. Rex Ransom arrived alone.

I found him lying down in his room with the shades drawn. "Stewart Hoag, Mr. Ransom," I said to the dim shape there on the bed. "We spoke on the phone."

"Oh, yeah, the writer. Sorry, musta dropped off—trip kind of wore me out." He reached over and turned on the bedside light.

It was some kind of mistake. This wasn't Rex Ransom. Not this bald, shriveled old man with no teeth who lay there on the bed before me with his shoes off. His color wasn't too good—unless you consider gray good—and he'd lost some weight. The skin on his face and neck fell in loose folds, and his polo shirt was a couple of sizes too big for him. So were his slacks. His belt was cinched practically twice around. He sat up slowly, put on his glasses, and lit the stub of a cigar that had gone out in the ashtray, his hands trembling. The cigar didn't smell too good, but it smelled better than his socks did.

He got to his feet with a groan and offered me his cold, limp hand. He was no more than five feet four in his stocking feet. "I know, I know," he said quickly. His voice was thin and slightly nasal. "You always thought I was a lot taller. That's 'cause I'm big through the shoulders and chest." He looked down at himself and frowned. "Used to be, anyways. And I wore lifts."

I was staring. It was so hard to imagine him as the Masked Avenger, that fearless doer of good who rode so tall and proud in the saddle. Now I knew why I hadn't seen him in anything for so long. And why Merilee had said, I hope he doesn't disappoint you.

"It's an honor to meet you, Mr. Ransom," I finally said. "I carried your lunch box."

"One of my kids, huh?" he said with a gummy smile. "Yeah, you look about the right age." He went into the bathroom. A moment later he returned wearing his teeth and his toupee. It was a bad rug. The hairs looked sticky and dead and didn't match the color of his sideburns. "Made two fifty a week to do that lousy show. Low point of my career. Christ, *television*. Wasn't until I had the job I found out they was gonna put me up on a goddamned horse. Damned horse hated my guts, too. Always tried to throw me. We used two different Neptunes, y'know. First one broke a leg doing some damned fool stunt, had to be put down. Nobody knows that. Go ahead and put it in your article. I don't give a shit anymore."

"Actually, I'm not writing an—"

"Hey, you got a pooch!" he exclaimed, noticing Lulu for the first time. "I love dogs. Landlady won't lemme keep one." He bent over and patted her. "Jeez, her breath . . ."

"Your landlady's?"

"No, the pooch."

"She has strange eating habits."

"It was the war, y'know," he declared, chewing on his cigar.

"The war?"

"Old man Goldwyn, he was gonna make me a leading man. I was on my way up when we wrapped this picture. Then I had to go into the service. None of that public relations fly-boy crap, neither. I fought hand to hand in one lousy, stinking Pacific jungle after another. Killed three men. Woulda killed three more for a decent meal. When I came back, it was all different. They wanted dark and brooding—Greg Peck, Vic Mature, Bob Mitchum. I was an old face. Nothing worse in this business. Best I could get was two-line bits. Bartenders, cops, cabbies, maybe a few weeks here and there in a horror picture. . . . Hey, you want a drink or something? They said I can order room service. Food, booze, anything."

"I'm fine, thanks."

We sat in two club chairs by the window, which over-looked the tennis courts. No one was using them.

"That lousy series, it's all I got, y'know," Ransom went on. "On in reruns all over the place. I don't get a nickel off residuals, but I still do the sci-fi conventions, mall openings, junior high assemblies. I put on my costume and my mask, sign a few autographs, make a few bucks. My kids still love me. And I love them. They're my family. I got no one else." He shook his head. "And now they won't let me do it no more."

"Who won't?"

"These sons of bitches. Same studio that's doing this *Oh, Shenandoah* thing. Seems they're making this fifty-million-dollar *Masked Avenger* special-effects movie with some twenty-three-year-old weight lifter playing me. They want the public to think of him as the Avenger now, not me, so they're hassling me about making my appearances. Like I'm some kinda threat to 'em or something. All I make is a few bucks. I'm just an old man trying to get by. I got a one-bedroom apartment in Studio City, an eight-year-old car, no pension, hemorrhoids hanging from me like a handful of table grapes. And now they want to take it away from me. I tell ya, I'm so pissed off I didn't want to come to this thing. But what the hell, they're paying my way with a little something on top, so I can't afford not to. What kinda story you writing, kid? What can I tell ya?"

"I'm not a reporter, Mr. Ransom."

"Make it Mike. That's what my friends call me. My real name—Mike Radachowski."

"I'm working for the Glazes on the sequel to *Oh, Shenandoah*, Mike. Right now I'm collecting anecdotes for an introduction. I wondered if we could talk about Sterling Sloan's death."

"Sure," he said easily. "Some kind of stroke, wasn't it?"

"I don't think so. And I don't think you do, either."

He examined his cigar butt. It was cold. "What makes you think I know anything about it?"

"I have an idea you do."

He kept on examining his cigar. He looked worried now. "Sloan died a long, long time ago. What does it matter now?"

"It matters."

"I'd like to help you, kid," my boyhood hero said slowly. "But I really can't say nothing about it."

"About what?"

"The studio . . ."

"The studio is fucking you over."

"I still gotta make a living."

"They just said you can't."

"That's true," he admitted. He hesitated. "I don't know . . ."

"Why don't you do what I do when I'm in doubt?"

"What's that?"

"Ask myself what the Masked Avenger would do."

"That was comic book stuff," he scoffed.

"If we kept on believing what we learned in comic books, we'd all be a lot better off."

He looked at me curiously. "Y'know, you're kind of a strange young fella."

"Yeah, I'm what's known in the *New York Times* crossword puzzle as a oner."

"I don't know . . ."

"Trust me, Mike."

"Trust you? I don't even know you."

"Yeah, you do. I'm one of your kids."

"Look, I hate to let you down, seeing as how you are, but . . ." He thought it over. "What exactly do you want to know?"

"What you saw and heard."

"You mean gossip?"

"Okay."

He relaxed, relieved. "Well, hell, that's no problem. I can tell ya right off—it was a horny set. So what else is new. Errol, he was shtupping Laurel Barrett under Sloan's nose. Helene, Jesus, I had her, Dave Niven had her, we all had her—except for Sloan, who turned her down cold."

"Because of his wife?"

"Naw, on account of he had something else going. At least, that's what we all figured."

"Who with?"

"That got to be a major topic of conversation, you wanna know the truth. Sloan was very closemouthed. Not one of the gang. Didn't like to drink with us, play pinochle. You play pinochle?"

"Who was the smart money on, Mike? Who was Sloan's girlfriend?"

He crossed the room slowly and got a fresh cigar from the nightstand. He lit it, puffed on it until he had it going to his satisfaction. Then he turned around. "Ethel," he replied, standing there in a cloud of blue smoke. "Ethel Barrymore."

"But she was—"

"Old enough to be his mother, I know. What can I tell ya— nobody's ever accused picture people of being normal."

"Any chance it was Alma Glaze?"

"The author? I doubt it. She wasn't exactly the cuddly type." He slumped on the edge of the bed and puffed on his cigar. "Still, you never know. Sloan was married to a great beauty. When a guy cheats, he always goes for something different. Coulda been. All I know is there was somebody, and I guess him and Laurel had some deal where it was okay for her to play around but not for him, on account of she let him have it but good."

"When?"

"That night. They had one hell of a fight in their hotel room the night he died."

"How do you know, Mike?"

"I had the room next door. Heard 'em hollering."

"What were they saying?"

"Couldn't hear no words."

"Then how do you know what they were fighting about?"

"What else do a husband and wife fight about besides money, and with their two paychecks money wasn't no problem."

"You're sure it was Laurel?"

"It was Laurel."

"And you were in your room when he was stricken?"

He nodded. "Getting dressed for the wrap party. Tux, studs, the works. I looked like a million bucks in those days. Rock hard, broads fallin' all over me. So I hear 'em goin' at it, a real doozy, and then . . ."

"And then?" I prompted.

"Then it got real quiet. I guess that's when the thing in his brain blew. Right away she comes running out in the hall screaming for Doc Toriello."

"As I understood it, he first complained of a terrible headache. She sent a bellhop out for some aspirin. Then Sloan got worse and *then* she called for the doctor."

He shrugged. "It coulda been that way. Sure. I don't remember so good."

"What really happened, Mike?"

He got up and went into the bathroom and filled a glass with water—an evasive maneuver. He returned with it and sat back down on the bed, mouth working furiously on his cigar. He said nothing.

I shook my head at him. "You've been holding the truth in a long time, Mike. You've kept your mouth shut, been a good soldier. And look what it's gotten you. Look how they've treated you."

He drank some of his water, smacking his lips as if it were good scotch. His eyes were on Lulu, who dozed at my feet. "I'd like to help you, kid. I would. But whatever a married couple does behind closed doors is their own goddamned business. And picture people—we don't tell stories on each other."

"Okay, Mike." I sighed heavily. "Only, you're really letting me down. . . ."

"Aw, don't pull that," he whined.

"I'm sorry, Mike, but it's true. You're letting one of your kids down. One of those eager, fresh-faced kids who grew up in front of the television set believing every single word you told him about truth and justice and tooth decay."

"That's low. That's awful fucking low."

Lulu stirred and looked up at me funny. I think she was having trouble imagining me as eager and fresh faced.

"People are getting murdered, Mike, and you're the only one who knows why. I can come back with the sheriff if you want, but if I do, everyone is going to find out you talked. Tell me now and no one will. You have my word."

"Jeez." He got up and started pacing the room, rubbing the lower half of his face with his hand. "The law. Jeez."

"What's it going to be, Mike?"

"You won't tell anyone where ya heard this?" His voice trembled.

"Not a soul."

"Okay, okay." He slumped back down onto the bed. "I was . . . I was dressing, like I told ya. And that's when I heard it."

"Heard what?"

"The gunshot," he said quietly.

"Gunshot?"

"Yeah."

"She shot him?"

"Blew half his head off. I pulled on my pants and went over there. Door was unlocked. He was on the floor. Blood all over the rug, the wall. Laurel was covered with it, screaming hysterically, the crazy fucking bitch. In and out of the bin after that, but they never prosecuted her. Whole thing got buttoned up nice and tight."

"Who was in on it?"

"They all were. The sheriff, Doc Toriello, the local doc, the hotel, funeral parlor . . . Money changed hands all the way down the line. Lots of it. Melnitz, Goldwyn's hatchet man, he took care of it. It was like it never happened. He came into my room later that night and told me just that—it never happened. I said okeydoke, you're the boss." He shook his head in amazement. "She was the star of a major motion picture. They could get away with murder in those days. She sure as hell did. And that's the story, kid. Kind of glad to be telling somebody about it, you wanna know the truth."

"What exactly was Laurel doing when you first went in there?"

"She was hysterical, like I told ya. I called the desk first thing. They got hold of Toriello."

"Was she holding the gun?"

"Uh . . . no."

"Did you actually see the gun?"

"No."

"Did anyone tell you for a fact that she did it?"

"Nobody said *nothin'.*"

"Then how do you know it was actually Laurel who shot him?"

"Nobody else was there," he replied. "Who the hell else could it have been?"

"A third party. Someone who arrived before the shooting, then hustled out before you got there."

He shook his head. "No chance of that. I could hear their door from my room. They didn't have no visitors."

"You said you were dressing for the party."

"Yeah?"

"Did you take a shower?"

"Sure I took a . . ." His eyes widened. "You're right, kid. I was in the shower two, three minutes washing my hair. Had a whole head of it then, thick and blond. Somebody coulda knocked and gone in then. I wouldn't a heard. Only, why are you so convinced it wasn't Laurel?"

"Because Laurel Barrett is long dead. No one here would bother to kill two people now, fifty years later, if she were Sloan's murderer. Someone local shot Sloan. Had to be. And someone local is still trying to keep it buttoned up." I got up out of the chair. "Thanks, Mike. You've been a big help. And it's been a genuine thrill to meet you."

"Sure thing, kid. Glad to have ya."

I started for the door, stopped. "Would you do it for me, Mike? Just once?"

He grinned at me. "Do what?"

"You know what I want."

He did indeed. Because something was already beginning to happen to him there on the bed. The blood was pumping harder in his veins. His chest was filling out, his shoulders broadening. He cleared his throat, and then he did it. He cried, "Neptune, *awaaaaay!*" His old cry. The one from long ago. He puffed on his cigar. "How was that?" he asked.

I tipped my cap. "It'll do, Mike. It'll do." I left before he started shrinking again.

Cookie Jahr would know. She had been there in the sitting room when Fern freaked. She knew who was in Vangie's room with Sterling Sloan. Whoever it was had shot him that night in his hotel room. That's why those pages had been torn from Alma's diary. Cookie knew. She was the one outsider who did.

Her room was down the hall from Mike's. Her door was

open a few inches. I called out her name. There was no answer. I tugged at my ear, not liking this. People don't generally go out and leave their motel-room doors open. Not unless they've gone for some ice. I was standing ten feet from the ice machine. Cookie wasn't getting any ice.

Lulu was already heading straight for the car. She wanted no part of it. I called after her. I told her that after everything I'd done for her these past nights the least she could do was stay by my side when I needed her. Reluctantly, she returned to me. We went in.

Cookie was stretched out on the bed looking right at me. She had a cigarette going in the ashtray on the nightstand next to her. She was a frail, birdlike woman with bright yellow hair. She wore a floral-print blouse, white slacks, and a bright pink silk scarf. Whoever strangled her had used the scarf.

Chapter Fifteen

olk Four reached over and turned off his radio when it started squawking. We were sitting in his cruiser out in the parking lot of The Shenandoan, Lulu between us on the front seat sniffing gleefully at the tools of his trade on the dash. She likes sitting in police cars. Polk kept watching her. I don't think he liked her sniffing at his things. He certainly hadn't liked what I'd had to tell him—that his granddad had covered up a shooting. Cookie's body had been taken away. Polk had told the swarm of entertainment press she'd died of natural causes.

"No one saw anything?" I asked.

"Not a chance," he replied grimly. "Not with so many people coming and going. Plus the door at the end of the hall by her room opens directly onto the parking lot. She'd only been dead a few minutes when you got to her, too. So darned close. Now we may never know what happened."

"We'll know. We'll just have to work a little harder. You find out anything?"

"I might have." He glanced at me. "Except it goes no further than this car."

"Agreed."

"Your friend Pam was right. Frederick Glaze does have a rather serious . . ."

"Pain in the assets?"

He nodded. "In fact, the U.S. attorney's office has been quietly preparing to indict him."

"For?"

"Defrauding the Internal Revenue Service. Operating an illegal tax-shelter scheme involving some fifty-eight million dollars in bogus securities trades over the past three years. The way I had it explained to me, he claimed to be trading in government securities, only there were no actual transactions. Just fictitious pieces of paper. And hundreds of thousands of dollars in illegal tax benefits for his grateful, and unwitting, investors. It seems he's now scrambling to make good on what he owes the IRS and keep his name out of the papers and his butt out of jail. That accounts for where all of his money is going. Of course, the investors will have to pay back what they owe, too."

"Did he drag Shenandoah's holdings into this?"

"Some of them."

"Did Mavis find out?"

"She found out." The sheriff cleared his throat. "As a matter of fact, she was actively cooperating with the investigation."

"She was willing to testify against her own brother?"

"She was indeed."

"Hmm. Interesting, Sheriff. Who's Frederick's lawyer?"

Polk straightened the cuffs of his khaki shirt, not that they needed straightening. "His brother, Edward."

"Is Edward involved in the swindle, too?"

"No, he's clean. A conservative investor, Edward is. Just puts it in the bank. While we're on him . . ." Polk pulled a small notebook out of his shirt pocket and opened it. "He married one Danielle Giraud on August twenty-eighth, 1952 in Washington, D.C. She was attached to the French consulate. Marriage was annulled one month later. She married in '55, had two kids. Died in '84. Husband is still alive. A law professor, lives in Alexandria."

"Have a phone number for him?"

"Why?"

"I happen to be a very thorough ghost," I replied, writing it down. "Ask anyone I've ever worked for—if you can find one living."

Polk leafed through his notebook. "I also rechecked the medical examiner's report on Franklin Neene. It still turns up suicide. There was no sign of a struggle—he wasn't conked on the head or anything. No trace of drugs in his bloodstream— other than alcohol, but not so much that he might have been unconscious at the time of his death. The amount was consistent with what he'd consumed the night before. There's nothing to suggest it was anything other than what it appeared to be—suicide brought on by severe depression. Consequently . . ."

"Agreed. We focus elsewhere."

Polk bristled. "Who's *we*?"

"You're right, Sheriff. It's your investigation."

"Thank you," he said crisply.

We sat there in silence a moment.

"Have you spoken to Polk Two?" I asked him.

He stared straight ahead out the windshield. "I'm waiting until I have more facts."

I tugged at my ear. "Want me to do it?"

"I'll do it," he snapped in reply. "It's my job and he's my granddad. Just give me some time."

"Okay, fine. But you'd better hurry up, Sheriff. We're starting to run out of live bodies."

"Darn it, Hoagy, this isn't easy for me!" he raged. "I'm out here all alone on a shaky limb investigating people I've known and loved my entire life! One thing I don't need right now is your cheap sarcasm!"

"You're right again. Sorry, I don't mean to be hard on you. Seeing dead people just does strange things to me. Always has. I appreciate the effort you're making. I really do. And if Mercy survives this in one piece, I'm sure she'll thank you, too." I glanced over at him. He was staring grimly out at the parking lot. "Was that any better?" I asked gently.

"I'm trying, Hoagy," he said miserably. "I'm trying real hard to like you. For Mercy's sake. She thinks so highly of you. But it's no use. I just plain don't."

"It's okay, don't take it so hard." I patted him on the shoulder. "I'm used to it, pardner."

"And *don't* call me pardner!"

Polk Two had told me the Hotel Woodrow Wilson was once a fine place. It wasn't anymore. Now it was where Staunton stashed whatever it didn't want to look at. Its old geezers scraping by on social security. Its single mothers on welfare. Its discharged mental patients. Now it was one step up from the street, and a short one at that. The lobby had all the ambiance and charm of the Port Authority Bus Terminal. It certainly smelled just like it. Two musty old guys were dozing on a torn, green vinyl sofa. A gaunt, toothless black woman was screaming at her three dirty kids at the elevator. Signs were taped up all over the wall behind the reception desk. No credit. No overnight guests. No pets. No loitering.

The clerk was a thirtyish weasel with slicked-back black hair, sallow skin, and sneaky eyes. He looked down at Lulu, then up at me. "Can't you read?" he sneered. "No animals."

"They let you in here, didn't they?" I said pleasantly.

He curled his lip at me. "What are you—some kind of bad dude?"

"I like to think I am," I replied. "But no one else seems to."

"Well, what do you want?" he demanded coldly.

"Some information."

"This ain't the tourist information bureau."

"Tell me, does it wear you down being such an asshole or does it come easily to you?"

The weasel reached under the desk and came up with a nightstick. I reached in my pocket and came up with a twenty-dollar bill. I won.

"What do you want to know about?" he asked, the bill disappearing in his palm.

"The old days. Fifty years ago."

He yawned. "What about 'em?"

"Who worked here."

"How should I know?"

"Are there any employment records that go back that far?"

"All gone. Place has been under different ownership for years."

"I see. Any chance someone's still around who might remember those days?"

"Could be," he said vaguely. He was angling for another bill.

"I already gave you twenty," I pointed out. "And I can be back here in five minutes with Sheriff LaFoon."

"Okay, okay," he said quickly. "No sense being that way. I'm trying to think . . ."

"Yeah, I can see that. It's kind of like watching a Lego toy."

"Try old Gus," he growled. "He's always talking about how ritzy this shithole was back before the war. He worked here, I think."

"And where would I find Gus?"

"That's him over there," he said, indicating the two old guys nodding on the sofa.

One had a walker parked in front of him, the other a runny nose that was dripping freely onto his legs. "Which one?" I asked.

"The one without the walker."

"I was afraid you were going to say that."

I pulled a battered old armchair up in front of Gus and sat

down. He stirred slightly but didn't waken. He was a burly old man in denim overalls, a faded flannel shirt torn at the elbows, and work boots. He needed a shave. Old men don't look hip when they're unshaven. They look like bums.

"How's it going, Gus?" I asked him.

He shifted on the sofa and grunted. Slowly, he opened one rheumy eye, swiped at his nose with the back of his hand. The other eye opened. I offered him my linen handkerchief. He took it and wiped his nose and his eyes with it, then carefully wadded it up and offered it back to me.

"You keep it," I insisted. "All yours."

His eyes focused on me for the first time. After a moment he said, "I know you. Sure I do."

"Sure you do," I agreed. "I used to play Smitty on the *Donna Reed Show.*"

"No, you didn't."

"Okay, you got me. I didn't."

"You're Bob Dilfer's boy," he said, pointing a bent finger at me."

"I am not."

"Are too. Went down to Lauderdale to work construction."

"I did not."

"Got married."

"Well, that's another story, and an ugly one."

"How's your pappy?"

"We don't talk much anymore," I replied.

Gus nodded. "Know jus' what you mean. He can get ornery. Specially when he got liquor in him."

I glanced over at his dozing pal with the walker to see if we were disturbing him. We weren't. "There was a fellow who used to work here before the war, Gus."

His face lit up. "Billy."

I leaned forward. "Billy?"

"That's your name—Billy. Knew I'd get it."

"I never lost faith. A bellhop, Gus."

"Lots of bellhops here in those days, sure. Fine ladies and

gents coming and going. They all stayed here. Roosevelt, Dewey. Harry S Truman. I once fetched Harry a fifth of bourbon. A fine gent. Tipped me ten bucks, he did."

"How about the movie folk?" I asked.

"Them had deep pockets all right," he sniffed, "but short arms."

"There was one guy who did real well by them though, wasn't there?"

"Weren't me."

"Who was it, Gus?"

His bleary eyes got a faraway look. "Hit the jackpot, he did. Got hisself a fancy new car. Fancy new job."

"Here at the hotel?"

"Naw, he got hisself into the easy pickings."

"Where did he go, Gus?"

Gus yawned, scratched his stubbly cheek and didn't answer me. I took out a twenty and laid it on his knee.

"I don't want your money, Billy," he said, staring at it.

"I know. It's a gift. Buy yourself something."

"Like what?"

"Like a handkerchief. Where did he go, Gus?"

Gus took the money and folded it carefully and stuffed it in the pocket of his overalls. Then he scratched his cheek again and told me where the lucky bellhop went.

I found him mowing the grass.

I brought Polk Four with me. I knew I'd get nowhere without him.

"Have a word with you, Roy?" I called to him.

He looked at me, then at Polk. Then he spat some tobacco juice and climbed down from the tractor mower and waited silently for one of us to say something.

"When did you come to work here, Roy?" I asked.

He stared at me blankly.

"About fifty years ago, wasn't it? You were working at the Hotel Woodrow Wilson when they offered it to you. Good pay, room and board. Glazes sure have taken fine care of you, haven't they?"

He kept on staring, jaw working on his tobacco.

"Fern wondered why they kept you around all these years," I went on. "Now we know why—to keep you from talking about Sterling Sloan's murder, right?"

He froze. Then his pale, deep-set eyes shot over to Polk Four. "Polk Two know 'bout you being here?" His voice was thin and reedy, almost a whisper.

"Let's leave my granddad out of this," Polk replied calmly.

"I'd call him, if I was you," Roy warned.

"I'd sit down and have a talk with Hoagy and myself, if I were you," Polk countered. "How would that be?"

Reluctantly, Roy said, "If you say so, Sheriff."

"I say so, Roy. I do indeed."

Roy shut off the mower. We sat on the low stone wall that edged the vegetable garden. The peacocks strutted around us, watching us. Lulu growled at them from next to me and got honked at for her trouble. She burrowed into the ground at my feet and kept quiet after that.

Polk took off his broad-brimmed hat and placed it on his knee. "Want to tell us about that night, Roy? The night Sloan died?"

Roy watched the peacocks a moment, shifted his bony rump, spat some juice. "Manager, he sent me up there from the front desk," he began slowly. "Said to get 'em whatever they needed. Said something funny had gone on up there. He looked real nervous about it."

"Why did he send you?" Polk asked.

"Thought I know'd how to keep my mouth shut," Roy replied.

"Evidently a keen judge of character," I observed. "What did they need up there, Roy?"

"Towels. For the blood. Blood everywhere. Him on the floor with his brains spilling out. She were screeching her head off. Rex Ransom were there, only him went back to his room to be sick."

"That's my Rex," I said. "Did she have the gun?"

Roy shook his head.

"Did you see the gun?" I pressed.

He shook his head again. "Me and the house detective got him up on the sofa. Movie doc got there in a minute. Weren't much he could do though. Didn't have to be no doc to see that. Then this producer fella got there."

"Melnitz?"

"Never know'd his name. He pulled Polk Two aside and them two talked real quiet. Were the producer did most of the talking—one of them real persuasive types. Another doc come, signed some papers. I stuck around, in case they needed anything."

"And did they?" asked Polk.

"Later that night," Roy replied. "Two, three in the morning when the guests were all asleep. House detective got a van from somewheres. Him and me took up the rug, cleared the furniture out, all them bloody towels. Drove it all out to the dump and ditched it there. He told if I were smart and forgot what I seen, I'd do okay for m'self, and if I weren't, I'd be right sorry."

Polk stared down at his trooper's hat, his brow furrowed. "Who paid you off, Roy?" he asked, his voice quavering slightly. "Was it this Melnitz?"

Roy cleared his throat. "Were your great-granddad. Were Polk One. He called me to his big fancy law office next morning, give me five hunnert bucks. And a job out here. In case I got loose lips, I reckon. I took it. Sure I did. We all did. Times were bad. Them movie people could afford it. They wanted to pay money to cover the thing up, crazy not to take it."

"Laurel Barrett didn't shoot him, did she, Roy?" I said. "The Glaze family wouldn't have taken care of you all these years if she had. It was someone a little closer to home, wasn't it?"

Roy stared at me.

"Who else was there that night, Roy?" I asked. "Who else was in the hotel room?"

Roy glanced nervously at Polk.

"Tell us, Roy," commanded Polk.

Roy spat some juice into the dirt.

"Who was it, Roy?" demanded Polk. "Tell us, or so help me I'll haul you into—"

"Hidin' in one of the bedrooms," Roy muttered. "I saw 'em in there talking with the sheriff, real upset. Door was half closed, but I saw who it were. It were Miss Alma. Alma Glaze were in there."

Chapter Sixteen

Pam brought me out my costume for the VADD Ball. My red velvet coat, waistcoat, and knee breeches were on a hanger. The rest was in a long white box—white silk stockings and black buckled shoes, white linen neckcloth and ruffled cuffs, black felt tricorne hat. There was one other box, squatly shaped.

"What's in that one?" I asked her as Lulu sniffed over all of it.

"Your wig, dear boy," Pam replied, smiling. "Freshly powdered."

It had a little pigtail at the back of the neck, held together with a black ribbon.

"Isn't all of this a bit silly, Pam?" I asked, trying it on in the mirror. I looked a little like Norman Bates's mother. I certainly looked more like her than I did Tom Jefferson.

"Of course it is. That is the point—it is a charity benefit."

"I could just wear my tux."

"You could not," she huffed.

"I don't look terrible in my tux."

"I'm well aware of that. However, this is a costume ball, not a Friars' Club roast," she reminded me airily. "Please, Hoagy. It's all been decided, and I've way too much to do to argue with you."

She did have a little to do. A thousand guests would be arriving by horse-drawn carriage that evening right after the movie. Trucks had been pulling up all week with party tents, tables, chairs, portable dance floors and toilets, floodlights, food, liquor, flowers. An army of carpenters and electricians were still putting it all together on the north lawn, while an assembly line of caterers was inside glazing the hams, baking the rolls. It was enough to send an average person bouncing off the ceiling. Pam was merely a bit flushed.

She started out the door. "A favor, Hoagy?"

"Sure, Pam."

"The family wishes for Gordie to appear at the ball, being the poster child and all, and the poor thing has the glums over it. Hasn't said a word or eaten a morsel all day."

"What makes you think I can bring him around?"

"He does happen to—"

"Like me," I acknowledged sourly. "I know."

"A lad of keen intelligence but questionable taste." She smiled. "Would you take him his dinner? Chat with him?"

"Soon as I get into my costume."

It took me a while. I had to climb into my breeches and stockings, put on my collarless muslin shirt, my neckcloth, my cuffs. It wasn't easy, and I wasn't happy with the way any of it looked until my coat was on and my hat was positioned rakishly atop my wig. I cut quite a figure in the mirror now. Erect. Commanding. Utterly Jeffersonian. I couldn't wait to see how Kissinger looked in his.

Lulu sat on her chair, watching me intently.

"Impressive, no?" I said.

She started coughing. She doesn't know how to laugh.

"Hey, I haven't made fun of your taste in men, have I?"

Stung, she got down from the chair and started her way

mournfully up the staircase. I knew where she was headed—under the bed. Bowser hadn't shown last night. She'd been in a snit fit over it all day. Okay, it was a low blow from me. But hey, she started it.

I know Pam was impressed when I went into the kitchen to pick up Gordie's dinner. The place was mobbed with caterers. She didn't even seem to notice them.

"Truly magisterial, dear boy," she exclaimed, checking me out from head to toe. "And how are the shoes?"

"I've worn more comfortable bowling shoes," I replied, hobbling over to her. "Women's bowling shoes."

Charlotte came in from her office, frazzled and rushed. But not so rushed she couldn't stop and stare. And start snickering at me.

"Ignore her," Pam told me. "You're a stirring sight."

"I'm just glad Merilee isn't here to see this," I grumbled.

Pam opened a drawer and pulled out the Polaroid. "One must capture the memory," she declared, snapping my picture.

"I'll take that film."

"Nonsense. It goes in tomorrow morning's post."

"I'll get you for this, Pam. You owe me now."

"Yes, dear," she said patiently. She handed me Gordie's tray. "The carriages for the theater leave in thirty minutes. Don't be late."

I heard my phone ringing as I hobbled across the courtyard toward Gordie's rooms. It was Polk Four. He sounded very, very down.

"I tried, Hoagy," he said, his voice low and choked with emotion. "I really tried."

"Tried what, Sheriff?"

"Granddad. I-I went out to see him. Told him everything we know. Laid all my cards out on the table. Even told him we know he was involved. . . ."

"And?"

"He was very calm about it. Didn't get upset or anything. Just said that for the good of the valley and for my own future

I should leave well enough alone. He said it's one thing for some outsider to try digging up old bones, but another for me. He said he was disappointed in me. Like I'm some kind of little boy. I'm *sheriff* of this county! Three women have been murdered! I asked him point-blank who it was he phoned that set those two boys on you. He refused to tell me. I don't know what to do now. I may have to nail him for obstruction of justice if we're going to get anywhere. I don't know, Hoagy. I sure don't . . ." He trailed off, was silent a moment. "It's all starting to sink in, you know?"

"What is?"

"Who I am, what I stand for—it's all corrupt. Everything that the LaFoons have built in this valley is corrupt."

"This from the man who was so sure that justice had the upper hand here."

He breathed heavily in the phone. "I've never been so depressed in my entire life."

"And you'll stay that way if you keep on thinking like you are."

"What do you mean?"

"I mean you can't deal in absolutes, Sheriff. Not when you're talking about people. Your family wasn't as clean as you used to think it was, and it's not as dirty as you think it is right now. The truth is somewhere in between. It always is. I don't know what else I can tell you, except that life sucks. But I think you're already catching on to that."

I hung up and went next door. Gordie flicked off the TV when he heard me knocking. He asked who it was. I told him. He said I could come in. I did.

If the kid was gloomy, you could have fooled me. He started giggling the second he saw me.

"What's so funny?" I demanded, setting his food down on the coffee table.

"*You* are."

My close personal friend Sadie seemed to think Gordie's

dinner was for her. She started hungrily for it. I scooped her up.

"I am not funny," I said, putting her down on the sofa. "I'm a piece of living history. You can learn an important lesson from all of this."

"Like what?"

"Like don't ever get talked into going to a costume ball."

Gordie's face darkened. He withdrew from me.

"Aren't you going to eat?" I asked him.

No reaction.

"Looks great," I observed. It did, too. Fried chicken, mashed potatoes, greens. I wouldn't get to eat until after the movie, and *Oh, Shenandoah* is one long movie. "If you don't eat it, I will."

Still no reaction.

"Suit yourself." I sat down, stuffed a napkin in my sleeve and calmly went to work on a wing.

"Do I gotta go, Hoagy?" he finally said.

"Don't want to, huh?" I said, munching.

"More than anything in the whole world."

"Then don't."

He brightened considerably. "Really!"

"Really. It's their thing, not yours. You didn't sign on as a performing seal. Anybody says different, you tell them to talk to me."

"Gee, thankth, Hoagy," he said gratefully.

He glanced down at the plate with interest. I nudged it over toward him. He went for the drumstick.

"What were you watching?" I asked as we ate.

"My favorite movie ever," he replied eagerly. "Theen it maybe a hundred timesth. Wanna watch?"

"You bet."

He reached for the remote control and flicked the tape on. James Garner and Donald Pleasence were emerging from a tunnel into the darkness. McQueen was helping them. The climax of *The Great Escape*, one of my three favorite McQueen films. The other two are *The Magnificent Seven* and *Bullitt.* I'd hate to have to pick one over the others. The Germans were on to them now. The searchlights came on inside the compound, machine guns fired, all hell broke loose. Off our heroes fled into the woods, each to pursue his own artfully conceived date with destiny.

If only real life were so neat. If only Sterling Sloan's murder made such sense. It didn't. The damned pieces still wouldn't fit together, no matter how hard I tried to make them. Say Alma Glaze was Sloan's mystery lover. Say he wanted to break it off when the picture wrapped and she didn't, so she showed up at his hotel room with a gun and blew his head off, the lover scorned. So far so good. Goldwyn's people and Alma's own people would be equally eager to cover it up. Only, who ran over Alma a few months later, and why? Why had Fern screamed? Whom had she seen in Vangie's room with Sloan? Not Alma—it was Alma herself who reported the outburst in her diary. Who had torn those final pages out? Why? And why had all of this reared its ugly head now, five decades later? Who was still being protected?

Lots more questions. And these answers weren't so easy to grab on to. Every time I reached for them they seemed to slip farther and farther away.

"Oh, boy, here'th my favorite part," exclaimed Gordie, breaking into my wondering.

McQueen was on his own now. Coburn had found a bicycle, Bronson a rowboat. Garner stole a plane. The others tried the train station. Not McQueen's style. He was looking for his own brand of transportation. It was while he was getting it that it suddenly happened—it all became clear to me. Horribly, finally, clear. So clear that I sat right up, stunned and dumbfounded. What can I tell you—sometimes it happens that way.

I wish I could say I was happy it had. I wasn't. The truth is, I felt lousier than I had in a long, long time.

·   ·   ·

"We have to talk, Frederick," I said into the phone after he said hello.

"Is that you, Hoagy?" he inquired in his husky, elegant voice.

"It is."

"I'm just climbing into this ridiculous costume . . . ," he groaned. "Go right ahead and talk. What's on your mind?"

"I know it was you who hired those two goons to get your mother's diary off of me." I waited for him to respond. There was only breathing from his end. I plowed ahead. "You were going to sneak it to the tabloids for a lot of money—money you desperately need. Taking it off me outside your office was your best shot. Once I had it with me at Shenandoah it would have been too obvious that an insider was behind it."

"I see," he finally said. He sounded weary and defeated. He sounded old. "And what else do you know?"

"I know it was you who Polk Two phoned after I visited him at his house. It had to be you—you were their contact. You sent them out there to kill me."

"Now that's not true, strictly speaking," Frederick protested. "I only meant to scare you. Get you to concentrate on your work and forget about this other business."

"And I know why. It's time for all of this to end, Frederick. I've no desire to hurt you or anyone in your family. Merely to see justice served. It's time for us to talk."

He breathed in my ear some more. "Yes. Okay," he said heavily. "I'd prefer to do it in person if you don't mind."

"I don't mind. Where and when?"

"Hell, let's do it right now—I've already seen the damned movie two hundred times. I'll come out there. We can go to the ball after we talk."

"That'll be fine. My quarters?"

He hesitated. "I'd rather we make it somewhere more private. Shall we meet at the gazebo? In half an hour?"

"See you then, Frederick."

Lulu didn't want to come with me. She was still sulking

over the crack I'd made about Bowser. She only agreed to come when I begged her forgiveness. And mentioned the word *caviar* several times.

It was dark out now. The batteries in my flashlight were about dead from all of our late-night strolls. I found some fresh ones in the kitchen utility drawer, and put them in while the caterers rushed in and out with their fragrant trays.

"And what are you up to?" Pam wondered, watching me.

"Taking a small stroll."

"Where?"

"I don't know. Just felt like breaking in my new shoes."

"Must I remind you that the carriages leave in—"

"Please, Pam. You've stripped me of what's left of my dignity. Leave me my secrets." With that I straightened my tricorne hat and hobbled out the door.

The great north lawn was ablaze with the party-tent lights. Waitresses were setting the banquet tables. Musicians were testing their microphones. The peacocks were honking. A couple of old-fashioned movie-premiere kliegs stabbed way up into the black sky overhead, adding to the good old colonial effect. Lulu and I took the path that bordered the lawn, then plunged into the woods alongside the cemetery. It was dark and quiet in there. I could see only what was ahead of me in my flashlight beam, hear only the clopping of my shoes. Briefly, I thought I heard footsteps in the woods behind us, someone following us. But when I stopped, I heard nothing. And my flashlight beam found nothing. Lulu whimpered. I shushed her and moved on, sorry for the moment that Bowser wasn't with us. I could use someone like him, someone with no class or breeding. Someone who'd happily sink his teeth into a nice meaty leg if I asked him to.

I saw the weak flicker of a light up ahead. It was an oil lamp sitting on the pine table under the gazebo. Frederick was there already, seated at the table, smoking a cigarette. He stood when he heard me. He was dressed for the ball as I was, though he had a cape of peacock-blue silk over his outfit, and gold braid on his tricorne hat. I don't know why I didn't get gold braid on mine. I'll bet his shoes fit, too.

"Ah, here you are, Hoagy," he rasped pleasantly.

"Frederick," I said.

"Not exactly." He dropped the cigarette on the rough wooden floor and stepped on it. "Horrible things. My fingers will stink of nicotine for a week. . . . I'm afraid you've fallen for a trick we've played on people since we were boys, Hoagy. I do Frederick and Frederick does me. Drove our teachers crazy. I think I do him better. Just my opinion. You see, Frederick was in the shower when you phoned. I'd stopped over for my costume and answered it for him. Naturally, you assumed you'd reached Frederick. Your tough luck, I'm afraid. If you had gotten Fred, you might have lived." Edward reached under his cape and pulled out a revolver and pointed it at me. "But you got me."

Chapter Seventeen

"**K**ind of the wrong period, isn't it, Edward?" I said, my
eyes on the gun. "A dueling pistol would be so much
more appropriate."

"You'll forgive me the historical inaccuracy."

"I'll try. But I'm making no promises."

"You've gotten too close, young man. Much too close. And
I have survived too long to be brought down now, particularly
by some washed-up writer."

I glanced down at Lulu. "Are you going to take that from
him?" In response she yawned and curled up under the table.
Bowser. I needed Bowser, crashing through the woods, saliva
dripping from his fangs. "Mind if I sit down, Edward? My feet
are killing me."

"Please do."

He stayed where he was, the gun on me. "You know the
truth, of course. That's why you wanted to speak with Frederick."

"Yes. I was off course for the longest time. Mavis and her
damned collarbone kept throwing me. That business in your

mother's diary about how little Mavis took a horse out one day, and fell, and was missing until Sterling Sloan found her in the pasture across the way. It seemed odd to me. Supposedly, Sloan rarely left his trailer. What was he doing out there with Mavis? And why was she still afraid to get back up on a horse so many years later? Because she broke her collarbone as a child? That didn't sound like Mavis to me. Some other form of childhood trauma seemed more like it. Like, say, the great Sterling Sloan trying to hand her his shlong. And maybe trying to do it again in Vangie's room on the last day of filming. I figured maybe *that's* what Fern saw, and what Alma walked in on. And I figured Alma shot Sloan because of it—the protective mother taking the law into her own hands. It all fit together, Edward. Except it didn't. Because if Alma killed Sloan, then who ran *her* down several months later on Beverley Street? Laurel Barrett? Possibly, except she was out of the country—I checked. And then there was now to factor in. Okay, Fern and Cookie were killed to keep things covered up. That part worked. But why kill Mavis? If all of this had been done to protect her, then why kill her? That made no sense. And it got me nowhere—except back to you."

"And how, may I ask, did you arrive at me?" he inquired calmly.

"You tipped me off yourself the day Fern died. We were all sitting there in the old house while Polk Four attended to her body. You were pretty upset about it."

"It's true, I was."

"So upset you messed up. You turned to Frederick and said, 'I keep thinking of the night mother died. I was at Fern's when I got the news, remember? She was the one who actually told me.' Frederick got somewhat curt with you and changed the subject. None of which meant much to me until later, when I interviewed Polk Two about that night Alma died. He told me all three of you kids were home when she was hit. A small discrepancy, but it stuck with me. And it didn't go away. Just got bigger and bigger. What had you been doing at Fern's?

Why had Frederick gotten so snappish about your mentioning it? The answer was plain—Fern was your alibi for that evening in case Polk Two ever got around to checking up on you. Only he never did because Frederick covered for you, said you were home. And Polk Two accepted it. I guess he just didn't believe that you could murder your own mother, even though he was fully aware that you'd murdered once already. You murdered Sterling Sloan—the man you loved."

Edward lowered his eyes. The gun never left me. "It's true," he said softly. "I loved Sterling. I've never stopped loving him."

"It was *you.* You were Sloan's mystery lover. Fern saw you two together in Vangie's room. That's why she screamed. It must have come as quite a shock to a teenaged girl back in those days to discover that her Romeo, her Sweet Prince, was gay."

He was silent a moment. "It happened for me," he began slowly, "that very first night I saw him standing out there in the rain. I felt something I'd never felt before, not for any girl. Even Fern. She and I were so close. We gave each other our souls. But I'd never felt the *hunger* for her that one read about. The physical part, that was never real for me somehow. Until I met Sterling. He was . . . I suppose he was the very man whom I most wished to become. Brilliant, artistic, sophisticated. He was a soul in torment, a man locked in a loveless marriage. That simply made him all the more romantic. It was merely a business arrangement, their marriage. Good for both of their images. Laurel went her way, he went his. At least he was discreet about it. . . . I was so terribly flattered when he showed an interest in me. Of course, being a naive small-town boy, I had no idea *why* he was so interested. Not until the two of us were together in his trailer one afternoon. He got one of his terrible headaches and asked me if I'd massage his neck. As I did, I-I felt it happening to me—I felt myself coming alive. And then he looked at me and I knew he felt it, too. He took my hands in his and led me over to the daybed. We kissed.

Gently, tenderly. And then he undressed me. I was powerless
to stop him. I didn't want to stop him. It felt so right. For me it
was. For me it was love." Edward's eyes moistened in the
lamplight. "I loved him, don't you see? I've never loved anyone
else in my entire life."

"You did try though," I suggested.

"I did," he acknowledged. "Years later, after I had finished
law school, taken a job in the Justice Department in Washington." He chuckled softly. "I suppose I was the only murderer
on the staff."

"Oh, I wouldn't be so sure," I said. "You took a wife."

"Yes, Danielle. A sweet, lovely woman. I hurt her badly."

"Indeed you did. Her husband told me all about it on the
phone this afternoon. How she'd been married once before,
briefly, to this man who'd wanted so desperately to conform.
But he couldn't. It was clear from the first night he couldn't.
Your marriage was annulled—on the grounds of nonconsum-
mation."

"I wasn't being *me*," Edward explained. "Only with Sterling was I me."

"And he broke your heart, didn't he?"

"Such a tired old story," he murmured. "Such a cliché. But
what did I know? I was eighteen years old. I thought he loved
me as I loved him. I believed him when he said he would take
me with him to Hollywood, to London, to wherever. That he
would divorce her." Edward gazed out the gazebo at the
woods. He seemed very far away now. The gun didn't. "How
was I to know I was nothing to him? I was just some boy he'd
diddled on location, one of the dozens he'd fucked and forgot-
ten through the years, a bimbo. How was I to know? I didn't.
Not until he told me. In Vangie's room, that last day of filming.
That's when I found out. He said he wanted me to stay behind.
He said he was no good for me, that I'd be better off forgetting
about him. I couldn't believe what he was telling me. *Wouldn't*
believe it. I threw myself into his arms, sobbing, begging, cov-
ering him with kisses. . . . That's when Fern saw us. That's

what she saw. I heard her scream, saw her run away. A moment later Mother came into the room. Sterling and I were merely standing next to each other by then. But she *knew*. Somehow, she *knew*. Not that she said a word to either of us. She merely said, 'Excuse me,' in that stiff, proper way she had and walked out of the room."

"And put it in her diary—the pages you tore out."

"Her lawyer, Polk One, did it, actually. Before he sealed it and put it in the safe."

"And that evening you went to Sloan's hotel room and you shot him."

"I went up there to tell that evil bitch Laurel she had to let him go. I wouldn't believe him, you see. I wouldn't believe he didn't love me. I-I set Laurel straight, face-to-face. I told her Sterling was mine, not hers. I told her there was no love between them anymore and she should be sensible and divorce him. I thought I was being very adult, very mature. And she . . . she simply rolled her eyes at me and called to him in the bath: 'Oh, Sterling, dear, one of your little friends is here!' As if I were some irritating stray that had followed him home, some petty nuisance. And when he came out and saw me there, I realized from the way he looked at me that I *was*."

"So you shot him?"

"Never. I would never have. . . . I-I shot her. I shot Laurel."

"And you missed?"

Edward shook his head. "Sterling jumped in front of her at the last second. He took the shot. She screamed. I heard her screams in my ears as I ran out the door, down the hall, out of there."

"Your mother was summoned by Polk Two as soon as Laurel told him what had happened. Alma put the fix in for you. Both the townspeople and Goldwyn's people were only too happy to oblige her. No one wanted a scandal."

"Precisely," Edward agreed bitterly. "Mother protected her precious little boy. The studio protected their colossal investment. They weren't about to jeopardize it because of some faggot killing. Toriello dreamed up the aneurysm story, symptoms and all, and everyone went along with it. It was all covered up. Buried. And it would have stayed that way if it hadn't been for Sam Goldwyn. The greedy bastard had a hit on his hands and he knew it. Even before the movie came out he knew it. Right away, he began pressuring Mother to write a sequel. He even tried telling her how to write it—De Cheverier has to win the duel with John Raymond at the end, he said. After all, Errol Flynn was still alive. Sterling Sloan wasn't. Well, Mother didn't like being bullied by anyone, especially Goldwyn. She told him that if there ever was a sequel, she would write it in her own way and in her own time, thank you. He offered to buy up the rights to her characters and commission his own film sequel without any book. She declined. That should have been the end of it. Except he wasn't through, Goldwyn. Not so long as there was a gutter left to climb down into. He put it to Mother this way: Let me do my sequel or the whole world will find out that your son murdered Sterling Sloan and got away with it. Goldwyn figured that would break her. Break any mother. But he was wrong about Alma Glaze. Because she didn't care about me, not as much as she cared about her fool creation. She told him fine, go ahead and tell the world about Edward. She sold me out. Told me so to my face. She had a choice to make and she made it—she put her book ahead of her own son. I ask you, Hoagy, what kind of woman would do that? Only an evil one. Miserable, horrid, *evil* . . . I did the only thing I could do. I killed her. So Goldwyn could have his way. So that what had happened would stay private. Sterling and me . . . that was nobody's business. Nobody's." He chuckled softly. "Ironically, it was only after I'd killed her that I learned about the codicil she'd added to her will. I hadn't known. None of us had. Only her trusted legal advisor, Polk One. She did it to punish Goldwyn. Oh, the bastard thought about contesting it. Taking the estate to court. But the war was on by then. Wartime was no time for long,

ugly court battles. Or big-budget Hollywood epics. So he quietly dropped the whole thing, moved on. . . . It was right,
what I did. I've never been sorry that I killed her. Not sorry in
the least."

"How nice for you. May I ask you how you did it?"

"You may. I overheard her on the phone with Polk One. A
Saturday afternoon, it was. She wished for him to come out to
Shenandoah at once. I suppose to talk about the codicil. He
couldn't make it. She said she'd come into town that evening,
meet him at his office at six. He agreed. After all, she was a
rather important client. I moved swiftly, seizing the opportunity. I made a date for eight that evening with Fern. As soon as
Mother left for town, I stole a bottle of bourbon from the liquor cupboard and did the same. I left my car near Fern's
house, took the bourbon with me, and went hunting through
the neighborhood for a car. I found one with its keys in it just
a few blocks away. No one saw me take it. It was suppertime,
the street was deserted. Polk One's office was on Beverley
Street. I parked down the block and waited there for her to
come out, my hat down over my face, my collar turned up.
And when she did, she got what was coming to her. She flew
fifty feet through the air when I hit her. God, it felt good. I kept
right on going, until I was outside of town. I left the car there.
Poured the bourbon all over the seats so Polk Two would think
a drunk had done it. Then I ran to Fern's. I was only a few
minutes late for our date. I was there when I got the news
about Mother. Frederick phoned me. He knew I'd be there.
And he knew why."

"Did Mavis?"

"Mavis was a child. She knew nothing about Sterling's
death. And she never knew I killed our mother."

"And Polk Two never suspected you?"

Edward smiled. "If he did, he never said anything. You
must understand that Polk Two was never anything more than
a Glaze-family lapdog. His position as sheriff, his seat in Richmond, depended on staying in our good graces."

"I see. Why did Frederick let you get away with it? Why did he cover for you?"

"He's my twin, Hoagy. I don't suppose you can understand just how close that makes us, closer than any other two human beings can possibly be. Frederick loves me, and I love him. We've always watched out for each other, stood by each other. He is the only person I've ever completely trusted, just as he trusts me. Oh, we have our small differences. I happen to think he lacks personal discipline when it comes to money and women, for instance. But I'd still do anything for him. I'm helping him right now—trying to extricate him from his financial misfortune."

"That's certainly one word for fraud." I sat back and crossed my legs. At my feet Lulu paddled in her sleep, small whimpers coming from her throat. Dreaming of you-know-who no doubt. Edward stood there motionless, the gun still on me. "All of which brings us to the present, Edward. And to three more murders. You had to kill Cookie. Polk Four and I were starting to sniff around, and Cookie was the one living outsider who could name you as the person who'd been in Vangie's room with Sloan. Like you said, you've survived much too long to be brought down now. But Fern and Mavis were another matter entirely. How much did Fern actually know?"

"She knew of my relationship with Sterling, of course," Edward replied. "As to the circumstances of his death, Mother's death . . . Fern drew her own conclusions. Not that she ever said anything to me about it. Not then, not ever. We never talked about what Fern saw that day in Vangie's room. Or about anything else ever again. Oh, she was always cordial toward me, just as I was to her. But anytime I happened to look deeply into her eyes I saw . . . *pain*. Fern drew a line between us, and I was never, ever, to cross over it. It was an unspoken contract between us."

"Which she was prepared to break. My first night here she told me it was time for the truth to come out. Only, why kill her? I mean, I was prepared to ignore her. I just took her for a jolly, slightly paranoid old crank—*until* she was murdered. That made me think maybe she *did* know something. It was dumb for you to kill her and arouse my suspicion that way. Just as it was dumb for you to kill Mavis. What was the point? To get at her money? The estate goes to Mercy, not you and Frederick. There was no point, and that stumped me. Because if there's one thing you're not, it's dumb. You're a bright, sensitive, and extremely gracious psychopath. I couldn't figure Fern and Mavis out. Not until tonight, when I realized there was only one way it made any sense."

"And what way was that, Hoagy?"

"You didn't kill them. You had nothing to do with either murder."

Edward spread his feet slightly, took careful, steady aim at the center of my chest. "You're a gifted man, Hoagy. You should have stayed at what you know, writing. You're not as good at this sort of thing. Just good enough to die."

"Killing me won't solve anything, Edward. Polk Four knows too much. He'll follow the same trail right to you."

"And when he does, he'll do what he's told, just like Polks One, Two, and Three before him. The Glazes are the power in this valley. We *are* this valley. Young Polk, he has his sights set on the governor's mansion. He'll never make it there without our backing, and he knows it. I'm not worried about him. It's you I worry about. But my worries end here."

So here it was. The end. Staring at me from six feet away. I stared back at it. I wasn't afraid. There was no fear. Only regret. Because I was going to die here and now with nothing to show for my life, nothing except for two novels, a weird dog, and my independence. I was sorry I'd never see Merilee's green eyes again. Sorry we hadn't built a life together, only a truce. Sorry I hadn't said hello to my father in more than five years. He'd never hear me say it now. If only I lived I'd do something about that. But of course, I wasn't going to live.

Edward pulled the trigger. The gun made an odd sound

when he did. As if it had fired twice at once. But I barely had time to register that thought. Almost instantly I felt a searing pain in my head, and the rough wooden floor of the gazebo was rushing up at me and I was hurtling down toward it, and then there was only blackness.

Chapter Eighteen

It was Pam's face I saw first. She was standing over me looking very pale and grim. I was lying in a bed, the one in my slaves' quarters. I was dizzy. My head felt heavy and thick. I reached a hand up to it, fingered it. Something cottony was wrapped around it.

Pam wasn't alone. A crowd of people stood circled around me. Most of them wore costumes. Polk Two, Frederick—at least I hoped it was Frederick—Richard, Charlotte, Mercy. Charlotte and Mercy wore elaborate silk gowns over hooped petticoats, and wigs piled high under peacock-feathered hats. More damned peacock feathers. Polk Four stood there in his uniform. The weary old doctor who had signed Fern's death certificate was there, too. They were all staring at me, looking very serious. Everyone was there. Everyone except—

Two shots. Not one. Two.

I tried to speak, but my throat was too dry. Pam held out a glass of water with a straw in it. I drank some. "Lulu . . . ," I got out hoarsely. "Luluuuu . . ."

"Here she is, dear boy." Pam bent down to the floor next to

my bed and hoisted her up onto the covers, where Lulu began to wriggle and whoop and lick my fingers. "Safe and sound," Pam assured me. "As are you."

Polk Four leaned forward. "You have Pam here to thank for that, Hoagy," he explained. "She tailed you out to the gazebo. Overheard the whole thing. She shot him just as he was about to fire at you. His shot went wild. Your wig took most of it."

"My wig?" I swallowed. "I admire your definition of a wild shot, Sheriff."

"Just got a shallow little groove over your left ear, son," the doctor informed me. "It bled quite a lot, but it's nothing serious."

"You wouldn't be saying that if it was your ear." I turned to Pam. "I thought I heard someone behind me on the path. "That was you?"

She nodded. "When you left the kitchen, I took Fern's gun from my nightstand and followed you out there."

"But why?"

She reddened slightly. "You do have a tendency to get in over your head sometimes, dear boy."

"I sure do wish you'd filled me in, Hoagy," Polk Four said crossly. "Instead of making the hot-dog play."

"I honestly didn't know that's what I was making. You saved my life, Pam."

"Why, yes. I suppose I did."

"I owe you one."

"You could take me home with you when this is over."

"Please, Pam. Not in front of all of those people."

She smiled. No one else did. They didn't have much to smile about.

"Edward is . . . ?"

"Edward is dead," Frederick said quietly. He looked drawn and grief stricken. His eyes moistened. "We came into this world together. We've never been apart." He choked back a sob. "Not ever."

"I'm sorry it had to happen, Frederick," I said. "Only how could you do it? How could you cover for him all these years? He killed two people, one of them your own mother."

"He was my twin," Frederick replied simply. "Right or wrong, he was part of me."

"That works for you. Maybe." I turned to Polk Two. "But not for you, sir."

The big old man shifted slowly in his costume, hands gripping his canes tightly. His blue eyes were bright and clear and unapologetic. "I was an employee," he declared. "I was paid to do a job, and I did it. Nothing I was particularly proud to do, but I did it. People always make the mistake of thinking a politician leads. He doesn't lead. He follows."

"You agree with that?" I asked Polk Four.

"Not entirely," the young sheriff replied stiffly.

Polk Two let out a deep, hacking cough. "Now that Edward is gone, I believe it's best we put this whole sorry business behind us. Not make a big public spectacle out of it. Be bad for the valley. Bad for everyone. It's from long ago, and it's over now."

"Not entirely," I said.

"That's right," Polk Four agreed. "Pam swears she heard you say that Edward *didn't* kill Mavis or Fern."

"He didn't," I acknowledged. "Wasn't involved in their deaths at all. Merely an unfortunate chain of circumstances for him. Not to mention the two ladies."

Mercy frowned and shook her head, baffled. "But if Uncle Edward didn't kill them, who did?" she wondered.

They all seemed to stop breathing as they stood there staring at me, waiting for my reply.

"Steve McQueen," I said.

Polk Four frowned and glanced at the doctor, who leaned over me and stuck a light in my eyes. "I did sedate him," he murmured. "I'm afraid we may be losing him."

"You are not," I insisted, waving him away. "Remember *The Great Escape*, the McQueen movie?"

"I've seen it on television," replied Polk Four, baffled.

"What of it, lad?" inquired Richard, equally baffled.

"Remember how he got away?" I asked.

Polk Four scratched his chin. "He didn't get away. They caught him at the end. Brought him back, and his friend tossed him his baseball mitt as he was being led to the cooler."

"Right, right. But when he was on the run, before they caught him. Coburn took a bicycle, Bronson a rowboat, Garner a plane. And McQueen . . ."

"Wasn't there a car chase or something?" asked Mercy.

"No, that was *Bullitt.* He stole a motorcycle off a German —by stretching a wire across the road. The guy ran into it and went flying."

"A *wire.*" Polk Four swallowed. "Okay . . ."

"McQueen happens to be Gordie's hero," I said. "And *The Great Escape* is his favorite movie. He told me he's seen it a hundred times."

"Wait one minute," declared Richard, incredulous. "Are you actually suggesting it was that little orphan boy who murdered Mavis and Fern?"

"Ever since Fern fell down those stairs," I said, "I've been wondering what the hell she was doing upstairs in the old house when she was supposed to be serving up our lunch in the kitchen. She was chasing after Gordie. He was playing games with her, getting her mad at him. He got her to chase him into the old house, then up the stairs, and then he hid. When she went in one of the bedrooms to look for him, he tied a wire across the top of the stairs and ran down them, making sure she heard him. She chased after him and being blind as a bat, tripped over the wire and fell headfirst down the stairs to her death. Then he quickly gathered up the wire and hightailed it out to his room before I found her. Got to hand it to him— he's a clever little guy."

Polk Four gaped at me, aghast. "B-But why did he do it?"

"He hated her. He thought she was going to take Sadie away from him."

"Who is Sadie?" asked Pam.

"His cat."

"I didn't know he had a cat," said Richard.

"He used the same technique to kill Mavis," I went on. "He knew her patrol route. He tied a wire around two trees and hid. Then removed it after she'd gotten thrown. He killed her because she insisted he go to the VADD Ball. He didn't want to. The kid lost his whole family. Suffered a major emotional trauma. He needed someone to care about him. He needed help. What he got was a billboard and a room outside next to the garage. So he's withdrawn, drifted away. Drifted so far he sometimes can't tell the difference between what he sees on TV and what's real. He worships McQueen in *The Great Escape.* He dresses like McQueen does in the movie. He sits and tosses a ball against a wall like McQueen does. He's even tunneling out in the middle of the night like him. And when Gordie gets real upset at someone, he solves the problem the way he thinks his hero would."

No one said anything.

"I'll be darned," Polk Four finally said under his breath. "Guess I . . . I ought to take the poor little guy into custody."

"Don't be too hard on him, Sheriff," I said. "He honestly doesn't know what he's done. And if it hadn't been for Gordie, we would never have found out who killed Sterling Sloan." To Pam I said, "How's the VADD Ball?"

"In full swing," she replied.

"I want to go," I declared.

"You're hardly up to it, dear boy."

"I have to go," I insisted.

Polk Four frowned. "And why is that, Hoagy? What else is left?"

"Kissinger. I have to see Kissinger."

The doctor leaned over me again. "I believe we *are* losing him."

And this time they were.

Chapter Nineteen

Edward Glaze's death made kind of a nice capper to the *Oh, Shenandoah* golden-anniversary festivities. At least all of the press who were around seemed to think so. They had loads of good, dirty fun with the story—the whole story. The deaths of Sterling Sloan and Alma Glaze fifty years ago. The deaths of the three women during the past few weeks. Polk Four insisted on a full and complete disclosure. Polk Two wasn't happy about that. After all, it didn't make him or the Glazes look too good. But Polk Four insisted on it. He showed me a lot of class by the way he handled the situation. He showed everybody a lot. Made quite a name for himself. Don't be too surprised if he does turn up in the governor's mansion one day soon.

I asked him to do me one small favor. I wanted him to impress on the media just how crucial the courageous testimony of actor Rex Ransom had been. The sheriff complied. Rex got a lot of attention as a result. Appeared on Letterman. Landed a lucrative series of denture-cream commercials. Even got carte blanche from the studio to keep on appearing around the country as the Masked Avenger. I never heard from Rex again, but I still watch the Masked Avenger in reruns. And he's still my hero.

The Major League Editor started calling me again. Not just to breathe down my neck either, although *Sweet Land* and how it was coming along did come up. She wanted me to write a book about the scandal after I finished up. Major advance. Major upside. Major excitement from her end. "True-life crime has become the fiction of the nineties," is how she put it, burbling. I turned her down. She immediately offered it to Frederick. He immediately accepted. He needs the money. He's still looking for a ghost. If you're interested, you can contact him care of Shenandoah, Staunton, Va. I forget the zip code. He's also looking for a new lawyer.

Gordie was placed in the children's ward of the state mental hospital in Charlottesville for observation. A team of child psychiatrists interviewed and tested him. It didn't take them long to diagnose that he needed permanent care. At the insistence of Mercy Glaze he was transferred to a private children's mental hospital nearby. The cost, seven hundred dollars a day, will be paid by the Glazes. His case will be reviewed every couple of years. He may get out someday. For now he has his own room and bath, and there's a baseball team.

Our last night at Shenandoah, Lulu woke me at the usual time for our usual date. She was particularly anxious. I'd been packing all evening—she knew we were leaving. I was anxious myself. I didn't know what she was going to do. Would she choose Bowser over me? Would she stay behind? Would I let her? Did I have a right to interfere? I didn't know.

Roy was still pulling wall duty. And still asleep on the job. He didn't hear us approach. Didn't see Bowser burrow under the wall and start toward us. Didn't see Bowser stop and turn and casually wait for his companion to burrow under it, too.

She was a collie. A real fox, too.

Lulu was so stunned she sounded as if she were going to choke.

Bowser wasn't particularly happy to see her. He sniffed at her coolly, as if she were a bad memory. The collie showed Lulu her teeth, the bitch. Then the two of them kept on going across the pasture. I guess they were just crossing Shenandoah on their way home. Or maybe he'd purposely gone out of his way—just to rub Lulu's nose in it. That's the sort of guy he was. Lulu sat there at my feet and watched them go, whimpering. Then she began to shake and tried to climb up my leg. I picked her up and carried her back to our quarters and gave her a bowl of milk with a slug of Macallan in it. She lapped it all up and fell instantly to sleep.

I didn't say it. I didn't say I told you so. It wouldn't have done any good, and she'd have bit me.

Polk Four stopped by in the morning to see us off. I was loading up the Jag when he pulled up in his cruiser, clean shaven and crisply pressed as ever. Still, he looked different to me. Not so certain of himself and his mission in life. That'll happen when the earth moves under your feet for the first time.

"Want to hear something funny, Hoagy?" he said, striding over to me.

"Desperately."

"I thought this whole business would drive Mercy and me apart. Send each of us running for cover. It hasn't. If anything, it's brought the two of us closer, in a way we never were before. It's as if we share something."

"You do. You've both joined the so-called real world. Welcome to it."

"Thanks." He stuck out his hand and smiled. "Thanks, pardner."

I shook it. "So long, pardner," I said, smiling back at him, liking him.

Pam came outside then with Mercy and Frederick. Richard and Charlotte followed. Those two seemed quite shy around each other now. She also seemed a little less drab to me now. There was a hint of color to her cheeks, a liveliness to her step. Maybe it was just my imagination. But I do know Richard's nervous tic had vanished. He was at ease. He was also sober. He carried Pam's suitcases. There was only room for one of them in the trunk. The other we'd have to ship north with the rest of my stuff.

"I'll be sending you more pages as soon as I have them," I informed Mercy. "Partly for your research assistance. Mostly for your approval. You're the boss now. The book won't get into print unless you like it."

"I know I'll love it," she assured me.

"Don't say that. I'm a writer like any other—I need someone to put their foot on my neck and keep it there." Polk Four frowned at this. "Figure of speech, Sheriff," I explained.

Mercy drew herself up. "Very well," she said sternly. "I'll expect several chapters by the end of the month, and they'd just better be up to Grandmother's standards."

"That's more like it, boss."

"Thank you." She giggled, made a quick, awkward step toward me, and kissed my cheek, blushing furiously. Then she lunged for the security of Polk, who put his arm around her, proud as can be. God, they were sturdy.

I shook hands with Richard and Charlotte and wished the two of them luck. Frederick as well.

"Absolutely sure I can't talk you into taking on this book of mine next?" Frederick asked me.

"Positive."

"That's too bad. Think they'd let me have a woman writer?" he wondered.

"I don't see why not," I replied.

"Yes, I think a woman's sensitivity would be a genuine asset," he mused aloud, nodding. "Any suggestions?"

"One. Keep your hands to yourself."

He turned to Pam, a mischievous glint in his eye. "Sure you have to leave, dear? Seems like we're just getting to know each other."

"Quite sure," Pam replied curtly.

We got into the Jag. Lulu and Sadie curled up on the floor together at Pam's feet, Sadie using Lulu as a pillow, and Lulu letting her. She was so depressed nothing bothered her. Actually, the two of them seemed to be growing on each other. Because of their shared diet, Sadie thought Lulu was a cat and Lulu thought Sadie was a dog. I wasn't about to break the truth to either of them.

Frederick's eyes hadn't left Pam. He waved good-bye somewhat wistfully.

"The man's an absolute beast," she murmured to me.

"We all are, Pam," I said, starting up the engine. "It's just that some of us are better at hiding it. I'd have thought you'd have no problem handling him."

"As would I," she admitted, sighing. "Except that when they're as terribly handsome as he is, I have a frightful time saying no. In fact, I can't."

"Why, Pam," I gasped, shocked. "You slut."

"It's high time you found out," she said. "After all, we are going to be living together."

Everyone waved good-bye. We waved back. Then I let out the Jag's parking brake and eased it down the twisting drive and out the front gate. We started for home.

I don't ever want to see another goddamned peacock again as long as I live.

I found Gordie sitting outside on the lawn, glumly tossing his ball against a retaining wall and catching it with his mitt. There were other boys out there playing ball, but he was ignoring them. The hospital had nice grounds, lots of grass, and trees and walking paths. You almost didn't notice the fence.

He lit up when he saw me. "Hey, Hoagy! How ya doing?"

"Just fine, Gordie. Heading up to Connecticut. I wanted to say good-bye."

"Can I come with you?" he begged. "Pleath?"

I shook my head.

"How come they're making me live here, Hoagy?"

"I guess they think it's for the best."

"How come?"

I took the ball from him. "Go deep. I'll throw you one."

He eagerly trotted off across the lawn. I wound up and sent one high through the air toward him. He picked up the flight of it right away, drifted back and to his left, and punched his mitt. He was there waiting for it when it came down.

I joined him, rubbing my shoulder. We walked.

"I'll be keeping Sadie for you," I told him.

"They won't let me have her here."

"I know. I'll take good care of her. She's still your cat. When you're ready for her, just let me know. I gave them my address at the desk in case you ever want to write her. Or me. Okay?"

"Okay." He glanced over his shoulder to see if we were alone, then looked up at me slyly. "Keep a theecret, Hoagy?"

"Sure."

A sneaky grin crossed his face. "C'mere. Wanna show ya thumthin'."

He led me into the trees over by the fence, behind some bushes. "You may sthee me thooner than ya think," he whispered, kicking at the undergrowth with his foot.

There was a big hole in the earth there under one of the bushes. He was digging. Tunneling out.

I must have gotten a whiff of pollen. My eyes were suddenly bothering me, and I had trouble swallowing. I grabbed him under his arms and hoisted him up, hugged him tightly to my chest.

He squirmed in my arms. "Hey, what'd you do that for?" he demanded, horrified.

"I don't know." I put him down.

"Well, don't do it again."

"Okay, I won't."

"I'm not a baby, y'know."

"I know. Sorry." I stuck out my hand. "See you, Gordie."

He shook it. "Sthee ya."

I started walking away.

"Hey, Hoagy!" he called after me.

I stopped. "Yeah, Gordie?"

"Take it thlow."

I smiled. "Slow's the only way to take it."

I went back to the car without looking back.

We cleared Washington by lunchtime and beat the rush hour out of New York onto the New England Thruway. It was nearing dusk when we crossed the Connecticut River into Old Lyme. Lulu jumped into Pam's lap and stuck her large black nose out the window as we made our way up Route 156 into the rolling hills of Lyme. Spring was happening all over again up here. The forsythia was ablaze, the apple trees and dogwoods blossoming. It would be nice to go through spring for a second time. This one might even make up for the first one.

Lulu started to whoop when I turned off onto the narrow country lane that dead-ended at those old stone walls flanking the dirt driveway. I stopped for a second to take it all in—the lush green fields, the fruit trees and duck pond, the snug old yellow house and chapel, big red carriage barn, Merilee's beloved old Land-Rover. Lulu, impatient, jumped out and sped up the drive without us.

She found her mommy out behind the house turning over her vegetable garden. She had on rubber boots and old jeans and a flannel shirt that once belonged to me. Her waist-length golden hair was in a braided ponytail, and she had mud all over her face. Lulu was whooping and moaning. Merilee knelt in the rich soil, stroking her. She looked up at me a bit warily when she heard me approach.

"Thought I'd finish the book here, if you don't mind," I said.

She turned back to Lulu. "I don't mind."

"I can stay in the chapel," I offered.

"If you wish," she said, her eyes still on Lulu.

"I don't."

"Then don't," she said. "Stay in the chapel, I mean."

"Okay, I won't."

"Good."

We both watched Lulu.

"It turned sour on her," I reported. "He dumped her."

"The brute."

"I did what I could, but she desperately needs a mother's touch right now."

"My poor baby," she said, rubbing Lulu's ears. "She's lost her innocence."

"It's true. She's already started reading Erica Jong."

Merilee looked up at me. "Hoagy?"

"Yes, Merilee?"

"Hello."

"Hello yourself," I said.

She got to her feet and started toward me. She stopped, peered at something over my shoulder. "Is that . . . *Pam* in the car?"

"She needs a place to stay. I figured you wouldn't mind."

"Mind? Gracious, I just hope I'm worthy of her."

"You'll more than do."

"But I look terrible," she said, brushing herself off.

"Just awful," I agreed, grinning.

She came up to me and kissed me and fingered the bandage on the side of my head, her brow creased with concern.

I took her in my arms and held her. "Just a minor brush with death," I said, getting lost in her green eyes. "How's Elliot?"

"Hmpht."

"What's that mean?"

"That's for me to know and you to never find out," she replied primly.

"What did he . . . ?"

"He got fresh."

"He got what?"

"You heard me. The big fat gherkin knocked me over and . . ."

"And what, Merilee?"

"Never mind."

"Did he put his snout where he shouldn't have?"

"*Mister* Hoagy!"

"You can't blame the fellow, Merilee. You put him back in the pink. It was just his way of saying thank you."

"That's not what Mr. Hewlett said. He gave me a severe tongue-lashing."

"Elliot or Mr. Hewlett?"

"Stop it. He said I shouldn't have gotten so close to him, what with his age and the time of year and all."

"Don't sell yourself short. You're also a lot better looking than what he's used to. Smell a hell of a lot better, too. So what did you do?"

"Stick around for a somewhat tardy Easter supper and you'll find out," she replied wickedly.

"No . . ."

"Mr. Hewlett said it was the proper thing to do."

"Well, well. This is a whole new pioneer side of you, Merilee."

"It is. Producers had better watch themselves around me from now on, or risk the consequences. Ex-husbands, too."

"I'll remember that."

"Do so."

There was some business going on at our feet now. Sadie was rubbing up against my leg and yowling.

"And who might this be?" Merilee wondered, picking her up and cradling her in the crook of her arm. Sadie dabbed at her sleeve with her paws and began to make small motorboat noises.

"Don't ask me. Never saw her before."

"Hoagy . . ."

"Her name is Sadie. She's kind of on permanent loan. Not

a terrible mouser. Every farm should have one, don't you think?"

She smiled at me. "I thought you hated cats."

"I do." I sighed. "It's a long story, and not a pretty one."

She gave me her up-from-under look, the one that makes my knees wobble. "I've got time."

"I haven't. Excuse me." I started for the house.

"Where are you going?" she called after me.

I went in the back door into the big old farm kitchen. I still had half a bottle of Glenmorangie in the cupboard. I poured two fingers in a glass and added some well water from the tap and drank it down. Out the window I could see Merilee and Pam cheerfully getting reacquainted out by the duck pond. I made myself another stiff one before I picked up the wall phone. I dialed the number from memory. My hands shook. My heart was pounding. It rang twice and then I heard the voice. And then I said it.

I said, "Hello, Dad."